THE FOLLY ON THE HILL

The Book Of Imaginari - Part One

Richard Hayden

First paperback edition March 2021
First Kindle ebook edition March 2021

Paperback ISBN: 9798703642283

Book and cover design by Richard Hayden & Naomi Clare
Images by Richard Hayden

Twitter: @r_c_hayden
Instagram: @r_c_hayden
Facebook Page: Richard Hayden Author (@rchaydenauthor)

Dedication.

This is an Amazon Kindle Direct Publishing first edition of The Folly On The Hill, which is part one of three in The Book Of Imaginari.

The series would not exist without the love and support of my friends and family. To get to this point has been a rollercoaster of edits, changes, late nights, long days, updates, and more.

To those that have read draft after draft, I thank you. I would like to thank by name; Amy, Imelda, Jane, Janet, Jo, Josie, Lesley, Martyn, and Steve, though there are many more that have known about this project in some way, these people have contributed in no small way to this adventure.

Most of all though I would like to thank Naomi, without her inspiration, love, and support, I would not have got any further than chapter one. In many ways, Imaginari belongs to us both, and now I am sharing it with the world.

To everyone that has helped or has been aware of this project, however small, thank you.

I hope everyone enjoys reading it, as much as I have enjoyed writing it.

Richard.

CONTENTS

CHAPTER 1

Many centuries ago.

It was a night of typical darkness. The sun always set with a grim finish to the day at this time of year, winter. As if it too could not wait for the longer summer days to arrive. This night was even darker though, gradually as the days crept towards the next full moon the nights had grown a deeper shade of purple. Out of the darkness a dark-haired man moved slowly through the shadows, a gentle shuffle to his walk. The shuffle was partly due to his apparent age, the years had not been kind to him, but also because of the reticence as to what could be at the end of this journey. He had spent the last few weeks moving around the village setting up for what may, or may not, happen next. He had a feeling that what he had been discussing with four other members of the village was important, so important in fact that he had not been back to his own dwelling for some time.

This was a simple time. A time where people led simple lives, a time when villages survived and thrived on the generosity and love of its occupants. It was also a time, when the unknown, unexpected, or unplanned was feared and spoken of in hush tones around the fires of people's homes. Abijah, the village shaman, did not fear such things though, wary and ponderous yes, but not fearful. He had seen the predictions in the stars, fire embers, and the tree's over the past six months. He knew what had to be done, and when. As he rounded the corner and started heading towards the peak of the hill that his village sat on, he became aware of people in front of him. He smiled a small knowing smile. They had listened to him. As he reached the peak of the hill, he could see the faces of three people glowing orange by the dancing flames of the campfire they had lit. Three, not four he frowned to himself. As he approached, one of the three turned to acknowledge him.

"Evening Abijah," said a fair-haired lady to the left of the fire.

"Evening Philippa. Do we have you to thank for the bread this evening?"

The lady replied, "Yes, the last batch before, well, before whatever happens tonight, happens. So, tuck in, I thought we should be fed before the end arrives."

"Thank you. Evening to you as well Thomas and Isabella. I'm so very glad to see you all here this evening. But where is Elizabeth?"

Both shuffled on the spot, clearly agitated with the situation. "She is on her way, we are led to believe. She needed more time to prepare. She has more at stake in this than we do," Isabella replied sheepishly.

"We all have everything at stake tonight - if we fail, there will be no tomorrow to regret it. We must not fail, and we cannot succeed unless we are all in agreement," Abijah retorted.

There was a silence as thick as the night itself, even the trees seemed to stop rustling.

"As I said to you all before, we have prepared the essentials to allow us to complete our task this evening. If we succeed, there is much more work to be done to ensure it remains secure for centuries to come. This is our duty to the village and to the world. We were fortunate..."

"Fortunate?!" Thomas, the only person to have been silent so far interrupted. "Fortunate?! How is that the case? We are the ones who have had to shape these, *things*, and we are the ones who are going to stand here and do something so horrific we need to do it at night! And if we succeed, we then have the pleasure of building a castle on top a hill where there is no stone to be seen! How are we fortunate Abijah?"

There was another silence, only broken by the crackling of the fire. Then, after a brief but sharp intake of breath, Abijah replied, "I cannot tell you why we are here, or why this is happening now. What I can tell you is that we have a sacred duty to create the structure he has designed and ensure the rituals around it are upheld. We will be the first members of the Key Council, we who have created the five totems for our huts in this very village. For when they are all in place and we have completed our task tonight, we will be keeping a great evil at bay to keep the world safe. Yes - a building is needed. A design to keep our totem's focus secure and true. This is only after we have succeeded though, for if we fail, I fear the darkness will last for much longer than these long winter nights."

There seemed to be a reluctant acceptance at this. The notion that it had to be tried to be believed seemed to have sunk in. The group of four looked at each other in turn, waiting to see who was going to talk next or challenge the idea of what they were doing. Nobody said a word. Nobody moved.

There was a loud snap from behind them. The four whirled round to focus on the direction of the noise, startled at its intrusion in the silence. They were no longer alone. A woman with long dark hair and tired looking skin was walking towards them, carrying a bundle in her arms.

"You are very jumpy - anyone would think that you were scared or something!" Elizabeth exclaimed. "I'm the one who has had to carry the burden so far, I'm looking forward to the relief."

She lay the bundle down in the middle of them all, near the fire. The dancing flames revealed the face of a baby, wrapped in several blankets and bundled up tightly to protect her from the cold. She stirred a little but otherwise seemed quite content.

The group stepped back a little, as if feeling they were too close to the child, almost in fear.

Abijah began, "So, we all know why we are here?"

They nodded.

"We have all prepared our totems and left them in the precise agreed location in our huts?"

Again, silent nods of agreement.

"Then, I think it is time. Would you like me to...."

"No," Elizabeth interrupted. "I want to. It was I who brought this down on us all, it is I that should start the beginning of the protection."

They all looked at her, not knowing what to say. At the same time knowing that anything they did say would be almost meaningless.

"Very well," Abijah replied. "I have marked the spot on the very crest of the hill, three marked stones all in a line. Ensure that her chest is over the middle stone and that her head and feet line up perfectly with the other two. This is crucial. She must be laying north to south. As soon as you have put her down, come back here and do not return, no matter what happens next, until we all agree it is safe to do so."

"I understand. And her name Abijah, is Joanna."

"God speed, Joanna," Abijah stated, attempting to comfort Elizabeth.

"God speed," the others repeated, feeling that joining in was the right thing to do.

Elizabeth stooped to pick up Joanna, turned, and started to walk up the hill to the crest. The wind had picked up a little now, blowing at the blankets as if trying to rip them off the girl. With every step, Elizabeth's heart felt heavier and heavier in her chest. Tears forming at the corners of her eyes as the realisation of what she was about to do kicked in. She knew what was about to happen, or at least what Abijah had said was about to happen, but she did not know how. Perhaps more importantly, she knew how it would end. She climbed the last few steps and held Joanna close to her chest in a tight, almost suffocating hug. She looked up and took in the night. It was clear, stars all around. On the ground around the hill, she could see small flickers of fires in villages, the stars and moon reflected in rivers and mile upon mile of darkness. She felt the darkness was reflected in her heart. It was time. She lowered to her knees and lined up next to the three marked stones, they had been pushed into the ground so they would be flat to the touch. She kissed Joanna on the head, whispered a note of love and affection, and lowered her onto the stones just as instructed. Chest over the middle, lined up north to south. She stood. Nothing happened. There was a pause, a moment where all she wanted to do was pick up the child and run. Run as far and as fast as she could to get her away from this madness. She knew she could not run away from this though. With one last glance down, she turned and started to walk back down the crest to the fireside with the others, tears streaming down her face. Thomas and Isabella greeted her and pulled her into a hug. They all waited. Nothing. The night was as still and quiet as it had been all the way through their meeting, the fire, dying down now, crackled quietly. They all stared up at the crest, the wind gently blew the sound of a crying baby towards them. It sounded distant and lost in the night. Elizabeth took a few cautious steps forwards.

"Why is nothing happening?" she asked, to nobody in particular. There was no reply.

They were all thinking the same thing. Had they got it wrong? Had they misunderstood the signs? Were they in the wrong place? They waited. Abijah was the most concerned as he had led the group to this place, it would be he that they blamed. Still, they waited. Nothing. Only the sound of the wind in the trees and the baby's cry in the short distance.

Elizabeth took a step forward. Nothing. Feeling braver, she took two more. Still nothing. She turned to face the others, all of whom shrugged with a look of puzzlement. She turned and took a few more cautious steps before calling back, "Nothing is happening, I'm going to go and get her."

Before anyone could respond to this, she had already started to move. Abijah looked up, he stared. He wondered where had all the stars gone. The sky had gone completely black. As if someone had turned out the lamps. He had also noticed that the fire had shrunk right down. He glanced up at Elizabeth who had started to make her way up the hill. He called after her, "Wait! You're too close! Something is about to happ..."

But it was too late. Before he could finish his warning, the sky was torn apart with a blinding bolt of light. It tore from above and came down to meet the earth where Joanna lay. The force sent Elizabeth tumbling back down the crest of the hill and flung the rest of the group onto their backs. The power of the impact uprooted trees, extinguished the fire, and forced everything outwards in a circle with the child at its centre. Gaping up at the sky, the group was now lying in stunned silence, unable to move through fear and wonder at what they could see. A grey spiral, a vortex of cloud had formed around them in the sky, turning faster and faster. Without warning there was another bolt of light, striking in the same place, but this time the light was reflected five times outwards as if in a star shape, beaming out sideways from where the child lay over the heads of the group. The beams of light scorched the Earth, burning through trees, grass, and bushes as if they were kindling, with the child at its centre. At the same time, rocks and boulders seemed to be pushed up from the ground causing it to shake and crack. To anyone nearby who happened to look up at the hill, this would have been quite the spectacle. Five beams of light scorching their way down the hill, only stopping when they reached a barrier. A purple bubble of energy that seemed to be containing the chaos to the very top of the hill. Then, as quickly as before, the beams of light seemed to get brighter and force their way back to the child in the centre. With a loud bang, they combined to shoot up into the centre of the cloud spiral. The light was blinding, everyone shielded their eyes from it as the intensity grew. Then as if being chased away, it lifted itself up into the sky like a rope being pulled up from above through a hatch in the centre of the spiral. Then there was darkness. Elizabeth lifted her head towards the heavens. She could make out the spiral clouds, she could also make out the fading image of a face in the clouds. An image of a face contorted with pain and anger, then it vanished. The clouds cleared, and the stars winked back into view. They sat up, stared at each other, and then up towards the crest of the hill. The wind had returned now, a gentle touch as though comforting them with what had just happened. Around them, there were gentle fires where the light had cut through trees. Rocks and boulders had appeared where previously there were none and the Earth felt torn and scorched. With haste Abijah began to move towards the crest of the hill. He moved past Elizabeth much faster than he had moved for weeks up to the crest; stepping over rocks that were not there before. He reached the point where the light had hit the ground, the point where Joanna had been left by Elizabeth. He looked down, there was nothing there. Nothing except the scorched earth and a precise point where the light had hit the ground on the centre stone, exactly where Joanna's chest had been. It was surrounded by a small circle of burnt Earth, otherwise the grass was green. Blown and bent outwards in a circle, but green and apparently untouched. As he looked up, the stars glinted brightly as if nothing had happened at all, he could hear the others coming to join him. Elizabeth was the first to arrive, she collapsed to her knees and wailed in despair.

"It's for the best, we have just done something remarkable and saved everything," Philippa comforted her, but it was of no use.

The pain and despair in the eyes of Elizabeth was clear, and untouched by the words of support from her friend.

The group stood silently, looking up at the sky, with Elizabeth at their knees sobbing.

After a short while, she stood and turned to face the group. "We better make sure this was not for nothing. We need to finish what we started and ensure that this never happens to another being on this Earth. We must start work on the lock. The five keys are in place but will be powerless when winter starts again. The keys must stay in their place for all eternity, but we must build a lock to stand the test of time with them." They all turned to Abijah. He lowered his eyes from the heavens to look at them all, regarding them all individually.

"I agree," he stated matter of factually as if deciding on what to have for supper. "We must begin work on the building at once. The girl's life must not have been in vain. We must prevail." He gestured around them at the ground, "Rouse the villagers, The Man has provided the stone for us to build this lock, we must do so."

They looked puzzled, "The Man?" Philippa asked.

"Yes," Abijah replied. "The keys will be secured and passed on through generations, but for the lock the Man Of Mow has provided. We must build his structure here, in Mow Cop on this spot with his stone. It will act as the lock to keep the world safe, keeping a great evil at bay, and most of all, ensuring that this never happens to another family again."

CHAPTER 2
Today.

"As you can see the mouldings are very tasteful and have recently been painted to bring them into line with the colour of the walls and floor."

Eleanor Fields, Ellie to her friends and family, had become accustom to phrases like this, for this was the seventh house they had visited in two days. Two days of travelling, hotel stays, and house viewing. Not exactly what a fifteen-year-old would long for. She would much rather be at home in the city, hanging out with friends, shopping, watching TV, or busying herself with her new favourite hobby she had picked up from her grandma - cross-stitch. But no. As any teenager will tell you, as much as your family love you and you love them, what mum and dad need to do will trump anything you want to do. They were house hunting because her mum, Katherine, has a new job that means they need to move. Ellie was happy for her mum, she had always admired her drive and passion to do what she wanted to do, but did it really mean moving so far away from home? According to her phone, it was nearly two hundred miles back to their home and would take nearly four hours to drive it. How am I going to see my friends again? She would wonder, she did not have many, but they were very close. Ellie had to admit this was the only negative, the area they were looking to move to looked pretty and it would be nice to be able to go outside and look at green instead of grey concrete. Ellie was sure there would be somewhere she could go, shop, and lots to do that is new, 'you'll make friends easily' she had been told many times over. She flicked her long blond hair over her shoulders, sweeping her fringe to one side at the same time and stared out of the window for a moment.

It was summer, the kind of summer where it gets so hot people grumble about it being too hot, and that its 'never been this hot before', even though it had been the year before and every weather report seemed to say the same thing, hot. Ideal weather for driving around looking at houses, Ellie thought sarcastically to herself. She was prepared for a day in the sun, wearing a skirt and a summer top that kept her cool whilst also looking reasonably presentable. They were all standing in a living room, Ellie's parents; Nicholas and Kathryn, Ellie, and the estate agent who Ellie thought was trying too hard. Wearing far too much makeup and perfume. She had no idea if the house smelt funny because all she could smell was the flowery fragrance of the woman. The house was quite big, certainly larger than their town house they currently had; her dad Nicholas had explained that they could 'get more for their money up north', whatever that meant. Ellie glanced at the piece of paper she had been given with the details of the house, they all had one, it was nice that she was being included even if it was not going to matter what she thought of the house.

The agent continued, "It is available immediately with no onward chain. All the furniture will be taken away, so you can put your own stamp on it, the sellers wanted to leave it in to help with people visualising the house with furniture in. One living room, kitchen, utility room, dining room, entrance hall, study, and garden downstairs. Upstairs has four bedrooms, one with en suite, one bathroom, and a storage cupboard There is also the loft space which is another bedroom, it also has its own bathroom and excellent views..."

This last statement caught Ellie's attention, a loft bedroom, that could be interesting, she started to think. If the views were as good as everyone claimed, it could be worth a look. " Can we see the loft room?" she interrupted.

"Of course," the agent replied politely, "would you like me to show..."

Ellie turned and headed for the stairs, not bothering to hear the end of that sentence. "I'll find it, surely it's just upstairs?"

she called back in her trademark sarcastic tone.

As she moved quickly up the stairs, she could overhear her dad, "At least she is showing an interest in this one..."

The voices tailed off as she climbed the stairs. The landing was a landing, nothing too exciting. Ellie peered inside the bathroom and the main bedrooms. All very spacious and clean. Considering how recently this one had been put up for sale, everything seemed remarkably neat and tidy. All the rooms had been decorated in light pastel colours, the previous owner clearly loved boats, the water, fish, and the like. Every room had at least two pictures, a model, and some form of furniture or ornament related to this theme. There was not any water nearby that she knew of, she concluded that maybe it was a hobby or interest from a distance. She moved along the landing, towards the door that she had guessed would lead to the stairs to the loft room. It opened easily, revealing the staircase behind; well-lit and painted a brilliant white. She had half expected it to be broken, run down, and unloved. Ellie walked up the stairs. The room was beautiful, painted a pale-yellow colour with matching furnishings and trim. A vintage wardrobe stood in the corner, with a dressing table next to it with a large mirror and chair, the sort that film stars supposedly used in the sixties. There was a huge four poster bed that dominated the room, beyond which she could see into the bathroom, like everything else here, it seemed lovely. The best thing about the room though, was the window. Big and round set into an alcove with a bench, the sort that would allow you to sit with your feet up and read looking out of the window. Ellie moved quickly over to it, excitement growing inside her.

This would be a wonderful place to sit, read, stitch, and think, was her immediate thought.

She leaned on the seat, the soft cushion wrapping itself around her knee as she did so. Picturing herself sat there looking out of the window pondering, looking at the colours of the trees changing in autumn, stitching the time away. Boys, would she ever sit here with a boy? Ellie had never really had a boyfriend, at least not a real one, but Sophie her friend from school had and she had said it was the best thing, Ellie did not understand how. She had not given it a lot of thought, she would take it as it came and see what happened, it did have the potential to be a romantic bench seat though. As she continued to look out of the window, a castle was suddenly in her line of sight, standing proud on top of the hill. Little more than a ruin these days but with a single tower in the middle and a wall coming off to one side. Ellie concluded that with the arch it did look picturesque with the clear blue sky behind it.

"Admiring the castle?"

Ellie jumped and turned. Her dad had walked in the room, standing there looking proud with his summer shirt and shorts, sunglasses on his head causing a tuft of grey to stick up.

So weird, Ellie thought to herself. He was followed by Ellie's mum and the agent of smell herself.

"Yes, well, the room as well. It's gorgeous dad, and this seat, come see!"

She beckoned her father to her, he obliged with a warm smile. They sat together looking out of the window, staring up at the sky.

"My two favourite beans," her mother said as she walked over. She always knew how to make her family smile, even if it was a wry one from Ellie. She headed over to the window, her heeled shoes clopping over the wooden floor, putting a hand each on a shoulder of her husband and daughter. They all looked for a moment at the world go by and listening to the gentle breeze blow through the trees.

The silence was broken by the agent, "This room is incredibly special, the previous owner treated it as their main room, they would often sit and look out of that window I'm told, just as you are now actually. And just to correct you, it is a folly, not a castle, built in the seventeen hundred's as a summerhouse, the only bits left are a single tower and wall now, wonderful views though. Staffordshire on one side and Cheshire on the other, you'll never need to buy fireworks again," the lady joked.

This did not go down as well as she expected and was not really acknowledged. Because the three people it was aimed at, were too fixated on the structure itself. Ellie was beginning to like the idea of living in a village with a castle, who even knew what a folly was, she thought to herself, castle is much cooler. They stood up to leave, turned and started to walk back towards the stairs, Katherine and Nicholas talking adult stuff with the agent, Ellie stopped and turned to face the window once more. It really was beautiful, it had an odd frame she had just noticed, it was round yes, but it had been split into triangles, as if someone had drawn an 'M' in straight lines within a circle. Odd design, she pondered, but it does add to the character of the room, and with that, headed down the stairs to pretend to listen to more grown-up talk.

After another half an hour or so of listening to the estate agent, with a final look up at the house, they were in the car pulling off the driveway to head to the hotel. As they wound their way along the country road, Ellie looked out of the window at the scenery, the folly was visible occasionally, demonstrating its dominance over the surrounding area, but Ellie was also paying attention to the trees, fields, and farms that flew by.

"It was bigger than I thought," Nicholas said factually, "plenty of room to write in the study with a view over the fields. Loads of living space although may need some work to make it more 'us' don't you think?"

"Yes, definitely has potential," Katherine replied. "It's easily the best we have seen, and the most expensive."

"Paying for a view I guess," he agreed. "What do you think?" he asked his daughter.

No answer, Ellie was distracted by the people in village, it was as if they were all looking at them all at once. Nearly every house they passed had someone either looking out of the window at them, standing in the garden leaning on the gates, or was walking along the path.

Very odd I don't remember seeing many people out and about on our way into the village, Ellie mused to herself. Maybe it's just me imagining it, after all, we are the new people...

"HELLOOOOO," he said louder this time, startling Ellie out of her trance.

"Sorry dad, what was the question?"

He considered her for a moment, "What do you think of the house?" he asked again.

Ellie contemplated, serious or sarcastic were the two options available to her she pondered. "Other than the fact it is miles away from home, and my friends, and my life, and everything is changing, and it could all be rubbish?"

He stared at her in the mirror, "Yes darling, other than that. What do you think?"

Ellie glared back at him, "I think the house is beautiful." She conceded, her eyes softening.

Looking into her dad's eyes, those deep blue penetrating eyes that could melt her heart she could not lie. She also knew this worked the other way around, she had her father's eyes, but it also meant she could never lie to or mislead him. He always knew. It was a beautiful house, in a beautiful place. Right now though, it was not home.

"Of all the ones we've seen, it's the one that I like the most, it's the one I could cope with and might warm to," she stated.

There was a knowing look and smile between Ellie's parents, as if they knew she would warm to the idea of moving eventually. Ellie was irritated that they knew her so well. The rest of the journey to the hotel was conducted with a mixture of songs and conversations on topics other than houses.

After dinner in a small pub, they agreed to retire to their hotel rooms. Ellie did not mind this tonight; she had some thoughts that she wanted to explore. After going up in the lift and walking along the corridor together she announced, "I'm going to read up on a few things about Mow Cop."

Her parents stopped and turned to face her, amused looks on their faces.

"Ok," Nicholas replied simply, looking at his wife with a small grin.

"Glad to hear you are interested in what could be our new home, come through if you need anything," Katherine reassured.

It was nice having joining rooms, but having her own privacy was the best advantage.

Ellie walked forward to hug and kiss her parents' good night, then entered her room. Closing the door behind her, she began to plan her evening of research, but first, a bath.

After soaking for a little while, planning out the way she wanted to do things this evening, Ellie got out of the bath, into her pyjamas and settled at the small writing desk in the hotel room. Laptop powered on in front of her, phone at the ready with headphones in, music of choice ready to play, cup of tea, and a kit-kat. Bliss. The only thing missing was some stitching to be done, but that could wait. She could not really research and stitch at the same time anyway. The focus of her evening was going to be the village itself, as beautiful as it was, something felt odd about it. She could not shake the image of everyone watching them as they left, as if they were being 'checked out' as newcomers. Probably nothing in it, but she needed to know about the village and its people. The first few hours passed without anything of real interest, usual stuff. Population, two schools, many churches, and pubs as well as multiple walks. Even the castle, or folly, as the internet confirmed, seemed unremarkable. But that was just it. The fact it was apparently so unremarkable made it remarkable. It was when she started digging deeper that things got interesting. Whilst looking on a chat room site, she noticed an entry titled 'The truth about Mow Cop and its mysterious Key Council'. This was then followed with a list of things that the writer claimed about the village:

Don't believe the other sites. Don't believe the hype. Don't believe anything other than what you read here. The folly was NOT built as a summer house in the seventeen hundreds, it goes back way before that. Who would build a summerhouse with one tower and a single wall pointing off of it? There is evidence of a settlement and a prehistoric camp all over the hill, the facts point towards the folly being built way before it should have been possible to do so. The stones used to make it are available on the hill, but there is no way they could have cut them and shaped them

as they did. There is also the fact that the single wall (yes, it was
always a single wall) sits exactly on the North/South line, why?
It is very precise! So precise that it can be checked using modern
technology today, perfect north to south! This surely cannot be
a coincidence? There are documents that talk about a secret soci-
ety, a ritual that was performed on the hill and the folly is part of
it, some sort of ancient lock protecting us from something, but
what? This has always been scoffed at as voodoo mumbo jumbo,
but look at the facts: Nobody ever leaves that village, they move
in or are born there but never leave until the day they die. They
have their own council, the Key Council. Keys to what? Keys go
in a lock! That council act in secret and never tell us what it all
means. The only people that know are those in the council, and
they are chosen by the houses they buy. The legends of the Man Of
Mow are strong in the area, are they connected? There are some
who believe the Man Of Mow is linked to the folly which is in fact
a lock that it looked after by the Council of the Keys to protect us
from...

Ellie stopped reading. Mainly because she was processing the
first part, but also because the site only showed that much of
the text, and when she attempted to click on the link, it was
blocked. She exhaled, that was a lot of information to take in.
She did not really know what to do with it either. It was the
only thing she had found, the only trace of anything odd happening in that village in the whole of the internet as far as
she could tell.
Ellie spoke aloud, "Did that make it any less true? Fact is fact
after all. Surely it would have been reported on if that were
true, if there was a council looking after some sort of keys
then surely everyone would know? Was it being covered up, or
was it simply not true?"
So many questions were now spinning through her mind,
most of all, did it change her view of the house? It wouldn't
matter if it did, she concluded, mum and dad will have the
final say and I'll just have to go along with it, maybe I should
keep this to myself for now, they wouldn't believe me anyway.
Glancing at the clock in the corner of her screen, five past
one in the morning. Deciding it was probably time to go to

bed, she saved all her findings, powered down the laptop, and moved to the bed. Lying there in the darkness, thinking about the Man Of Mow, the folly, the village, and the house, she decided to keep it to herself for now. It was a pretty house, maybe needs updating, but very pretty. That window though, she could not get the image out of her mind, the image of the 'M' in the panes of glass within the circle. She concluded that it was nothing, and that she really needed to sleep. She drifted off into a dreamless sleep.

A few weeks later, back at home in the city, Ellie returned home from the shops to find her mum and dad sat around the kitchen table looking at something.

"What's going on?" she asked as she walked over to the table.

"The paperwork for our new house has arrived!" Katherine exclaimed excitedly, "we are just checking over it before we sign".

They had all agreed that the house was gorgeous and was their combined favourite, Ellie had demanded the loft bedroom which had been agreed to, they had arranged her new school and her dad's work, everything had moved rather quickly. Ellie had decided to keep her little research project to herself.

"Have you seen this clause here?" Nicholas asked. "The bit about us, by buying the house, also agree to take ownership of 'the third obelisk of the Key Council, and will agree to keep it with the house and sell it on with it or pass it on to any heir that may live there', how crazy is that?"

"Yes, I had," said Katherine almost dismissively. "I'm sure it's nothing, it will be something silly in that village where every house has something they need to keep and move on, probably used at village fates or something, I'm not worried about it."

Ellie considered this and thought to herself It does match that one article I found, something about keys and a council. Nothing about an obelisk though, what even is an obelisk?

"Well, if you're happy, I'm happy," he concluded. "We can just give it to Ellie, and she can look after it," he said, looking at his daughter with a glint in his eye and a smirk. "Surely every girl of your age wants an obelisk in their room, don't they?" he chuckled.

Ellie tilted her head and mocked laughter at her father.

"Yes dad, it's what we all want. We will sit around in groups and chant and tell stories about boys," she retorted sarcastically.

His face changed at this, he loved his daughter very much, but the talk of boys had started to increase of late and it made him nervous. His baby girl was growing up! "Yes, well, maybe, you'll have to see. We don't even know what it is, how big it is or anything. Apparently, it will be at the house when we get there in 'the place it needs to be', whatever that means."

The conversation quickly turned to dinner after this, and then over dinner the conversation moved on again to Katherine and Nicholas' work, if Ellie was excited about starting a new school, and what they all thought of their new house. Ellie was looking forward to starting a new school, but most of all she was looking forward to sorting out her new bedroom, her bathroom, and her new life.

CHAPTER 3

Ellie spent as much time as she could with her friends, she wanted to make the most of their time together before moving day arrived at the end of July. There were multiple shopping trips, Ellie's parents had been especially generous lately, probably compensating for dragging me away, she would often think to herself. The thing she enjoyed the most though, was hanging around the local park, they would often just sit or lie on the grass and chat about nothing in particular. The focus of conversation was nearly always her new life. She was always asked questions about the house, when she would be back, do the villagers talk funny, and what the school uniform was like. Ellie would like to think that this last question is an intellectual one, but most probably more related to working out if it would clash with the colours she 'should' wear according to Sophie. It was a glorious day, the sky was clear and a brilliant blue, they sat in a circle on the grass, picking at it whilst they chatted and watched the world go by.

"I wonder what living in a village is like. I mean, what do they do all day?" asked Tina. "It must be so boring sitting around all day chatting with nothing else to do," she mused.

The others looked at her.

"You mean, exactly like we are now?" Sophie pointed out.

"No, what we are doing is different. We have chosen to do this, we could do loads of better things if we wanted to," she retorted.

"Thanks!" Ellie chimed in, "nothing like feeling special is there?"

They all laughed, except Tina, the irony seemed to be lost on her.

"Seriously though," Sophie continued. "What will it be like? What will you be doing all day? What are you excited about?" This was a fair and better question, considering her reply Ellie lay back on the grass, her long hair splayed out around her head and shoulders. She could have stayed there all day, in that moment. Bliss. "Well, once we have moved in and settled, it'll be back to school in September. Hoping to make some better friends," she looked up.

They all immediately threw little clumps of grass at her.

"Ok, ok, I give!" she screamed with laughter. "Only teasing. I'm hoping to make some friends very quickly, think it could get very lonely otherwise. There are loads of walks to be done though, the village is on a hill with a castle at the top..."

"We know!" Sophie loudly interrupted, cutting her off.

Ellie lifted herself up onto her elbows and looked at her, "But what you don't know, is there may be some kind of cult going on in that village."

They stared for a moment. Ellie had not intended on telling anyone about the article she had found, expecting nothing but laughter and teasing if she did. The words kind of just fell out of her mouth before she could stop herself. They were still staring at her.

"You need to explain this," Lara said, curiously.

Ellie knew she had a decision to make, she could either laugh it off now as a joke or tell them the truth of what she had found. She opted for the safest bet, to laugh it off. "I'm joking silly! They will be odd is all I mean. Country folk. Everyone knows everyone and chats, talks, and is polite to strangers in the street. Will be odd to adjust to, like a cult."

There was a pause, had they bought it?

"Ellie. That's your new neighbours you're picking on!" Tara exclaimed, giggling.

"You do need to keep in touch though. We want to know everything and see as much as you can share," Sophie said.

"Of course," said Ellie. "You can come visit too one day, once we are all settled."

"Only if we can go boy hunting," Sophie said.

Ellie chuckled, "You never stop do you? Can't we just hang out, catch up, and walk to explore?"

"My dear Ellie," Sophie said. "You have so much to learn. One day you will lift your head out of the cross-stitch world you live in and smell the aftershave!"

They all laughed again, this is what Ellie would miss, just chatting and passing the time with her friends, this sort of time could never be forced or created, it had to evolve and grow naturally. The best friendships grew over time and could not be forced.

"I need to head back soon, I have packing to do, and I want to stay in the parent's good books."

"I'd want to stay in your dad's good books too," Sophie said with a wink.

"Gross! Do not ever talk about my dad like that," Ellie shouted, pushing Sophie to the ground. She was laughing though, clearly enjoying poking fun at her friend's expense. "You're such a cow."

The others simply watched and giggled.

"That maybe so, but I did arrange something from all of us to you, Ellie."

Ellie was a little taken aback. Sophie was never the one to be sentimental and certainly has never been the first to start any kind of gift process. Sophie reached into her bag and pulled out a jewel covered photo album, in a heart shape on the cover was 'Ellie's Book' written in calligraphy style text with black ink. Ellie took the book, stunned into silence and opened it.

"We have all put in photos and stories of our favourite memories," Sophie explained as Ellie turned through the pages.

With each page turn, she was confronted with a picture of herself and her friends, doing something silly, going somewhere crazy, or just hanging out exactly as they are today. She was stunned. Looking up from the book, tears in her eyes she leant forward and pulled Sophie into a hug. The others piled on and before any of them realised, they were in a four-way group hug all crying their eyes out on each other shoulders.

"We have left some blank pages in there for you, so you can add more in as you hang out with your new friends," Tina sobbed.

Ellie replied, "They will be new, but they are new in the sense of more, not replacements. I could never replace you lot. Can we take a selfie now, to go in the book to mark our last night?" They agreed, even though they were all thinking the same thing, we've been crying and look awful.

This is what Ellie wanted to capture, the truth and rawness of the moment. She pulled out her phone, gathered them all around and took the picture. Despite Ellie needing to go home to pack, they all decided to go for food after this, they needed the energy and lift after all the emotion. They picked up their things and walked out of the park arms linked as a four like they had done so many times before.

The afternoon moved on into evening, and they started to say goodnight and goodbye, this was the last time Ellie would see her friends before the move. They all had various combinations of jobs and holidays coming up, not to mention the packing and organising that was needed to be done by Ellie herself. There were tears, more so as she worked her way around the group. Tina, Lara, and Sophie in order all hugged her tightly, wiping more tears away as they did so.

"Anyone would think one of us was dying. We can see each other again soon," Ellie stated.

With one last group hug, they went their separate ways. Sophie joining Ellie, Tina and Lara going the opposite direction. Sophie and Ellie walked in silence; arms linked through the streets. The shops were closing now, and the bars were starting to get busy. They were not old enough to drink and stay out, but they still knew the places that people liked to be in the evenings. Ellie took out her phone to look at the selfie they had taken as a group this afternoon. She smiled; it was perfect. Sophie in the middle - the ringleader, Tina and Lara at her side leaning in to be as close as possible, and Ellie in the foreground, smiling the biggest smile of them all. If she was with friends, she was happy. At the time she had not noticed the dark figure in the background. Covered in shadow of the trees but with a clear pale face, it is always hard to tell in photos, but Ellie was sure that the figure was staring at the group. As if looking straight at them. Creepy, she thought to herself. She scrolled through some other pics she had taken that afternoon. The figure, or at least one that looked a lot like it, was in nearly every single one, always watching the group of girls as they chatted, walked, and generally relaxed. Very odd and creepy, that's one thing I won't miss about living in the city, everyone staring all the time, she concluded to herself.

"Do you think it will change you, living in the country I mean?" Sophie asked, snapping Ellie back to reality.

She put her phone away and replied, "Not sure, I hope not. I like the way I am and would still hope to be the same after living somewhere else."

"Really? Nothing you would want to change?"

Ellie was puzzled by this, "What do you mean want to change?" she asked.

"You can be anyone you want to be now. You're starting a new life in a new place where nobody knows you. You can be anyone you want to be!"

"You mean, like start talking with an accent or something?" she chuckled.

"Sort of," Sophie replied. "Think about it. You can start any new hobby you like, show an interest in anything, change your likes and dislikes. Be anyone you want to be! Maybe even make yourself cooler like me," she smirked.

Ellie pushed her a little at this, "You're terrible! Not everything and everyone has to be about you Soph." She knew that Sophie meant well, but she was very self-centred at times. She did also have a point though. This was a new beginning. An opportunity to be who she wanted to be; the problem was she was not exactly sure what she wanted to be. "Maybe I'll just colour my hair or something," she stated.

"Not exactly what I meant," Sophie replied. "But it's a start."

They had been walking for a little while now and were nearly at the point where they would part. "I guess this is it then," said Ellie, fighting back the tears as she said it.

"I guess so," Sophie agreed. They turned to face each other, "Stay in touch, that's an order," she instructed.

"I will," Ellie sniffed, it was all she could do not cry right now. They hugged, said one last goodbye and parted ways.

Ellie's house was not far away, just a short walk. She decided for one last time to walk slowly and steadily, breathing in the city as she went. She moved along the street, thinking of her friends, the adventure she was about to embark on, and what may happen. Longing for something amazing to happen. She looked up at the sky, it was turning a gentle shade of orange as the sun set, the only blemish being the buildings in the way, something that would soon not be a problem for her. She carried on walking, still looking more up than forwards as she began to daydream.

"You really should watch where you are going," a deep voice said.

With a start, Ellie looked in front of her, she was about to walk into someone who was staring straight at her. She stopped walking, a little startled by the man. She could now see it was a man based on his facial hair and lack of clothing on his upper half.

"I'm sorry?" Ellie replied. "I was walking, you were standing still, and you are staring at me! Who are you? What do you want?"

Silence.

The man stared at her. "I was sent to check, I was summoned to check as someone who could be used and wasted, someone that would not be noticed."

"Well, that didn't work did it?" Ellie replied, anger seeping into her voice now. "You nearly let me walk into you, and I think I would notice that. Now, who are you and what do you want?"

He smiled, it was not a pleasant smile, but more a knowing smile that suggested he was fully aware of what he was doing and saying, he knew he was in control of the situation. After a few seconds, Ellie stepped to the side to go around him, he stepped across to block her.

"I have come to check if the prophecy will hold. To see if instructions will be honoured. We need to know that what is needed will be done and that what is done is upheld."

Ellie frowned, "You are making no sense, and I'm leaving now." She took a step forward past the man who turned and followed her with his eyes as she moved away. As she passed him, he bumped into her in the same way you would in a crowded street, but this one was empty. She wanted to scream for help but was shocked into silence.

He called after her as she moved away, "You will be tested, we will all be tested. He will test us. You are coming to us, you have chosen us, and you have chosen to support our cause. You will hold a key to our future," he stopped, apparently expecting a reaction.

Ellie did not oblige although she did glance over her shoulder to make sure she was not being followed. He smiled the same creepy smile, turned, and sped away. Ellie walked at pace in stunned silence. Nothing like this had ever happened to her or her friends before, she always knew it could happen as the city had some unusual people in it, but she had not seen it this close. The heat seemed to have left the street, she shivered, partly from the cold but mostly from the shock of what had just happened. Forcing herself to move faster, she began running towards home. It was not far, but it was far enough for her to have worked up a sweat and be panting by the time she clattered in the front door with a crash. She closed the door behind her and lent against it, breathing heavily, sweat dripping down her forehead and back. She did not ever remember feeling this scared. If ever there was anything needed to give her the push to accept the move to the village, this was it.

Entering from the living room her father exclaimed, "Are you ok Ellie? You look like you've seen a ghost."

She ran over to her dad, wrapping her arms around him into a tight hug. As he held her close, he kissed her on the head.

"Love you dad," she muttered into his shirt, though this was muffled by her tears as well. The emotion of the evening was just too much, saying goodbye to her friends, the creepy man on the street, all of it was just too much. She decided not to tell anyone about what had just happened, she did not think it was worth mentioning, and would only worry her parents. She pulled away slightly, still hugging her father she looked up at him. "I can't wait to start our new lives on the hill, in Mow Cop, we can be Mow Copians," she chuckled.

He smiled and chuckled back, clearly unsure of how to react

as her mood seemed to be shifting by the second. "Indeed, we can do whatever we want to do. Dinner will be ready soon, then we can settle on the sofa, why don't you go and get changed and come back down?"

Ellie nodded, she gave him one last squeeze and went upstairs to change. She was quick as she did not want to be alone. She threw her jacket into a clothes bag that was already packed and ready to go to the new house, her other clothes were put into the wash basket and she changed into her pyjamas. She went back downstairs into the kitchen where her mum was just about to serve dinner. In the Fields' household, everyone could cook, they took it in turns but they were all accomplished in the kitchen. Tonight, was fresh grilled meats, salad, and breads. Perfect for a summers evening. Ellie had calmed down now, her cheeks were no longer red, and she knew she could relax, safe with her family. They ate, discussing Ellie's day with her friends, she had brought the photo album down to show.

This moved her mother to tears, she left her chair to move round to hug her daughter, "I am so proud of you," she said. "So proud of how you have grown and how well you have adapted to this, I know it's scary and you will be lonely at first, but I promise it will be ok in the end."

Ellie hugged her back, "I know mum, I'm proud of you too. You show me how to be and give me the confidence I need. Love you."

They both cried. There was a lot of tears lately, except from her dad, he did not cry. That silly macho man thing Ellie often thought, but he was a big softy really. After eating, they spent the rest of the evening curled up on the sofa together, that and the TV were amongst the ever-shortening list of things that had not been packaged up for the move. After watching TV, it was time for bed. Ellie said goodnight and went upstairs. After getting herself ready, she got under the covers and settled down to sleep. She had put the photo album on the bedside table to look at whilst she drifted off, she did love her friends. She would miss them. But she was starting to realise there may be more positives to this move to the countryside than she first thought.

The days past by in a blur, moving day had arrived and it was time to say goodbye to the family home. Everything had been boxed up and labelled, the moving lorry had been loaded and left. They were leaving early to ensure they get to the new house in the morning. With one last look at the house, the three members of the Fields family got in the car and headed north for their new home. Their new adventure. The journey was long, they stopped a couple of times for a break, the excitement and emotion was too much for all of them. As they travelled up the motorway nearing the end of their journey, the hill with the folly came into view. Ellie looked out of the window at it, she had not really appreciated how far away you could be to still see it. According to the sat-nav, they were still forty-five minutes away and it was as clear as day, standing proud on top of the hill dominating all around it.

"Can see why it was built as a summerhouse," her dad stated. "Brilliant views for miles."

"Can we go up there this weekend?" Ellie asked. "I want to see what it's like up there, go exploring and stuff." She had wanted to do her own investigating into the folly for a while, and aside from looking pretty she felt there was more than meets the eye.

"I'm sure you will be able to soon," her dad said. "We have a lot to do this weekend though."

"I think she should go and have a look after helping us a little," her mum suggested turning to look at her daughter, smiling as she did so from the front passenger seat.

"What do you suggest?" her dad asked, clearly a little put out at being undermined like this.

"Well, the movers will do most of the work, so why don't we just get the car unpacked, work out where to put things and then she can go whilst they do the rest?"

Nicholas sighed a sigh that said he agreed, even if he did not really want to. Ellie smiled, she did not like her mum and dad disagreeing, but she did like it when it meant she could do what she wanted to do. Ellie was not a spoilt child, but she did know how to get her own way.

"That's settled then," her mum concluded. "Ellie, you can

help us with the car, then leave a note with where to put your bed and big stuff for the movers, then you can go to the castle. Deal?"

Ellie nodded enthusiastically. "I can remember the room, I'll draw a picture and note now so you know where everything needs to go," she stated excitedly. She spent the remainder of the journey drawing a map of how she would like her room laid out. What she ended up with was the bed and wardrobe in the same place as where the last owner had theirs, bed in the middle of the main wall, wardrobe in the corner, drawers opposite them. The last thing to be placed was her bookshelves, they needed to go near the window with the bench seat in, she longed to sit on that bench and read, stitch, and relax. That was going to be brilliant.

They arrived at the house. It was exactly as she remembered it. The room that would be Ellie's faced the back of the house, so the round window was not visible. Nicholas took out his phone to call the movers to see how far they were behind. Ellie and her mother moved towards the house to open the door together. They slid the key into the lock, turned it and the door swung open. They moved through the hallway into the living room, which was big but seemed odd without any furniture in it like the last time they had seen it. They checked all the rooms to make sure nothing was amiss. Eventually, Ellie moved into the back garden, she had not spent much time there when the visited the house before, and she was taking it all in now. It was a reasonable size, grass in the middle, overgrown flowerbeds to the sides, and a shed in the back corner. She peered through the shed window. It was dusty but mostly empty. She opened the door, which creaked as she did so. Inside there was a rusty lawnmower, some garden tools, and some paint. Nothing too exciting. She moved towards some shelves, they were laden down and looked like they would buckle under the weight on them at any moment. She left the shed and was now facing the house and could see something that she had not noticed before. A stone structure, like a tall spire, as she approached it came up to Ellie's head height. Quite tall for a garden sculpture, she thought to herself. It appeared uneven, as if it had not been carved as much as left to form over time. It looked heavy, made of solid stone as far she could tell. It intrigued her. She could not see any reason why it was here. It did not go with anything. It was not a bird table or anything remotely as useful as that. It had been there for a long time though, there was moss around the bottom of it and flowers had attached themselves to it. She reached out to touch it about halfway up, she rested her palm on the side of the stone. It was cold to the touch, not surprising really given it was made of stone and in the shade of the house. She slid her hand up the uneven but gentle to the touch stone towards the top. There was something therapeutic about touching it. As she neared the top, about ten centimetres from the peak, she had a sneaky feeling she was being watched. As if someone was waiting for her to do something. She focused on the stone, the sensation of touching it was comforting but intriguing at the same time.

"Ellie!" her mother's voice rang out, bringing her back to reality instantly. "Come and help us with the car so you can go exploring."

"Coming," Ellie replied, the stone will have to wait, she thought to herself, and with that, she went back to the car to help unpack.

CHAPTER 4

Unpacking did not take long. Or at least, the level of packing Ellie was required to do did not take long. She helped empty the car of boxes, put the small amount of food they had brought with them in the fridge and cupboards, and left her layout requests for her room taped to the wall at the top of her staircase. Yes, my staircase, she thought to herself excitedly, not many teenagers could say that. She felt a new level of confidence, independence, and maturity at the thought of this for some reason. She had an entire floor to herself, space that was just hers that, within reason, she could do what she wanted to do with. Standing in the middle of the room, surveying the scene, a small smile crept across her face, she was going to like it here. With that, she grabbed her rucksack and went downstairs. She was already wearing comfy walking clothes, shorts, thin breathable top, and trainers with her hair tied up in a ponytail. She also had her sunglasses, sun cream, water bottle, and some snacks. Downstairs, her parents were in the living room discussing the set up with the removal company who had just arrived in the truck with all their stuff. Ellie went into the kitchen to fill her water bottle and see if there were any more snacks worth taking. Having decided that there was not, she headed back down the hall to the living room. "I'm just off out then," she called.

"Hold on a second," her mum called back.

Ellie waited, after a minute or two she came over to her.

"Ok, have you sorted everything?"

"Yes mum. There is a map on the bedroom wall for the furniture, I have my bag with water, snacks, sun cream, and my phone."

"Ok, well, have fun and be careful. We don't want any incidents on day one!"

"Incidents? What do you think I'm going to do? Knock the castle off the hill or something?"

Her mum chuckled, "No, nothing like that. Just look after yourself and be careful is all. Keep your phone on, don't know what time dinner will be but it will probably be takeaway anyway."

They hugged, Katherine kissed her daughter on the cheek and with a wave to her dad who was busy discussing sofa arrangements, Ellie left to explore the new village she would now call home.

It was a glorious day, the sun was shining, the sky was blue and there was a gentle breeze. The Fields' new family home was on Fords Lane, a road that was nearer the top of the hill than the bottom, but a country mile is further than a city one, and it would not be a gentle stroll to the top of the hill. Ellie started off by walking up the road and then at a junction noticed that there was a public footpath that led up away from the road through some more rural looking land. She climbed, it was quite steep here and was soon having to put a lot of effort in to get up the hill. Ellie was reasonably fit, her efforts for the school football team as a midfielder last year had seen to that but this was tougher than she expected. After a while, she reached a bend in the path to the right, thankfully it flattened out a little, and she took the opportunity to turn and look around. The view was stunning, she could see for miles and miles of rolling countryside. The hill seemed out of place on its own, almost as if it had been pushed out of the ground at a single point. While the hill seemed lonely, it did mean the view was completely unobstructed. Ellie could see farmers going about their business, lorries and cars moving around on the roads below. Thinking to herself, I'm not even at the top yet, she pushed on. The path was now a small road with some driveways off it, some of the houses were huge and were all set up to take advantage of their part of the view. They all seemed to have been built at a different time, nothing matched. Ellie felt this added to the charm of the village. She reached a tarmac road and followed it to the left until another public path was posted to the right. A gravel road that was little more than a service road to the houses on it. This hill goes on for ever, was the thought most often crossing her mind, and she had a point. Through most of the walk she was able to see the folly, but it never seemed to be getting any closer. Standing proud on its hill surveying all below it. Eventually, the road stopped, and she knew she was nearing the end of her walk now. The ground had turned to grass, worn where it had been walked on but certainly had never seen a vehicle. The folly was close, and she could begin to see others walking round it at the top, like insects from this distance. She pushed on, until she finally had to walk up a steep bank past one final house and there it was. Towering above her on the crest of the hill, the folly. It looked smaller than expected. considering how visible it was from such a distance, Ellie recalled how it was visible from the motorway earlier, but still impressive. Clearly in ruins, its single tower stood tall with several window holes in view. Its single wall was slightly obscured by the top of the hill from this angle, but she could see the size of the stones that had been used to create it. Pausing only to take a few pictures on her phone, she moved around to a set of steep stairs that would take her to the very peak of the hill, the level that the folly sat at. First, she decided to take in the breath-taking views. In a compete circle, less the part blocked by the folly itself, Ellie could see for miles and miles. On all sides there were fields separated by roads, rivers, and canals. She could see trains, lorries, and other vehicles moving around. The world looked like a model village from up here, it completely staggered her. Then she turned to face the folly. The tower was indeed imposing from up here. The single wall with its single arch joined into it seamlessly, some steps running up next to it. She walked up the steps, the council had erected gates and fences to keep visitors safe, Ellie had not appreciated until now how high and how steep parts of this hill were. The folly had near vertical drops all around, it would be extremely easy for someone to fall if they were not concentrating. The folly had also had some fences put up, you could not enter the tower, and nor could you

climb on any of the walls or surfaces. Not that Ellie wanted to
climb but entering the tower could have been interesting.
She walked up to the gate closing off the tower from visitors
and peered inside. Dirty was the word that came to mind,
and not surprising really. Given it had no roof, open windows,
and was no doubt enticing for visitors to throw things
through the bars it was full of mucky grime and rubbish. Did
not do it justice at all. Why do people feel the need to post
things through every little box and hole they see, Ellie
thought to herself as she looked at some crisp packets and
drinks bottles. She looked up, craning her neck to see up the
tower, she could just see the sky through the top, the walls
were round all the way up with five windows spread around
them at about the halfway point. Turning, her attention was
on the single wall. From above, the folly would have looked
like an old-style lock, where the barrel sits at the top and the
teeth of the key slide into the vertical slot. The wall had a single arch in it, it was an odd design, it would never have been
wide enough to walk up and there was no sign of a doorway at
the top where it met the tower. It was not a particularly good
gateway or archway like you would see on larger castles, as
there was nowhere to walk to it from. It was on a hill. It was
literally a single wall, about the height of the average house
with a single archway in it attached to a tower. Built as a summerhouse, Ellie recalled from her research, and indeed what
the estate agent had said all those weeks ago. How? How was
this ever useful as that, Ellie tried to work out. She appreciated that it was a ruin, and parts of it had probably fallen
away but even so, it did not make sense. She walked back
down the steps to the level part at the top of the hill to look
up at the folly, whatever it was for it was pretty.
"Even as a lookout tower in medieval times, look out the
enemy will be here in a fortnight," she mused to herself out
loud. Taking out her phone to snap some more pictures, she
walked away from the folly towards the rocks and what she
assumed were cliffs. There were others climbing and sitting,
so it could not be that bad. After climbing over a few small
rocks, she found a nice sized one to sit on, and made herself
comfy. Looking out over the land below, surveying all before

her in the sunshine, she could get used to this. Taking her water from her bag she took a big gulp, it had been a tough walk, but it was worth it. Lying back on the rock, feeling the warmth against her skin where it had been in the sun, Ellie closed her eyes and listened to the world go by.

"You'll get sunburned if you stay here much longer," an unfamiliar male voice said.

Ellie opened her eyes, she still had her sunglasses on, so the owner of the voice would not know this. She looked up, there was a young friendly face beaming down at her, dark haired, sunglasses sitting on his small button nose in the middle of a round face; his white teeth shining through a genuinely nice smile.

"Sorry, who are you?" she enquired, at the same time as sitting herself up and turning to face the boy so he was not upside down anymore. She wanted to be friendly but firm enough to stand her ground should she need to.

"Simon, Simon Lesley," the boy said, tilting his head slightly as a gesture of welcome. "Mow Cop boy born and bred, surveyor of all things geek, and keeper of the sweeties." As he finished, he flashed a bag of sweets towards Ellie, a cheeky smile spreading across his face.

She went to take one.

"Uh-uh!" he said pulling the bag away. "Not until you tell me who you are lovely lady," his confidence and charm very apparent, he had clearly done this before.

"Eleanor, Eleanor Fields," she replied, mocking his tone. "New girl to Mow Cop, footballer, cross-stitcher, and stealer of sweets from cocky boys!"

She snatched the bag out of his hand.

"Hey!" he exclaimed.

"Well, that'll teach you to sneak up on girls and be cheeky," she took a single sweet. "I only like the cola bottles anyway," she smiled sweetly at him.

He smiled, Ellie took another cola bottle and gently threw the bag back to him.

Catching it, Simon laughed, "Well, you certainly know how to make an entrance don't you, where you from?"

Ellie concluded that this was a fair question, and if she wanted to make friends here, she had better start now.

"I'm from London, we have just moved here today, as in hours ago. Mum and dad are unpacking, and I've come to explore this beauty," she nodded towards the folly. "Clearly I fell asleep though."

She was right. The sun was still out but it had moved quite a way across the sky, Ellie could feel her skin was a little raw and tender as her clothes moved against it.

"Knew you were new here," Simon stated. "Could tell."

Ellie raised her eyebrows, "Oh, and how can you tell?" she enquired. This boy was treading a thin line.

"Quite simple really, I saw you walking out of your house with the removal van outside it, was on my paper round you see. Saw you leave and walk up the hill. I finished my round and was just enjoying the sun; I recognised your bag so came to say hello. Hello!" he smiled.

He did have a lovely smile, and he knew it, thought Ellie, but he was pleasant enough. "I see," she acknowledged. "So, I already have a stalker then do I?" she smirked.

"No, nothing like that. Honest!" he said, clearly alarmed.

"If you back pedal any quicker, you'll fall off the cliff," Ellie laughed. "I'm messing with you, it's nice to meet you," she offered her hand.

Smiling again, he took it, and they shook. "You too, Eleanor."

"Call me Ellie, all my friends do."

"Ok Ellie it is, Can I sit?" he asked, gesturing to the rock they were now both sharing.

"Of course, on two conditions though. One, I want to know about this folly and the hill, two, don't put the sweets away."

"Deal," he smirked. "Although I can only tell you what I know and hear about the hill, my family and I are not in the council, so we don't know everything."

He sat down; this last sentence had shocked Ellie though. Was this council a real thing, did they keep secrets from those not in it? She smiled, keeping her thoughts internal, wanting to keep him on side so she could learn from him.

He offered the bag of sweets, "What do you want to know?" he asked.

"Everything."

"Ok, most of this is stuff of legend and stories though, told so many times by different people, nobody knows what's true anymore."

"Ok, I just want to know as much as I can, imagine I know nothing."

Clearly seeing an opportunity to try and be funny, Simon began. "Ok, billions of years ago there was nothing, then one day, we all popped into existence..."

She pushed him gently with a giggle, he smirked.

"Ok, here is the real bit. The whole thing is based around the Man Of Mow, they are a set of rocks round the other side of the hill. Legend has it that this was once just a plane boring hill, until one day something happened that caused all these rocks to appear on top of it," he tapped the one they were on. "They are all from way down you see, scientists have tested them. From way below the Earth at ground level, never mind up here. Anyway, the legend has it that something happened, some kind of really bad thing happened, and the Man Of Mow was like a god type person, he pushed up the stones to protect us. To honour him, they were shaped into the Man Of Mow sculpture I mentioned. The council that is the council of keys are very secretive and have elected themselves protectors of us all. Acting in the service of the Man Of Mow." He looked at her to make sure she was still paying attention, seeing that she was he continued. "They are supposedly the keeper of the keys to the lock, the lock that is keeping us all safe."

Ellie was fascinated by this. "There is a sculpture of a man on the hill?" she asked, to make sure she was still following correctly.

"Yes, well, formation of rocks, sculpture is probably pushing it a bit. It's on the other side of the hill facing towards the future so they say." He looked at her, she looked perplexed, "You don't believe me, do you?"

She chuckled, "I do, it's just a lot to take in for a city girl isn't it? Legends, rocks, people that are made of rocks become legends. Rock legends in the city are the likes of singers and bands. Where does the folly fit in?"

Simon looked impressed, "Yes, it is a folly. Most new people don't know that. If you imagine looking at it from above, does it look like anything to you?"

She looked blank.

"A lock maybe?"

Ellie's eyes winded, "I guess it would look like a lock from above."

Simon continued, "Well, depending on what you believe, it is either a structure that is keeping our world safe from something else that hither-too has been kept at bay by the legends, tales, and characters of old. Like the Man Of Mow. Or..." he paused for dramatic effect. "It's a rundown building that someone rich built ages ago because they could. Given that nothing has ever happened, been heard of, or even been remotely interesting, I believe it is the latter."

Ellie agreed, as much as it would be more interesting to have the fantasy version, it was very unlikely. "So, it's most probably just a building that was once very pretty with amazing views that is now a ruin with amazing views?" she concluded.

"Pretty much," Simon agreed. "The Man Of Mow does look like a man from some angles though, has signs up naming him and everything. Want to see?" he asked.

Ellie could tell he was excited to show her, and she was genuinely intrigued. Glancing at her phone for the time, "Ok, you can show me now as I start to make my way down the hill. But I must warn you, if I find out you are part of some cult and all that other crazy stuff is true, and you try to bury me in rocks or something..." she paused, he was staring at her and in truth she did not really know what to say. "Then, you will, just owe me some sweets ok?" she laughed and stood up. "Now, where is this Man Of Mow bloke?"

Simon led her back passed the folly, down the stairs Ellie had walked up earlier and along a path by some more houses.

After about ten minutes, they had walked round an outcrop and the folly was no longer in sight. The view here was just as stunning though, out to the side that had previously been blocked by the folly.

"There he is," Simon stated proudly, pointing at what Ellie thought was just a pile of rocks.

"Where?" she asked with a tone of confusion in her voice.

"That's just rocks!"

"You have to look, really look," he took her hand and led her around the corner. As he did so, Ellie felt a twinge of excitement. He was lovely, and this was as if they had known each other for years. True enough, there was a fence around the pile of rocks and a sign that stated this pile of rocks was the 'Man Of Mow'.

"See it yet?" Simon asked.

"No, I see rocks."

"What about from this angle?" he was behind her now and was tilting her head gently to change her point of view.

This was an odd but nice feeling for Ellie. Then, there he was. The Man Of Mow, looking down at them as if he had been there the whole time. Not exactly a 'Man' in that he had been carved, but the rocks were stacked and shaped to give a body, shoulders, and a face including a nose.

"Yes! I see him," she exclaimed. "He is right there looking at us and the view, how did I not see that before?"

"It's all in the angle," Simon replied. "He is only visible if the angle, and the person, is right," He smiled at her.

Ellie smiled back, "Thank you for showing me this and telling me about the *legend* of the hill and stuff."

The emphasis that she put on 'legend' made him smile.

"It's been great to chat, Simon, keeper of sweeties," she offered her hand to shake it again, he took it.

"It has," he agreed, smiling. "Can I walk you home?"

Ellie had a feeling this was his plan all along, to chat and get to know her. Credit to him, it had worked. Normally she would say no, but he was easy to chat to, and as Sophie had pointed out, now was the time to change things.

"Of course, you can walk me home," and with that they turned and started to walk back down the path and down the hill.

As they walked, the conversation moved on from legends, rocks, and hills to more normal teenager conversations. Ellie learned that Simon was also an only child, was the same age as her and was at the high school she was soon to start at, Redwing High School which was a short bus ride away. This was a good thing; Ellie knew she would have to catch the bus but did not like the idea of getting on it knowing nobody. At least this way, Simon would be able to accompany her and introduce her to the school and the area. They carried on down the hill, the sun on their backs as they talked.

"Cross stitch?!" Simon teased. "Isn't that the thing that old ladies do with needle and thread?"

"I'll have you know it takes a lot of skill and can be very creative, I've made all sorts of hangings for the wall."

"Ok but still. Can I see them one day?"

"Is this your way of inviting yourself into my house one day? If so, you need to be nicer about my hobbies."

"Fair enough."

"But yes, it is what old ladies do. I learned from my grandma." Simon frowned at this; Ellie knew he had not meant anything by it though. They were reaching the last bend before turning onto Ford Street, Simon stated, "Next time you're up at the folly, face down the hill the exact way the wall sits. It cuts right across Ford Street, maybe not your house but close. That's cool."

"If you say so," Ellie did not really see what was cool about it though.

They rounded the corner, and she was surprised to see a group of people standing on the end of her driveway, talking to her mum and dad. They were standing in a semi-circle, with her parents at its centre as if they were presenting to them or something.

"I best stop here," Simon stated, a look of concern on his face.

"Why? My house is only just there."

"I know, but, that's the council I told you about, and mum says I'm not to speak to them."

This was odd, the boy who had seemed so confident not moments earlier, now appeared to fear four people in the street.

"Ok, if you say so Simon. Thank you so much for today, for the story, showing me around, walking me almost home, and of course the sweets."

She smiled kindly at him.

Simon smiled back, "My pleasure Ellie, give me your phone and I'll put my number in it, maybe we can hang out some time?"

"Sure," she gave him her phone and he saved his number in it, he handed it back.

"See you around new girl," he smirked, turned and carried on walking down the hill.

Ellie began walking down the road to her house. She really had enjoyed her day, already started to make a friend, learned so much about the hill, folly, and the Man Of Mow, all in all, a good day. The way Simon left was very odd though, there was no getting away from it. All over four people on the end of her driveway. As she got closer, she too started to have reservations about the four people deep in conversation with her mum and dad.

CHAPTER 5

Ellie walked the last hundred yards alone, her eyes not leaving the group that had congregated at the end of the driveway. Her mum and dad were facing four people, which appeared to be two women and two men all of whom were deep in discussion about something that she could not quite hear yet. As she got closer, voices became clearer.

"So, you will come to the next meeting?" the first man said, almost stating it as a decision.

"We will be there," her mother's voice replied, "all three of us as you have requested."

"Wonderful," a woman replied, the second from the end.

As Ellie reached the group, she was able to pass them silently and easily as they were all so deep in conversation, it was only when she passed them and turned into the driveway that her dad noticed she was back.

"Ellie, welcome home, we were just talking to the Key Council members, they came to say hello and invite us to the next meeting, isn't that lovely?"

"I guess so," Ellie replied. She moved between her mum and dad so was now facing the group of four. From left to right, she surveyed them, taking in as much as she could without being obvious. The first, a young-looking man with light coloured hair, fair skin and clean shaven, next to him were the two ladies. The first an older woman, a stereotypical grandma Ellie thought, white perm, frilly tops, and glasses on a chain that clattered against her necklace. The second woman looked younger, but her tall thin frame and skeleton like hands made it look as if her arms were older than her face. Finally, there was the old man to the right, he was bald with penetrating eyes that suggested he did not like to be messed with, he gave the aura of the leader, and he spoke with the most authority in his tone. It was he that Ellie had heard speak first, the one who had suggested they would be at the next meeting. The oddest thing about the group though, was not their age, hair styles, or even their clothes. They all seemed to be wearing typically normal summer clothing, shorts and t-shirts. The oddest thing was that they were each holding a wooden staff. Not a tall staff that reached their heads, but short walking stick style staff. All made of wood, all with the same handle, all of them were clutching them as if it were the most important thing in the world.

"Hello there Eleanor, sorry, Ellie," the old man to the right said.

She turned to look at him. "Only my friends call me Ellie," she stated coldly.

The man did not react, her dad did though.

"Eleanor Fields don't be so rude," he scalded. "I'm sorry Douglas, she just has difficulty with new faces."

Before Ellie could react to this, she was not happy that her father had not defended her, Douglas replied.

"Quite alright, quite alright," he said, in exactly the tone of voice Ellie had expected. One of age and boredom of the young. "I'm used to this sort of tone from the youngsters in the village. They see an old man and immediately jump on the offensive," he looked at Ellie, staring right into her eyes. "Yes, almost the same as the rest, but clearly has the potential for so much more when it comes to manners," he finished off. Ellie had never heard anything quite so rude in her life, at least not with her own ears anyway.

"Maybe," her dad replied. He was clearly agreeing with the man, Douglas, but there was a tone in his voice that suggested he wanted to move on quickly.

"Anyway, we best be carrying on, lots of boxes to unpack," her mum interjected, almost as if she were sensing the tone as well.

"Yes of course," the man on the left answered. "But one last thing." As he finished this sentence, he revealed from behind him another staff, identical to the ones being held by the four council members. "This is for you," he offered his hand with the staff in. Ellie's dad took it. The moment that he did, all four council members stated as one, as if it were a chant:

"The staff is accepted. The council accepts you, and you accept the council. If you need the council, it will be there, equally, if the council needs you, you will be there. The legend will carry on, the prophecy will be fulfilled, and the obelisk is safe in the hands of its new owners. The Man Of Mow will be pleased his legacy and protection will endure for eternity."

Then, with a bow and a smile that would have been pleasant if not repeated exactly on all four faces at once, they turned, and walked single file up the road behind the older man, Douglas.

The family were stunned. Rooted to the spot all three of them simply stared up the road after them and watched. Finally, Katherine spoke.

"Well, that was, er, a nice welcome," she said. With the shakiness in her voice that was less than convincing. "Let's go inside and have a cup of tea."

With that, they turned and entered their house. As soon as they were inside and the door was closed, all three of them burst out laughing. Ellie collapsed on the floor, her mum leant against the bannister and her dad the door. It took a few seconds before any of them could speak normally again.

"I have never seen or heard anything like that before," her mum said, in-between giggles.

"It was ridiculous, they were perfectly lovely and normal until that speech at the end," her dad agreed.

"I understand why Simon didn't want to come and say hello now," Ellie added. This caused the laughter to stop.

A small smile creeped across her parents faces as they looked at her.

"What?" she asked.

"Made a friend already have we, and a boy at that!" her mum teased, jabbing her in the ribs.

"Yes actually. I met him up the hill, he told me about the hill, the folly, the Man Of Mow and how he protects us and that the folly is a kind of lock and the Council of Keys are self-appointed guardians and everything," Ellie retorted, confidence all over her face.

"Well," her dad said, "Simon was certainly telling the same stories that those numpties were. There must be something in the water round here. Still, at least we know what the obelisk is now," he looked at the staff in is hand. He offered it to Ellie. "Here you go lovely."

"Wow thanks dad, a stick!" she replied with a sarcastic grin. This caused fits of laughter once more.

Eventually her dad lent the staff against the corner of the wall by the door, then they all filed into the kitchen for a cup of tea together for the first time in their new home.

The next week or so followed a similar pattern. Unpacking and sorting with a little bit of exploring and just generally settling in. Ellie showed her parents the folly and told them the same stories and information that she had been told. There were two things they all agreed on, first that the views were stunning from their new village, and second that the stories were crazy. None of them believed that what they were hearing was true, it could not be. As they worked on the house, the staff they had been given was moved into the garage, disregarded as anything important. The stone statue that Ellie had seen on moving day did attract some interest though. Initially, they tried to move it, they attempted to dig down beneath it to allow them to hoist it out and move it out of the way, but it went down too far. They concluded that there was no way it had been put there by the previous owner, it was too deep. They decided to make a feature out of it. Ellie and her mum went to the local garden centre and bought some bedding plants to go around the stone, removing all the moss and older plants that were around its base to try and tidy it up. Once done, it did not look too bad, as it was a light grey in colour, the bright coloured plants did make it look like a decent feature. Indoors they added homely touches; family pictures and selfies, old and new, along with new furniture and styling meant the Fields family had really started to make a house a home. In Ellie's own room, she had changed her bedding to match the pastel walls, her new bookshelf was near the window covered in her significant collection of books. She had spent many an evening on her window seat, reading or stitching, she had created a cross stitch picture of the folly, brilliant blue sky behind and the green of the hill below. Underneath she had written the date they moved in with the caption 'The Fields Family Folly', even though it was not theirs so to speak, she felt the naming worked. The amount of space she now had was fantastic, and she loved having so much space and time to do her own thing in. Something she was particularly pleased with though was a picture she had hung in the hallway on the first floor. In a local shop she had bought an ordinance survey map of Staffordshire, and then cut out the section that covered the village, with the folly right in the centre. Marking their new home with a little black cross, and underneath the image on the border had written 'We lived here'. It was presented in a beautiful frame and hung with pride.

"You really are very creative and thoughtful," her mum had mused when Ellie had hung it on the wall.

"Very tasteful," had been the reply from her dad.

Ellie did not mind that they had both been busy, she knew there had been a lot to do. She herself had been occupied and quite enjoyed sorting out the garden and her room. The shed she did not enjoy, it had taken several trips to the tip to empty it of the rubbish that had been left, and nothing remotely interesting had come of that little exercise. Occasionally she would exchange messages with Simon, and on a weekly basis she would have a video call with at least one of her friends from back in London. She enjoyed the video calls, she could show off her room, she even did one from the folly just to show Sophie the view from up there.

The summer holidays were coming to an end, Ellie was getting ready for her first day at her new school. She would only have one year to endure, pass her exams and then the choices were hers. She had arranged to meet Simon for the bus on her first day, he had agreed to show her around, introduce her as best he could and be her 'friend' for the day. She was beginning to warm to him, he was friendly, admittedly she did not currently have anyone else to compare him with but still. Her mum and dad had also not mentioned him much, they were leaving her to it which she appreciated, he was just a friend, but she did not really want to have to deal with teasing this early on. Finally, the time came to be ready for school, that night she packed her bag ready and got her new uniform hung on the side of her wardrobe. It was not that bad - black blazer and skirt with the school crest on, white shirt with clip on tie, black shoes with black tights. Ellie did not really wear makeup or nail varnish, so the rules around not having them were not really a problem to her. Typical school uniform really. She wandered over to the window seat and began to ponder what tomorrow would be like. Would it be a good first day? Or one of those horrendous ones where she felt like the outsider? Maybe they will think she is part of the cult? Would people avoid her the way Simon avoided the council? She hoped not. After a little while she decided to go to bed, drawing her curtains on the setting sun, she got under the covers and turned off her lamp, eventually she drifted off to sleep.

That night Ellie dreamed of her new school, that the day started well on the bus with Simon, but when she got to the school everyone was being split up. As she walked towards the main entrance there were two doors, one for 'Others' and one for 'Council Contacts'. Simon had to go through the door labelled for 'Others', and she had to go through the one for 'Council Contacts'. Once through, she saw there were only about ten people in there, all her age, but none of them with faces. She had to sit in a circle and listen to them as they chanted, it started as a rhythmic noise, drawing her in, and then expanded to be more of a song. It took her a while to register the words, but when she did, she recognised them immediately:
"The staff is accepted. The council accepts you, and you accept the council. If you need the council, it will be there, equally, if the council needs you, you will be there. The legend will carry on, the prophecy will be fulfilled, and the obelisk is safe in the hands of its new owners. The Man Of Mow will be pleased his legacy and protection will endure for eternity."

At first, Ellie tried to resist the urge to join in, but she found herself swaying along with them, gently left to right and then she began to chant along with them. As much as she tried to stop herself, she could not. Then she realised that all the others in the room were looking at her, even though they had no face she could tell, and they were all pointing their wooden staffs at her. Chanting louder and louder. Then they all stood up, and started walking towards Ellie, she tried to stand up, to run, to flee the room and escape but she could not move. Her body would not respond, all it would do was gently sway from left to right as she chanted the same lyrics over and over. As the group grew closer to her, the tips of their staffs almost touching her face, she finally was able to say something other than the chanting lyrics. She screamed, "STOP! I DON'T WANT TO BE IN THE COUNCIL OF KEYS!"

They stared at her. With a throaty cackle, the group stopped chanting and quickly thrust their staffs towards Ellie's face. Then she woke up. Covered in sweat, but safe, sat bolt upright in her bed.

Ellie, not surprisingly, did not get much sleep after that, her alarm woke her at six AM, by seven she was showered, dressed, fed, and ready to walk out the door. Her mum and dad had already left for work, leaving a note wishing her a good day. She picked up her school bag and lunch, then headed out of the door. It was a lovely morning; the sun was warming even this early. She rounded the corner to the bus stop and was pleased to see Simon there. As soon as he saw her, he smiled his trademark grin and beckoned her to him.

"Where have you been hiding?" he asked in his casual way.

"Nowhere, just been busy unpacking and sorting, you know how it is," Ellie replied. "You going to show me the ropes today then. Look after me? Make sure I don't get lost?"

"Of course I will."

She pointed at him, "Good. Because I have told my dad you will so if anything happens to me, it's you he is coming after," Ellie retorted with a grin.

The look on Simon's face changed slightly.

"I'm messing, why so serious Simon? That's it! That's your

name from now on, Serious Simon!" she grinned and gently pushed him.

His expression softened.

"The bus will be here soon," he said, clearly keen to move on. "We are the only people in the village at our school, so it will just be us until we get further down the hill."

"Sounds good, any tips for a girl on her first day?"

Simon considered this for a moment, "Just be yourself. Don't try to impress anyone, buy anything, or agree to join any clubs. Everyone will be wanting you in their clique, group, or team, just relax and enjoy it I say."

Whether he meant it or not, Ellie thought this was good advice. "I can do that," she grinned. Just then, a blue bus appeared around the corner, it stopped in front of them and they entered. Moving to take seats about halfway back. The bus wound its way along country lanes, stopping off every now and then to let on varying numbers of children, some the same age, and some younger than Ellie and Simon. Simon acknowledged a handful of them by name, introducing Ellie to them as he did so. Ellie noted that his close circle of friends were Annabelle Jones, Tyler Harris, Daniel Simmons, and Leopold Johnson. All of whom were very friendly and chatty towards Ellie, even if they did tease Simon a little for not mentioning her over the summer.

"Keeping her a secret, were we?" Tyler joked. He was a stocky boy, muscly, which would account for him being so prominent in the rugby team. He was impressed with Ellie's football credentials though, saying "You'll need to try out for the girls' team, they normally do the try-outs in late September."

"Back off it's her first day," Leopold defended. "She should at least be able to walk in the door before you sporty lot get hold of her." He smiled at Ellie, she reciprocated in kind. "I'm Leo," he said, "I'm not sporty but if you need any guidance around the library, I'm your man."

Ellie chuckled at this, it was as if everyone was competing for her friendship or something. It felt good, she had never been in the new girl position before, maybe Sophie was right - she could be anyone she wanted to be. The journey passed by with everyone asking questions about their summer, what they were looking forward to and dreading most, Ellie's main contributions were that of explaining where she was from and what she had done with her summer. She soon established that Leo was the smarter one, Tyler was the sporty competitive one, Annabelle was always happy and giggly, and Dan was everyone's friend, always down the middle in agreeing with people. A nice group of people to make friendships with. When the bus finally pulled up at the school and they disembarked, Ellie stopped and looked at the building. It looked exactly as it had in the pictures and websites she had seen whilst her parents sorted her move here. A long brown brick building with big imposing windows. It had steps leading up to the main entrance with a grass bank either side, in that moment Ellie thought it looked rather pleasant and picturesque. The group moved forward, Ellie was not in Simons' class, but Leo was with her so agreed to take her through to meet the group and main teacher, Mr Johansen.

"He's alright really Ellie," Leo comforted. Ellie had given them all permission to call her Ellie on the bus, it made her feel more welcome. They walked down the corridor to Mr Johansen's classroom. As they entered, they were greeted by a tall man with a beard. He had a friendly smile with contrasting serious eyes.

He spoke with an accent Ellie could not place, "Hello and good morning to you both! Leo nice to see you've had a haircut this year and you must be Eleanor?" He smiled at her kindly.

"Yes Mr Johansen," she said politely.

He beamed at her, "Welcome to Redwing High, I trust your journey up and move went ok?"

Ellie thought he seemed very friendly, but even though she was sure it was not, his accent sounded fake as if he were putting it on. "Yes, thank you, been here a couple of weeks now and have settled into the house."

"Wonderful, in Mow Cop I understand? Been up to the famous folly yet?"

"Yes, a few times. It's lovely up there."

"Indeed it is, a great passion of mine is photography and there are many great things to snap up on that hill." He made a gesture of a camera, as if worried that Ellie would not know what he meant by snap.

"Yes, I've taken lots myself, really love it up there."

The phrase 'love it up there' hadn't been one she intended to say, it just sort of happened, was it too early to say that? Nothing had happened to mean she did not love it, so she decided it was ok.

"Well, we will do a little introduction when the class is here, but please make yourself at home." He gestured to the room, "This will be your base for the year, claim a desk, a locker and make it yours - without ruining it of course. What's the rule Leo?"

Ellie had forgotten he was there for a moment, "Nothing that can't be moved or changed easily." He mumbled.

"Yes, Leo forgot this last year, didn't you?"

Leo nodded. His mumbling now made sense. "I wrote my name in permanent ink by mistake," he admitted.

Ellie chuckled. He was a funny boy.

"Indeed, he did!" Mr Johansen replied in a voice that said he was not too pleased. "I'm sure Eleanor here won't make the same mistake?" he looked at her.

"No sir," she replied with a stern look on her face. She had no intensions of upsetting teachers on day one. She turned and moved through the room to find a desk to sit at, Leo followed and together they sat down at one towards the back. It was a typical classroom layout, desks big enough for two set out in rows facing the front. Mr Johansen was a maths teacher, so the walls were covered in maths problems, posters, and quotes. Maths had never been a strong subject for Ellie, she could do it, but not with ease all the time.

The room gradually filled until it was buzzing with teenage chatter. Most of her new classmates came to say hello, and those that did not Ellie chose to believe this was only because they were too busy chatting to the group they walked in with. Every school was like that, every class had its cliques that would stick together.

When the bell rang at nine, everyone almost immediately fell silent, turned and faced the front where Mr Johansen was smiling down on them all.

"Hello, good morning and welcome back! This is the start of your last year here and this year will shape your lives..." he went on.

Ellie concentrated for the beginning, listening to the time-table, how lunch worked, and the list of after school clubs and teams. The usual stuff. She began looking out of the window, and for the first time noticed that the folly was visible. From where she was sat, she could see it on top of the hill. For some reason she found it alluring, she could not take her eyes off of it. She was already longing to be back up there, remembering the last time she was in the sunshine.

"Miss Fields?" Mr Johansen's voice broke her out of her trance. She snapped her head around to face him, "Yes sir?" she asked, not having a clue what was going on.

"Thanks for coming back in the room."

Everyone sniggered.

"I was just saying how today was your first day, and I asked if you wanted to say hello and introduce yourself?"

Ellie had expected this to happen, but due to her daydream-ing it had now caught her off guard.

"Yes, errr hi," she said, standing up. Why have I decided to stand up, she thought as she did so. "I'm Eleanor, just moved here from London. Live in Mow Cop," she pointed at the folly.

"We know where Mow Cop is, we live here remember," a small ferret looking girl said at the front.

"Be nice Rochelle," Mr Johansen interrupted; this wiped the smile from the girls' face.

Ellie continued, "Well, we moved here through the summer for my mums' work. Most of the summer was spent organis-ing and sorting the house out. I'm looking forward to spend-ing my year here though, speaking to you all, making some friends and stuff."

She smiled at the room.

Most of the faces smiled back and mumbled positive things like "Welcome", "We will look after you," and "Relax, we don't bite." There were of course a few negative ones, Rochelle at the front was going to be a problem Ellie felt, she sat down.

"Thank you, Eleanor," Mr Johansen said politely. "We look for-ward to learning with you." Then he continued the usual first day of the year information.

The day moved on, Ellie spent most of it learning people's names and where everything was. As quickly as she had learned that the four people she shared a bus ride with could be friends, she also learned that Rochelle, the ferret look- ing girl with a pointed nose, blonde hair, and a cackle like a witch that interrupted her earlier was probably not going to be friendly. Unlike her classmates, this was not her fifth year here so knew nothing in terms of layout of the school. At lunch, Ellie and Leo met up with Simon and the others. They all sat around a table in the canteen together discussing the morning's events. Ellie was really beginning to feel that she could settle in here. The six of them shared stories of teachers and classmates, it was a nice way to pass the time. After eat- ing, they moved outside, the group led by Simon showed Ellie around the grounds, the football pitch, tennis courts, and so on, it really was a lovely school, although Ellie did long for her friends from London occasionally. They sat down on the grass, it was a beautiful late summer day, they chatted, Ellie shared more about herself, her family and what life was like in the city. They were as fascinated by life in London as her friends in London had been about life in the village.

"So that's about it. We moved here, settled in, and I met Simon on the hill by the folly. He bribed me with sweets and here I am." Ellie smiled at Simon as she said this, she did have fond memories of the sweets.

"He never gives us sweets," Tyler interjected. "Git," he play- fully pushed Simon to the ground. They all laughed, even Ellie.

"Yes, well he gave them to me, and was a perfect gentleman until he saw the council on my driveway."

The silence that fell over the group at this was deafening. It was as if all the noise and air had been sucked out of their lungs and the school. All noise seemed to stop as they looked at her, staring. Tyler and Simon stopped wrestling, Simon lift- ing himself up to look at her.

"You've met the council?" Annabelle asked, a shaky nervous- ness to her tone. It was the first time she had not had a beam- ing beautiful smile on her face, Ellie really noticed that on this occasion.

"Well, they came to our house and spoke to my mum and dad, I only saw them for a minute or two. Why?"

"Nobody here has family on the council, they are seen as a weird group almost like a cult that nobody can chose to be a part of, nor can they choose to leave," Tyler stated, a similar nervousness to his voice.

"What do you mean, nobody can choose to leave?" Ellie asked, this sounded more like a wind up than anything else. "Are you trying to wind me up on day one? Pick on the new girl?"

"No, I promise you this is not a wind up, if we were going to tease you, we would pick on your accent or something more fun," Annabelle attempted to reassure.

"The council are just weird," Simon said. "They are closed off; they seem to choose their members for their meetings. Unless you are in the group, you don't know exactly what happens or why, we all know the stories, but nothing for real. Be honest, nothing good ever came from a closed off group did it? A group that is shrouded in secrecy and keeps everything hidden?"

He looked at Ellie with a piercing look, almost daring her to challenge him.

"I guess not, but they seemed harmless enough?" Ellie was less sure of herself now, she had little evidence to decide on this, but why would this group of people here and now lie to her?

"They go around, they choose their members whether they like it or not and pull them into their cult world. They worship the 'Man Of Mow' and all sorts of weird stuff," As Tyler said this, he waved his arms around theatrically.

"What stories have you heard then, give me some specifics?" Ellie challenged the group, they looked back at her, as if nervous of speaking out loud what they wanted to say.

Dan, who had been silent until this point, spoke first. "Ellie, all we know is the stories that are passed around through families. That group, the Key Council, have been around for hundreds of years. They get together, they chant, they talk about the Man Of Mow as if he is real, like they believe him to be a God." He paused. Looking around the group to see if anyone else wanted to take over, silence. He continued, "They believe in the legend that long ago the hill didn't exist. That it didn't exist until a terrible demon or spirit threatened the world. Back then, the villagers witnessed the creation of the hill, they believed that the Man Of Mow saved them. That he created the hill, in his honour they then built the folly and carved the figure on the far side of the hill as a tribute to him. The council that you saw are the chosen ones, the ones that carry this message on today," he sat back, as if exhausted by the revelations he was sharing.

"So, you're telling me, that the council that I met are the chosen group that carry on this cult message? Some crazy story about a legend of a man making a hill, that is honoured with a folly and a rock face? All because he supposedly kept us safe from something nobody remembers?" Ellie played it back exactly how it was in her mind. She expected at least a chuckle, nothing.

"Basically, yeah," Simon said plainly. "All we are saying is be careful, I know it sounds like a load of nonsense but ask anyone! They will tell you the same, they can't be trusted and are dangerous. Did you not feel anything odd from them? Nothing in your gut as you saw and spoke to them?"

Ellie considered this, given the reaction she had been given in the last few minutes, how much should she share? The chanting, staff, the mention of the obelisk in the house paperwork? She did not want to alienate the only group of people who showed any interest in being her friends so early on! "The older one looked at me weird, he commented that I had lots to learn when it came to manners. That wasn't great, oh, and they chanted some song and then walked off in a single file line. We were in hysterics for ages about that, strangest thing I have ever seen." This at least was true, but she decided to keep the staff and obelisk talk to a minimum for now.

"See," Tyler exclaimed. "Weird! Who chants and walks in a single file line? Nobody!" He slapped his hand down on the ground, as if he were judge in a court somewhere and his fist was his hammer, closing the issue for good.

The group chuckled a nervous laugh together, then Annabelle said kindly, "Just be careful Ellie, we don't want you to get caught up in something that isn't fair, or right is all."

"Thanks, I will," Ellie replied. She agreed that it was all a bit odd, and was thankful that they had talked to her about it so early in their potential friendship. The conversation moved on, Leo explaining how the textbooks they needed had changed and Annabelle explaining what her drama class productions would be for the year. All in all, a lovely school Ellie concluded. The bell rang indicating it was time to go back to class for the afternoon, they went their separate ways, Leo leading Ellie to French class, with them all agreeing to catch up on the bus after school.

The afternoon passed by with little incident, other than making a fool of herself with her apparent poor French speaking and being made to do an experiment in front of the whole class in Science which she did not appreciate. The teacher, Mrs Simmons, had meant well but it was embarrassing on day one. When the final bell of the day rang, Ellie made her way to the front entrance, down the steps and towards the bus stop. Leo was with her as he had been all day, he seemed excited to have a new friend. They were the first to arrive, but the others soon followed behind. After a short wait, the blue bus arrived, they got on and this time sat on the back row as a six, Ellie really felt like she could belong in this group of friends. As the bus once again wound its way along the country lanes back home, she watched as people got off gradually, as well as chatting occasionally she also could not stop thinking of the conversation around the council. Should she be worried, or could she just relax and let it go? She may not have a choice, her parents would no doubt be making that decision for her soon. Ellie and Simon were the last two left on the bus, they would be for the whole year.

"First picked up, last off," Simon said as they stepped off the bus together a little while later.

"I'm more used to getting a tube to where I need to be, much more efficient I think," she smiled.

"I would offer to hang out," Simon said regretfully, "but I need to get back tonight I'm afraid."

Ellie believed him, there was a small paranoid part of her that thought he was avoiding her after the conversation at lunchtime, but she decided to ignore it. "No problem, we will hang out loads I reckon anyway," she replied with a smile. She meant it. She had enjoyed her day with him and his friends, her friends, their friends. "Thank you for looking after me."

"No problem, I'll get you added into our chat groups as well, everyone liked you, so you can join us all now." He smiled, winked, turned, and started to walk towards home.

Ellie did the same, as she turned around the corner back down her street, she pondered the day's events. A good day she concluded. She entered the driveway, her feet crunching over the gravel, put her key in the lock and opened the door. Walking through the hall and into the kitchen where her mum was waiting for her, with a wide grin on her face.

"Ellie! Welcome home. Did you have a good day? Made any friends? I want to know everything. But you will need to be quick, anything you can't fit into an hour will need to wait. You have a council meeting to go to."

CHAPTER 6

Ellie was stunned. With all the thoughts flying around in her head it was all she could do to stand up right, not shout and scream, or run away from her mother at this revelation. This meant she had no time to contemplate what she would say or do, no time to work out what to share with her mum and dad, no time to talk to her friends some more about it. This was the definition of being thrown in at the deep end. Eventually, after what seemed like an eternity, she spoke, her mouth dry from shock making her voice croak. "I have a what?" was all she could manage.

"A council meeting, you remember. The group that came to see us and left us in fits of laughter? Well, we had our first invitation, and it is tonight. Your father and I didn't think it would come round so quickly, but it has. Isn't it nice to be included in things so early on in our time here?"

Ellie pondered, her mother had always been able to see the positive, if she had not heard all the other stories Ellie herself had experienced then why wouldn't she be excited to be included in the meetings? "Oh, that's err, great!" Ellie tried to fake enthusiasm; it did not work. "Why just me though?"

"It's not just you, it's all of us but I can't make it. I will drop you off and you will meet your father there. Whatever is the matter young lady? Here you were worried about fitting in, meeting people, being an outcast, and now when we get invited somewhere with minimal effort, you seem so uninterested anyone would think I just asked you to clean your bathroom. Which by the way could probably do with doing as well."

There was a cold look in her mother's eyes, Ellie did not wish to upset her parents, she loved them very much and had in-

deed been happy here over the summer, even made friends
and had a good first day at school.

"I know mum, I know," Ellie frantically tried to work out what
she should say. Everything? Nothing? Surely something was
better than nothing? Would she believe her if she did tell her
everything? "It's just, don't you think it is a little strange?"
Her mother stared her down.

"You know, strange that we have been invited before anyone
in the village even really knows us? Why would they want our
opinion or views when all they have to go on is a conversation
at the end of the driveway where, as far as I can tell, you and
dad were *told* to come to the meeting rather than *asked*?" Ellie
emphasised the words 'told' and 'asked' as much as she dared,
she had seen this look in her mother's eyes before, and it was
one that meant be careful.

"Well, that's one way to look at it isn't it," there was a harsh
tone to her mother's voice, Ellie knew there was more incom-
ing. "Or we could look at it that this *is* their way of getting to
know us? Inviting us to a meeting where we can see the sort
of thing that happens in the village? Understand the views of
the people, the events, the setup, the culture? Could it be possible that they just want us to feel welcomed?"

Ellie had no answer, her mother continued.

"The country is different Eleanor. Out here people talk, support each other, know each other, and work with each other.
If we refuse to go, we could get excluded from everything
and then we will be the outcasts in the village forever. Is that
what you want? Do you want us to be lonely and left out?"

"No, I Just..." before Ellie could finish, her mother interrupted.
"Well, we just need to go along with it. Honestly, you have
been brilliant and so supportive until now. Was that the plan?
To play along and then make it difficult for us? It won't work
Ellie, it just won't. We are here now, and we are going to make
this our home! Do you understand?"

Ellie was stunned by this. She had never dreamed that her
mother would take this so far so quickly, of course she did not
want to make it difficult. "No mum, I just thought it was a bit
odd is all. I love it here, I really do, I've had a great summer and
a brilliant first day, and I really feel that this could be home

for me." This was true, but she knew that it now had lost some of its credibility given the conversation they were currently having.

"Yes, well, maybe you should lead with that next time," her mum replied, clearly hurt by the whole situation. "It wasn't easy for us either you know, I've taken a huge risk bringing us here, it is all on me. If I fail, we fail, I need you all on my side we need to be a team to make this work Ellie."

Fear was seeping into her voice now; Ellie had no idea her mother felt under so much pressure.

"Mum, I am on your side. I think it's amazing what you have done for us, we are a team, we will make this work and I promise I believe every word I am saying, it just caught me off guard is all." Ellie knew she had to back down, there was a real danger of causing a major melt down between the two of them if she was not careful. She went and gave her mother a hug, which to her relief, was reciprocated. "Love you."

"Love you too, Ellie, more than you will ever know." They stood in silence for half a minute or so. "Now, why don't you tell me about your day before we go?"

With all the commotion, Ellie had almost forgotten that she had been to school, all the positive energy had been drawn out of her with the debate with her mum. She composed herself, sat down on a stool at the kitchen worktop, and decided to share some of the day's events. "It was a good day, Simon looked after me and introduced me to his friends. I think I will fit in well with them, a real nice bunch ranging from sporty competitive to smart and everything in between. They are all clever though. I spent most of the day with Leo as he is in my class, he is always reading it seems."

Her mum smiled at this, "See, we knew you would settle in."

"There is one girl who seemed to have a problem, Rochelle, Leo said not to worry about her as she is just one of those girls who likes to be all about 'me' and stuff." Ellie flicked her hair mockingly at this. They both chuckled, the tension from a few minutes earlier seemingly to have dissipated.

"Good, well, I'm glad you had a good day. Now, go and get changed ready for the meeting, your dad will meet us there."

Ellie stood, smiled, and left the kitchen. As she made her way up the stairs and along the hallway, she thought to herself did she do the right thing? Should she have told her mother about everything? Would she have believed her? By the time she reached her room on the top floor she had decided that she had made the right decision, she would go there tonight with as much of an open mind as she could muster and go from there. It could not be that bad, could it?

Ellie got changed out of her school uniform which she hung neatly on the wardrobe and into some leggings and a top. It was still quite warm so did not want to overdo it. She decided to put her hair up, felt it made her look more official and important. It also made her feel ready for action for some reason. She went downstairs and into the living room to wait for her mum who she could hear getting ready upstairs.

"Ellie, can you get that wooden stick thing out of the garage please, we need to take it apparently," Katherine called down. "Ok," Ellie called back, she did not want to touch it, feeling doing so was accepting everything that everyone had told her. Moving into the garage through the door under the stairs, she picked it up. Turning it over in her hand, she examined it, wondering who would own such a thing. It was plain. A simple looking staff made of wood, smooth all the way down. At its tip that touched the floor was a rubber stopper to protect it from the ground, it made it look like an upside-down pencil. Turning it over to examine the handle end, she noticed a small engraving. Near the top of the staff, on the rounded edge was a small symbol, about the size of her thumb nail. It was a circle, with a capital 'M' in the middle, but written in the way you are taught to write as a child with the sides straight going up at an angle leaning inwards. It would only look like an 'M' when the staff was vertical though, otherwise it looked like three lines forming triangles in a circle. Ellie tried to think where she had seen this before. She focused on the symbol, staring at it. The realisation hit her like a truck. The symbol on this staff matched her window. The round window above her seat in her bedroom, the only window in the house where the folly was visible. She ran out of the garage and up the stairs back to her room, she needed to be sure.

Panting, she held the staff up to compare it to the window. She was right. A perfect match. Why did this feel so connected to her? She was missing something she knew it. She sat on the end of her bed, the staff across her lap and put her head in her hands forcing herself to think. She knew there was something she was missing, something that made the connection. The window. The staff. The council. The house. If the first realisation in the garage had been like a truck this was like a train.

"The Obelisk!" Ellie shouted out loud. She had not meant to, but it was as clear as day to her now. The paperwork her parents were reading mentioned how they would own an obelisk; the council had chanted about the obelisk being safe with its new owners but only after this had been given to her dad. The symbol on it matched the window because the previous owner was in the council. She recalled the line on the chat room site she had seen, 'nobody ever leaves that village', it had said. She was starting to scare herself now, could all this be true, or was it just her mind running away with her? Here she was, holding a staff with a symbol on that matched her window, a staff that had only been given over to her dad after they had moved in and the council had seen them. Once they had, they chanted and said it was safe now. Ellie kept playing these facts over and over in her head. Was it true, or was she just filling in the blanks, adding two and two to get five?

"Ellie!" her mum shouted from downstairs, breaking her concentration. "Where are you it's time to go. Did you get the staff?"

"Yes, mum. Sorry. I was just, looking at something."

She did not know what to say, this had hit her for six as her dad would say being a cricket fan. What should she do? She looked out of the window, the sun had gone in now, behind some grey clouds, reflecting her mood perfectly.

"ELLIE!" her mother's voice rang out again, louder this time.

"Coming," without thinking, she stood up, went to her drawers and got out a jacket, threw it on and ran down the stairs clutching the staff, what should she do now?

She did not have a lot of time to think, no sooner as she had made it downstairs, she was ushered into the car by her mum and they started driving. Ellie sat in the front passenger seat with the staff upright between her legs staring at the symbol on the handle. It was almost hypnotising. The more she stared at it, the more she got confused and tied herself in a knot. Had they really come all this way and got drawn into a cult? She would rather deal with weirdoes on the street any day. They drove through the country lanes; it was only a five-minute drive but was still very twisty down the village roads. "You're very quiet, everything ok?" her mum asked.

Ellie, not for the first time today, was speechless. "Yeah, I'm fine. Just wondering if I over think or whether there is more than meets the eye at times. How do you tell mum?" Ellie did not expect a detailed answer, it was not even a real question, more just something to say to break the silence.

"Not sure I know what you mean? But I try to take things on face value for what they are as I see them, when I see them. Does that help?"

Ellie wanted to say no, as it did not. "Yeah, I guess it does," she pulled her eyes away from the staff and looked out of the window, it was a lovely late summer evening, the sun just starting to drop below the horizon.

After a few minutes driving in silence, they pulled into the car park of the village hall, a small building, clearly only made up of one room with a small reception area. It was also apparent that they were not the first to arrive, there were other cars on the car park, lights on in the hall, and faint sounds of talking coming from inside.

Ellie and her mum got out of the car, glancing at her phone Katherine said, "Dad won't be able to make it, he is stuck at work." She looked at Ellie, "So it's on you to fly the Fields flag tonight, ok? Can you do that for us?"

Ellie smiled a forced smile, "Ok mum, let's do it."

She did not feel she had a choice, knowing what happened at home in the kitchen, she could not challenge her mother again. This was far from an ideal situation though.

They linked arms and walked across the car park to the hall entrance. Ellie did not know what to expect, but she was not prepared for what greeted them as they entered the hall. The room was rectangular in shape, they entered at one of the shorter sides. The voices stopped as soon as they had been noticed in the doorway. In the middle of the room were a circle of chairs all facing inwards, they approached the circle.

"Hi," Katherine said, in attempt to sound friendly.

Ellie felt there was a small tone of nervousness in her voice, she was not used to her mum sounding unsure or nervous about anything. She squeezed her arm to try and reassure her. As they walked towards the circle they were greeted by Douglas, the council member who had challenged Ellie on her manners previously.

"Good evening to the Fields, well, two of them anyway. Will the third be joining us?"

"I'm afraid not, he has to work late, and I have to go, but Ellie is here and ready to join in." Katherine replied, keen to show her strength. "Will the rest of the village be joining?"

Ellie could tell there was now more hope in her mum's voice than anything.

"No, no. Just us. The Key Council is made up of five families, you are the fifth to arrive tonight so now we can begin. If we have one member of your family here, we can proceed. Having the youngest member is always our preference anyway. At least with only one of you here, we no longer need to choose," he smiled. Not a warm smile, but a more of a scheming smirk. "Please sit," he instructed.

Ellie turned to her mum, gave her a hug and whispered, "Love you".

"Love you too," she replied, pulling away. "Nice to see you all again, but I have to go. Have fun! Call us when you need picking up, Ellie."

She turned on her heel and left the hall. Ellie moved into the circle and headed towards one of the three chairs that had been left vacant for them, before Ellie sat, the younger man who had given her father the staff spoke.

"Please align your staff with ours on the floor."

Ellie looked, on the floor were four staffs laid out making the outline of a square, like a box. "Where does ours go, you already have a square?" she asked.

"The fifth to arrive is the wall, always, please put it on the corner facing your chair so it points towards you."

Ellie did so, she placed the end with the symbol on touching the corner of the square and the bottom end pointing at the chair she was going to be sitting in. Once done, she backed towards her own chair and sat down. Only then did she make the connection between the shape on the floor and what he had said. 'The fifth to arrive is always the wall'. It was a crude version of the folly, if seen from above. The box representing the tower, and the final staff the wall. She looked up and scanned the other members around the circle. Unlike on the driveway, where they had seemed odd but kind, they now seemed intimidating and forceful. Ellie was very much aware that everyone was watching her, it was as if she were on display and being examined. She could not remember ever feeling as uncomfortable as she did now, this was worse than standing up in Mr Johansen's class earlier.

"Hi, what happens now?" she asked timidly.

"Now, we welcome you and explain what it means to be a part of the Key Council. You will need to remember and pass on the messages to your family, for you are their representative here, the responsibility of the Fields family rests on your shoulders, Eleanor." It was the older woman who had spoken, the one who looked like a grandma to Ellie's eyes. She was sat two seats away to her right. "First though, we will tell you who we are."

Ellie shifted in her seat, "Ok, looking forward to it," she lied.

The lady continued, "I'm Beryl. I live in Church Street; I am in council position one. It is always I that will speak first to start the meetings off."

Ellie nodded, taking in her long necklace and glasses that sat on the end of her nose.

"I'm Kenny," the man between Ellie and Beryl stated. "I live in the lane behind Wood Street. It is a road that is hard to pass, but I like the privacy. I am in council position two, I always greet new staffs to the group," he gestured towards the arrangement on the floor.

Ellie looked at the floor, could this get any weirder? They all looked at her. Silence. Ellie waited for the next person to speak, then she realised it was her. They had sat her in a chair and gone in a circle and an order to her. She decided to go with it.

"I'm Eleanor, I live on Fords Lane, and I am in council position... three?" she finished the sentence with more of a question to the room to make sure she had it right than anything else.

"Yes, you are," Kenny jumped in. "As position three, you will always be at the centre and keep us balanced, two of us to your right, and two to your left," he smiled. It was not that friendly but was the friendliest yet.

Ellie questioned herself, had she really just said that? Like a robot in the room, was this her being inducted into the council without her realising?

The lady to her left spoke next, she was the younger of the two women but had the skinny frame that made her look frail and weak. "I am Hannah, I live behind the campsite, and there are no roads to my abode. I am in council position four, I am the one who will ensure our members are eligible," there was a glint in her eye at this, as if it were a threat or a suggestion of power and control. This made Ellie feel uncomfortable.

Finally, Douglas spoke. "I am Douglas, I live on Sands Road. I am in council position five. I am the instigator and leader of the council. It is I that will call meetings and lead us through the will of the Man Of Mow."

This was the first reference to the Man Of Mow, and it hit Ellie like a bolt of lightning. How many more would there be?

"Now, welcome Eleanor," Douglas spoke directly to her. "Now you know our names it is time to tell you of the legend, the story, the great message of the Man Of Mow."

"Man Of Mow," everyone repeated. This shocked Ellie, they really were a strange bunch of people. She focused, she needed to stay in the zone for her parent's sake, and she needed to tell them everything. After glancing round at the room, she focused back on Douglas.

"Are you ready to be shown Eleanor? To be shown how you fit into our world?" Douglas' eyes were penetrating, so intense they were exhausting to look at. She became aware that everyone was looking at her in the same way.

"Yes, I'm ready," she said in the most confident way she could.
"Good, then we shall begin. Our story begins hundreds of

years ago, when there was nothing here but a hill, a lone silent hill with a few small huts around it. It was a peaceful time, a time when everyone worked together for the better of the village. Our tale focuses on the creation of the council, the ones who created the laws that we abide by, the ones that summoned the Man Of Mow and begged his help to rid them of a terrible evil. This story has been passed on into legend through the generations, and we uphold it still today."

Ellie looked at him, it was an odd feeling, she was fascinated by what was being said but she also wanted to burst out laughing.

"There was a darkness over the village, animals were disappearing, people were acting strangely, and a nervousness was growing amongst the villagers. They sought the knowledge of their spiritual leader, for it was believed he would know the cause and how to protect them. He consulted the stars, the fire embers, and the trees to work out what the cause was. He decreed that the hill had become a gateway from our world to another, and something had come through from the other side. He did not know how or why, but he knew what they needed to do. He decreed that the man under the hill, the man who had pushed up from the centre of the Earth to create it had chosen them to protect the world. The Man Of Mow. He traced the chain of events back to the birth of a child. He calculated that the child had been born on the first full moon of winter, and it was at this moment that the creature had passed into our world. He believed, and indeed convinced the village of the same, that they needed to give up the child in order to protect the world. He gathered four people, the five of them together would be the first council. They decreed together that the child should be given up for the good of the people. They created five keys, five keys that we symbolise with our staffs here today, five keys that would help keep the creature at bay. One dark but clear winter night, they positioned the five keys around the hill in places specifically chosen. The child was taken to the summit and at the stroke of midnight a great storm stirred, blasting the hill and returning the creature to its own world, taking the child with it. The council decided that the keys would keep it at bay, but keys need a lock. They created the folly on the hill in this shape," he pointed at the floor. "This shape is a specific shape. It is the shape of a lock, the wall is exactly on the north to south line, and the exact angle the child was laid. It is that folly that keeps the gateway closed, that with the five keys around it keeps us safe, that folly and its keys keep the other world away from ours, and in doing so they created the Council of Keys. They must be at their strongest for the first full moon of each winter, for that is the time that darkness is stronger. We are the descendants of those people, passed on through generations to ensure the five keys are kept secure, for if they fail, it is believed that the lock will also fall, and evil will once again be a plague on this Earth."

He stopped, as suddenly as he has started and looked at Ellie. Ellie looked back; she was lost for words. She did not know what to say or do, this was completely bonkers. She chuckled, "You're serious? You believe that a child was sacrificed in order to protect us from a demon or something?" she looked round the room. Nobody was smiling. Her own smile immediately faded.

"This is no laughing matter, child," Beryl said sternly. "You must help us uphold the law of the Man."

Kenny interjected, "We know how this sounds, in truth, we all sat where you sat, and we all thought what you are thinking. It does sound crazy, but it also fits. I'm sure you know the rocks the folly is made of are not found on the hill? That the wall does sit perfectly north to south?"

Ellie, without thinking, nodded, "It does match what else I had heard, but that doesn't mean..."

"You doubt us?" Hannah interrupted incredulously. "You think that we would make this up and tell the same story over and over just for our own amusement?"

"No, it's just a lot to take in," Ellie defended, feeling she may have overstepped. "What exactly do you need from us, as a family I mean? How can we serve..." She braced herself, "The Man Of Mow?"

They looked at Douglas.

"You will need to keep your obelisk safe; you need to wear the emblem with pride, and you must attend our meetings," he stated to Ellie. "Most of all, you must believe."

"What emblem?" Ellie asked, "I haven't seen an emblem?"

"Yes, you have," Beryl replied. "Have you not looked at your staff? Or the window in the topmost room of the house you now live in?"

Ellie's mouth fell open, "You mean, the circle with a 'M' in?" she asked. Almost dreading the answer as she did so.

"Yes, but there is more to it than that. It is a 'M', but it is inside an 'O' and when viewed upside down, the 'M' becomes 'W', completing the symbol of Mow," the old lady concluded.

"M.O.W." Ellie repeated out loud, "The symbol of Mow is on those staffs and in the window of my room?"

"She finally gets it!" Hannah exclaimed excitedly, a smile on her face. "We all have the symbol somewhere, I have mine on my wrist," she showed Ellie her left wrist. There was a tattoo there of the symbol. "Douglas' is on the chain around his neck, Kenny's is on his ring and Beryl's is on her bracelet." As Hannah explained this, they all showed her the symbol, offering up arms and jewellery as if to prove the point. "You will have yours somewhere. Think Eleanor, think, focus on the symbol and it will come to you, they always do."

Ellie did as best as she could, she focused on the symbol, closing her eyes to allow her to think on this. She felt ridiculous, sat in a circle with these strange people, around some sticks closing her eyes to picture a symbol. She slid her hand inside her jacket pocket, she had gone cold for some reason. Her fingers on her right hand felt something in her pocket, a chain, a thin chain. She pulled out whatever it was and looked at it. A gold chain, thin and fine with a single charm dangling from it. A single gold circle, with a 'M' in it. Ellie could not believe what she was seeing. How had this got there? "This is some kind of magic trick isn't it?" she asked the group in hope.

"No, no trick, this is you being accepted into us," Hannah explained. "You finally see that you have been chosen, the Man wills it, and his will is the only way. You will be tested, we will all be tested, and he will test us. You came to us, you have chosen us, and you have chosen to support our cause. You will hold a key to our future."

This last phrase stunned Ellie. She could not figure out why, but she felt like she had heard it before, somewhere, but where? She could not take it in. It was too much, she was staring at the symbol dangling on the chain, absolutely stunned as to what she was holding and hearing. She lowered her hand, allowing the chain to gather in her lap. Ellie knew she was trapped, nobody would believe her, and her new friends would most likely freeze her out for this. She would become an outcast almost immediately. What would she do?

As if reading her mind, Beryl spoke up. "Do not worry child, we know what you are thinking. You are wondering how people will believe you? Or how you can share this? Or even how you can escape from us, the council? Am I right?"

There was a knowing look in her eyes, she was right, and she knew it.

"Yes, I'm feeling a little overwhelmed right now," Ellie answered. There was no point in lying about it, she knew it was written all over her face.

"Well, do not worry," Beryl continued in what she no doubt believed was a caring tone. "We are here to support and help you, on the noticeboard in the corner you will find a document that will help, go and look."

To Ellie, this felt like an instruction rather than a request. Without thinking about it, she stood and walked to the board on the wall near the corner, until now she had not noticed it. As she walked across the room, her shoes seemingly painfully loud in the silence, Ellie could feel four sets of eyes burning into the back of her head. She got to the table. It was covered in leaflets, letters, and flyers. Glancing over them they ranged from bus timetables and prices, to local gardener and dog walking services. There were window cleaners, decorators, plumbers, and babysitters, all advertising themselves to the village. Ellie scanned the board, it was so full with no obvious order to the posters that she did not know how she would find the one Beryl had referred to. She refused to give up, she would not give them the satisfaction of asking for help. Then, she saw it, right in the middle but slightly hidden behind a poster for a gardener and the opening times for the village shop. A single piece of paper with handwritten fancy calligraphy on. It had to be it. It was so out of the ordinary compared to the rest it just had to be. Ellie reached out and took it from the board, it felt old in her hands, felt older than it looked anyway, what she imagined parchment would feel like. She glanced down at the paper and read to herself:

The rules of council are as follows:

1. 5 members are needed at all times, meetings cannot begin until all 5 are present.

2. Members staffs must be placed in the lock formation, the 5th to arrive is the wall.

3. Only 1 person from each key family is required to attend meetings, where possible, this should be the youngest in the family to ensure longevity of membership.

4. Members of the council must always be available to it and its members.

5. Once chosen and inducted into the council, members may not leave.

6. Council property, including the keys and lock, must be protected at all costs.

We protect the will of the Man Of Mow, all council members agree to uphold his rule, beliefs, and follow his guidance. Most of all, all agree to protect the keys and the lock from harm. Any failure to follow these rules, or protect the keys and lock, may result in the lock being opened, and irreversible damage being done to our world.

Ellie lowered the paper. This was getting seriously out of hand, she thought to herself.

"Now do you see?" Douglas' voice called over to her. He had not moved, but the room caused it to echo and he had deliberately spoken loud and clear for real dramatic effect. "This is no joke Eleanor. This is real, you are with us now and us with you. We are the Key Council, and we will protect the keys and lock."

Ellie, turning to face the group, had nothing. Words failed her, she had never felt so scared, trapped, intrigued, and confused at the same time. She did not know what to say.

"It is up to you who you tell what to, you have all the informa-

tion, and you know the legends, the truth now. It is up to you,"
Kenny said, he seemed the most rational of the group, if that
was possible. "But they are binding, those rules are what keep
us safe, before you share them and anything else you have
learned tonight with anyone, think on this: will they support
you, or try to tear you down? Ask yourself that one question
and you will know what to do."

Ellie knew what that translated to. I can tell people, but will
they believe me, she thought. In silence, moving back to the
circle of chairs she realised the position she was in. She either had to go along with it or run. She did not really think
running would work. If only her mum or dad had been able to
come, if only they had been here to witness this. She looked
down at the piece of paper in her hand, without knowing
it, she was holding it in the same hand as the necklace and
charm, as if subconsciously she had chosen to pair them.

She was startled out of the mini trance she was in by the door
opening behind her, and footsteps moving across the hall towards the group. Everyone looked round, except for Ellie, she
was too focused on the paper and charm, mesmerised. Only
when a voice spoke, coupled with a hand resting on her shoulder did she look round.

"Sorry I'm late, what did I miss? Has Ellie been joining in with
the meeting?" her dad said, looking down into his daughters'
eyes.

Ellie had never been so relieved to see someone, she wanted
to stand up, hug him, and tell him they needed to run. But
she could not, either through her own decision making or the
sheer volume of pressure she felt under, she was frozen to the
spot. She quickly, and without really thinking about it, turned
the piece of paper over in her hand so the rules of the council
were hidden, and the paper itself covered the charm from
view.

"No problem at all Nicholas," Douglas said. "We have only just
finished introductions and were about to move on to item
two on the agenda."

Ellie looked at him, then around at the group. In an instant, the tone of his voice and atmosphere in the room had
changed. It had lifted as if they were in darkness and now

someone had turned on the light. Ellie, in shock at the sheer boldness of this man to change so quickly, started to speak. "Item two? What about introductions for my dad? Surely, he needs to know who is who and what is what before we proceed?" she was determined to get her father to see.

"Of course, how rude of me," Douglas replied politely, this was the politest Ellie had ever seen him. "Your family is the fifth member of our little gathering, to my left is Beryl, next to her Kenny with Hannah just there, and of course I'm Douglas. Together we are the Key Council, and we handle small things in the village."

He smiled first at Nicholas, then at Ellie.

Ellie noticed a flicker across his face, almost a flash warning to her as he did this. She knew she was beaten. They had clearly done this before, all the members of the council were now smiling brightly and pleasantly, welcoming and warming.

Nicholas sat down next to his daughter, "Right, well, all sounds good so far."

For a moment Ellie thought she may have a way out, all she had to do was get the piece of paper in her hand to her dad. Before she could act on this thought, Douglas intervened once more.

"My apologies Nicholas."

"Call me Nick."

"Of course, Nick, here is a copy of the agenda. I could see Ellie was about to give you hers, but we like to ensure everyone has a copy."

He stood and crossed the circle handing Ellie's dad a piece of paper. Unlike the one in her hand, it was crisp and new. Ellie's heart sank, she felt utterly deflated at this point.

"Ok, I'm up to speed. Do you use the staffs to make sure everyone is here or something?" he said. As he did so he held the paper at an angle that Ellie could see, it had nothing more than a council meeting agenda on. Listing item one as 'welcoming new members to the council'.

"Yes," Douglas replied. "It is an old tradition that symbolises that we are all here, when we should be," his eyes fell on Ellie, a small smirk crossing his lips.

Ellie, not knowing what to say or do, sat in silence, as the facade of the meeting carried on into the night, discussing homeowners' extensions and the villages' bus routes. She was the only one that had witnessed the initiation ceremony, that felt like the only thing could she describe it as.

CHAPTER 7

The meeting finished late though Ellie did not really pay much attention, she spoke when she was spoken to and answered a few questions, she was happy to sit in silence though. Happy to sit and try to work out exactly what she was letting herself in for. She sat there for nearly three hours, pondering silently about her plight, getting herself more confused and worked up by the minute. Allowing her eyes to move from the staffs on the floor, to her fellow members, to her dad, and back to the paper again. She had no choice. There was no way to signal to her father and he would not believe her after the meeting had finished. Why would he? Since he arrived the council had been friendly, inviting, and chatty. Normal. When the meeting finished, he shook hands with Douglas.

"Thank you for inviting us so early in our time here in the village, we really appreciate it, helps us settle in."

He put his arm around Ellie as he finished this statement, this made her feel even more uncomfortable.

"Of course, think nothing of it," Douglas replied, an apparent genuine smile on his face as he said this. "We are only happy to help induct new people to our little village and into our world."

He glanced at Ellie; she knew that last part was for her benefit alone.

"Ellie is normally chattier than this, what's up with you?" her dad asked. This was a problem, she could not tell the truth, but could not lie either.

"Sorry, I just felt it was more grown up talk so left it to people that know what they are doing." This was in part true. She had felt that way when they had been discussing bus routes and home builds, she had no interest in that at all. "I guess I was chattier when we were just talking about us, as people, and the things we like to get up to, to pass the time, that was before you got here dad," she stared at Douglas during this last part, she wanted him to know that she would defy him and be as strong against him as she could.

"Well, we shall see what the next few meetings bring, won't we?" there was a coldness to his voice as Douglas said this.

Ellie concluded that he had dealt with situations like this before.

After a few more pleasant goodbyes, Ellie was ushered to the door by her dad, across the car park, and into the car. Never had she been happier to be in a car. Nicholas got in the driver seat, started the engine, pulled out of the car park and headed towards home. It was dark now, the beams of the car headlights lighting the hedges on the side of the road as they went along. In her pocket, she clutched the necklace and symbol tightly. She dare not lose it, but she needed to decide what to do with it.

"So, did you have fun?" her dad asked, breaking the silence.

"Fun isn't the word I would use dad," Ellie replied, "It was, interesting."

Well, that was dull, she thought to herself, hardly a cry for help was it.

"Interesting eh? Should have told your face that, you looked positively zoned out at times this evening."

"Sorry, lots on my mind, I guess. Missing home, new friends, new school, wooden sticks," she held up the staff. "It's a lot to take in."

This was at least partly true.

"How was your first day at school then, friends? Enemies? Lessons? Anything exciting to report?"

"It was fine, made some friends who I think I can fit in with and stuff, lessons were ok, nothing too extraordinary there to be honest. As for enemies, not really, not yet anyway."

"Yet?"

"There is one girl, Rochelle, who may be a bit of a bully but nothing I haven't had to handle before."

She smiled to herself, this made her feel strong. Also, compared to the council, Rochelle would be a doddle.

He chuckled, "Don't do anything I wouldn't do."

They carried on the rest of the journey in silence, just the noise of the car for company. When they eventually arrived home, the house was in darkness.

"Your mother will already be in bed, we can tell her about our evening tomorrow, can't we?"

This was good news, at least Ellie knew she would have some time to process all this and work out what to do next. "Ok, dad. Tomorrow it is."

They got out of the car, walked across the driveway and into the house. Once inside, Ellie took off her jacket and went to go upstairs.

"Aren't you forgetting something?" he said, stopping her on the bottom step.

She turned to face him, he was holding the staff out to her, beckoning her to take it with her.

"Shouldn't this be with you? Council member?" he smiled.

Ellie knew that he meant well, and that he did not mean it the way it had sounded, for without knowing it, her father had sounded just like a council member himself. A creepy, self-indulgent weirdo. This was her dad though; he did not mean it that way.

She took the staff, "Thanks."

With that she turned and moved up the stairs to her room.

Once in her room, Ellie quickly got changed out of her clothes and into her pyjamas. She felt that changing was one way to get the feeling of intimidation off her. She picked up a fresh notepad, pen, the necklace, staff, and headed over to the window seat. The window that she now knew had the symbol of Mow in it for all to see. She lay the staff on the bench, then got on and sat next to it, legs outstretched but comfortable. Resting her notepad on them, holding the necklace between her fingers behind it, she began to write. She needed to record everything that had happened and been said. She started at the beginning, the staffs on the floor. She moved on to cover the way the council introduced themselves, the rules, the chanting, and finally right the way through to how they changed when her dad had arrived. At the back, she made notes on the staff, necklace, and the symbol. She drew a version of this next to it, large and filling the remainder of the page. Ellie was even able to write down the four streets that the council members lived in. Church Street, behind Wood Street, behind the campsite, and Sands Road. She lifted her head up from her notepad and looked out of the window. The folly was there, as always, on top of the hill, this time lit by the moon behind it. It looked pretty but foreboding at the same time, creepy and peaceful all at once. The wind rustled in the trees, the stars twinkled, and Ellie wondered if anything would ever be the same for her again. After a little while of staring through the window at the darkness, she decided it was time to go to bed. She moved the staff into her wardrobe, standing it at the back, put the notepad in her bottom draw behind some clothes, and left the necklace on her bedside table. She would decide on that tomorrow morning. Finally, she got into bed, turned out the lamp, and settled down to sleep.

Surprisingly, Ellie slept all the way through to her alarm going off the next morning. No dreams, no cold sweats, and she felt refreshed as if the previous day had never happened. Maybe it had not? She thought to herself, had it all been a dream? The thought of this sent a comforting warmth through her body, but it was short lived. She looked over at the bedside table and saw the necklace. To her dismay, it was not a dream. Ellie showered, dressed, and went down to make herself some breakfast, she had a little time before leaving for the bus. After eating some toast on her own, her mum and dad had already left for work, she went back upstairs to finish getting ready. She did her hair, ponytail again this morning, put on her tie, and was done. Heading over to the bedside table to pick up her phone, she saw the necklace again, as if was taunting her. She decided not to put it on today, nobody would know would they. She concluded that today was Friday and as such would be a good day. She was going to meet

Simon for the bus, then her new friends on the way to school, have a good day, learn something new she hoped, and come home to have an awesome weekend. Less the decorating that had been spoken about lately. She turned on her heel and headed out of the house.

The day was typically uneventful for a Friday, especially a Friday that was the second day back at school after the summer break. The teachers at Redwing High were quite relaxed, but they made sure that the pupils knew this would not last forever, and from Monday they would have to knuckle down and work hard. Ellie had decided not to share the previous night's events with her friends, she had concluded that it would be better to wait to freak them out for at least a week. Ellie had spoken to Annabelle as much as she could today, given they were the girls in the group, she wanted to get close to her. Annabelle was lovely, her glasses always sat well on her face and her smile was infectious. Ellie thought she was beautiful and was pleased to have been accepted by her into the group most of all. As she met Simon first and felt a stronger connection to him, she created a scheme to spend some time with him and get out of some of the decorating at the same time. Ellie was given homework for Maths, English, and Science in her first two days, a large portion of which needed to be done over the weekend. As such, on the bus on the way home, after the others had got off, she decided to chance her arm with Simon.

"Simon, what are you doing this weekend?" Ellie asked casually, not taking her eyes away from the passing fields.

"Not much, homework, bit of family stuff I think but nothing major, why? What's up?"

Ellie looked at him, "Nothing is up, I just wondered if you wanted to hang out, maybe do homework together, and go for a walk or something? What do you think?" she blinked, smiled, and flicked her hair through her fingers as she pulled it out of its ponytail. May as well try this cute thing occasionally, she thought to herself.

He stared at her, "Sure, that'd be great. When shall I come over?"

Ellie smiled; she had got what she wanted. "Well, I need to get out of decorating first, so, why don't we say tomorrow morning, I'll text you a time tonight and then we can go from there? Thinking homework first, then a walk? Sound good?"

"Sounds perfect," Simon replied, a cheeky grin growing across his face.

They spent the rest of the journey chatting about this and that, when they eventually made it to their stop and got off the bus Simon hugged Ellie goodbye. They were on hugging terms now it seemed, it took her by surprise, but she did not mind it. They went their separate ways. Ellie, with a little grin and cheeky skip to her walk, incredibly happy indeed. What she did not know, is that Simon felt the same way.

Ellie walked her happy walk home, all things considered it had been a good week, crazy council people not included of course. Being the first home, meant she also was not grilled on her obvious good mood, catching sight of her own face in the mirror, even Ellie had to admit that she was beaming. She made herself a drink of juice, then went upstairs to her room. She put her bag on the bed, took off her uniform to swap it for more comfy clothes. For the first time in a while, she decided she wanted to stitch. Unsure of what to stitch, she took her bag of materials, her phone, and drink back downstairs again and into the garden. It was a pleasant evening and she wanted to make the most of tanning herself on a patio chair with the sun on her back. She put some music on her phone and began. First removing some plain material and blue thread. Being her favourite colour, she nearly always started with blue. Looking round the garden for inspiration, her eyes fell upon the grey stone spire she had first noticed on moving day. It looked picturesque now, with the flowers planted by Ellie and her mother. As a crazy idea, for there was no other ideas around, she decided to stitch the grey spire. Complete with the sky above and flowers around it. It'll be quirky, she thought to herself. So, she began, starting with blue sky. This hobby was very therapeutic, but also time consuming as a lot of hobbies are. By the time her father had got home an hour and a bit later, all she had done was the sky and the grey stone itself.

"Hardly a masterpiece, yet," she had said to him as he came to say hello.

"Knowing you, it will be soon," he replied kindly.

She packed up her things and followed him into the kitchen, Ellie wanted to discuss food. "What's for dinner?" she asked, getting right to the point.

"What would you like? Chilli, fajitas, spaghetti, or beans on toast?"

This last suggestion was not a serous one, but Ellie's father suggested it every time he was asked what was for dinner. It was in reference to a time when this was the only thing Ellie would eat. She was six.

"Ha ha ha," she replied sarcastically. "What time's mum back? If we don't know, I say chilli. It can sit and stew then, it will get more flavour as it infuses."

This last part was said with a flourish, mocking her dad's favourite cooking show.

"Sarcastically said, but true. Ok, teamwork it is. You chop the veg, I'll get the pan on and start frying stuff. Deal?"

"Deal!" Ellie loved cooking with her dad and doing so in a kitchen as big as this one where there was actually space to move was so much easier and way more fun.

They worked together, chopping, frying, and mixing as they went to get the flavours right.

"The secret to a good chilli," her dad started to say.

"Is dark chocolate," Ellie interrupted. "I know dad."

She got some from the cupboard and broke it into pieces to go in.

"Indeed. I have taught you everything I know it seems, my young apprentice," he bowed as he said this, again mocking the same shows.

They giggled.

"Dad, how much work are we doing on the house this weekend?"

He looked at her, squinting, he knew there was a reason for this question. "Why? What are you wanting to do missy?"

"I have loads of homework, and I was going to ask Simon over to help me. Maybe hang out with him a little? Please? If I do that tomorrow, I promise I will help decorate all day Sunday. Pretty please?" she smiled her sweetest 'daddy please let me do this' smile.

He examined her for a moment, "Simon eh? Do I need to give him the father talk?"

"No. He's just a friend, really dad, just a friend."

"Hmmmmm. Ok. If your mother agrees then yes that's fine with me, but Sunday will be a full day, so be ready!"

Beaming, she hugged him, "Thanks dad. You know I just want to settle in and make friends, to make a life here."

"My turn," he said. Then changing his tone continued, "Yeah, yeah, yeah, I know," he said mocking her. They both chuckled at this together.

There was a strong love between Ellie and her father, they understood each other and were a team in every sense of the word. The evening flew by, and before long they were sat around the table as a family discussing their respective weeks whilst eating dinner. Ellie had started to discuss the topic of the weekend's plans with her mother.

"Well, given that your father has already said yes, I think I better say yes too," she exclaimed, shooting a look at her husband. Then it softened. "That said, I do actually agree and think this is ok, *if* you keep to your word and help us on Sunday, *all* day Eleanor."

Being called by her full name always made Ellie take note, it usually meant this was serious. She straightened her back up and looked at her, "Yes, I promise I will help all day Sunday. Thanks mum," she beamed at her parents.

Her mother smiled back, "No problem. Now, have we got everything we need Nick to decorate this weekend? Paint? Brushes? Sheets? All the fun stuff."

"Yes dear, we have it all in the garage, I picked it up this week," there was a mocking drone to his voice, Ellie chuckled to herself as she noticed this.

"Good, tonight I will start clearing the rooms, or at least moving everything into the middle of each."

They were going to decorate the whole of the downstairs this weekend, the idea being that it would be easier to do before they got too settled in and had furniture everywhere.

The meal continued, and the conversation moved on to work and school, to Ellie's relief, they did not quiz her too much on Simon or her weekend plans. After pudding, Ellie helped clear the table then announced she was going to go upstairs and work on her cross stitch, as well as some of her homework. After going upstairs, the first thing she did was message Simon:

Hey Si, all clear for tomorrow, homework, walks, and chilling! Wanna come over in the morning, say half 10? x

She threw her phone onto the bed and headed over to her window to finish stitching the stone in the garden, moving onto the green and brown ground around its base, it was starting to take shape, a bit of colour always helped. After about fifteen minutes her phone beeped a text alert.

Hey, yeup sounds good, I'll be there with stuff in hand to help us learn! Then we can go hang out somewhere. See you in the morning x.

Ellie smiled to herself, boys were still strange to her, but this one was cute and sweet. He could be a good friend indeed. She returned to her window; she was determined to make some steady progress on her design this evening. Ellie sat and stitched for a few hours, interrupted only by getting a drink or her parents coming to chat about this and that. She was quite happy in her own company most of the time. With a glance at the clock, it was now ten o'clock, she decided to call it a night. The design had taken some real shape, it had soil, plants, and some green all in there now. She left it on the bench, closed the curtains and got herself ready for bed. Setting an alarm for eight, she wanted to be up and ready for Simon, she turned off her lamps and settled down to sleep.

Ellie drifted into a sleep filled with dreams. She was in the classroom at school, surrounded by her new friends. Simon, Leo, Tyler, Dan, and Annabelle. They were sat in a circle, just like at the council meeting, except all wearing pyjamas.

"Welcome, Ellie," Simon said in a voice that did not sound like his own. "We are here to welcome you to the Council of

Friends, today, we induct you into our ways, and you accept us as we do you."

"I am ready," she heard herself say, in a robotic voice as if she was distant to herself.

Her five friends chanted together, "Welcome, Eleanor Fields, you are the sixth member of our friendship council, and as such, you must jump from this table to the next table."

Ellie looked down, she had now moved to be standing on top of a table, facing another table with a small gap between them. To her left were Tyler and Annabelle, Simon, Dan and Leo to the right, all clapping slowly and chanting "jump, jump, jump."

Ellie looked back at the table she needed to jump to, it seemed further away now.

"Mind the gap!" Leo screamed with laughter.

"Careful you don't fall into the bottomless pit," Tyler shouted. The chanting and teasing was getting louder.

"She's scared to do it, maybe she isn't worthy of us after all?" Simon joined in to roars of laughter from the rest.

The chant in the room changed, "Not worthy, not worthy, not worthy."

"I AM WORTHY," Ellie screamed, they immediately went silent. She took a deep breath, stepped forwards, and jumped. For a moment, she felt like she was soaring through the air. Her arms outstretched and her legs kicking off from the table below. A surge of positivity charged through her; she was going to do it. She would make the jump to the next table and be accepted once and for all. Then, disaster. She was falling, at first, she was falling level with the ground, as if she were going to land on it flat on her stomach, but then she twisted into a dive and was heading face first to the floor. She stopped. Frozen in mid-air, slowly rotating so that she was facing the ceiling. A she looked up; the faces of her friends came into view. All showing the same sort of look – disappointment. In turn, they all tutted, shook their heads and left.

The last to leave Ellie's view was Annabelle, she looked right into Ellie's eyes with her own deep brown eyes. "I have never felt so sad, disappointed, and let down all at once. Just when

I thought we could be friends; we could have had something amazing you and I."

With that, she turned and left Ellie's field of vision.

"No wait! I can do it! I am worthy, I am worthy! I can fit in, let me try again!"

But it was no use, they did not come back. Ellie started to turn towards the ground again, facing the hard-grey floor of the classroom. Then, without warning, she fell towards the ground. Ellie braced herself for the pain of hitting the floor. Then she woke up, covered in a cold sweat sat bolt upright in bed. It was three AM.

"Well, that was new," she said to herself out loud.

After sitting for a moment to adjust, she decided to get up for a drink of water. After doing so and getting back into bed, she turned over to try and settle back to sleep. Why did her dream focus on proving herself to her friends? Why did it focus on Annabelle? Why were they all in pyjamas? All these thoughts were pinging around her head as she slipped back to a restless sleep.

CHAPTER 8

The alarm woke Ellie at eight, she snoozed it. Then again at nine minutes past. And then eighteen minutes past. The clock said twenty-seven minutes past before she finally thought she should probably move. Lifting her head from the pillow, she caught herself in the mirror. Ellie did not like her first woke up look on a good day, never mind on a day when she wanted to be up and at it. Before moving from the bed, she briefly recalled her dreams from the night before, her friends initiating her, teasing her, rejecting her. The looks on their faces still made her shiver a little, the pure negativity in them was horrible. She shivered, and in doing so seemed to clear her mind a little of these thoughts.

"Shower, dressed, breakfast," she stated to herself out loud. "Lot's to do today."

Moving from the bed she headed to the bathroom to get ready. A short while later after showering, Ellie was dressed and sat at her dressing table doing her hair and makeup. It was only nine, she had loads of time so was taking her time to do what needed to be done. She looked to her right in the mirror and jumped, her dad had appeared behind her.

"You made me jump, dad."

"Sorry Ellie, didn't mean to. I just wanted to see if you were ok, we heard you calling out in your sleep last night."

Ellie did not know what to say to this, she knew of the dream but not that she had called out that loudly. "What did I say? I can't remember much of the dream," Ellie lied, she could remember most of it in vivid detail.

"You kept shouting that you were not worthy, that you would try again and could do it. Ring any bells?"

"No, not really. I remember being in a room, sat in a circle, then I woke up covered in sweat."

Ellie knew she had to tell her father something, he knew her too well.

"Ok, well, just a dream remember."

He moved across the room and smiled at her, perching on her seat next to her he put his arm around his daughter. "When did you become so grown up? You used to be my little Ellie-Bear, you'd tell me everything and I'd be able to fix everything."

Ellie snuggled into him.

"I'm so proud of you, but you will always be my girl, you can tell me anything," he smiled down at her.

"I know dad, you'll always be my hero." Squeezing him tight, she looked up, "But I need to finish getting ready now."

With a final squeeze, he stood up, "I know, you have a date," he winked.

"It's not a date, dad," Ellie replied indignantly pushing him gently, "Simon is just a friend that I am trying to get to know so I'm not lonely up here on this hill."

"Fair enough, well, I'll leave you to get ready. I need to get ready too anyway."

"To decorate?"

"No, to welcome Simon to the home, I've dug out my golf clubs and baseball bats to be stacked by the door. Just in case," he smirked.

Ellie knew he was joking, "Dad, honestly, this isn't the nineteen twenties you know, there will be no need for any bats."

"Ok Ellie, ok, I'm going now," he turned and headed down the stairs.

Ellie turned back to the mirror to finish getting ready. She did love her father, and his eccentric ways of showing affection.

Around nine thirty Ellie was downstairs and eating breakfast, Simon had already messaged saying he was still on for ten thirty and would be there around then. She could hear her mum and dad prepping the other rooms for a weekend of decorating. Looking out of the window, she could see it was a sunny day, perfect for going out later. She was excited about today, other than the homework bit of course. Ellie went back upstairs to make sure everything was tidy, could not have Simon seeing her room in a state. Fortunately, she was a tidy person generally anyway, so it was neat already. She did however decide to hide the necklace, just in case. She picked it up and moved it into her jewellery box. After she was satisfied that the room was ready, she moved to her window seat to do some more on her stitch design of the garden stone. She was not nervous about Simon coming over at all, but this would help settle and clear her mind. The time passed by, Ellie went into her trance that she goes into when stitching, peaceful, chilled, and focused. A short while later, there was a ring of the doorbell. Ellie quickly put down her work, and moved across the room, down both flights of stairs to get to the door first. She knew that her parents would not move that quickly to get to it, they were busy painting. She opened the door.

"Serious Simon," she exclaimed, beaming at him.

"Smelly Ellie," he shouted back. There was a moment's natural laughter between them.

"Come in, I'll introduce you then we can go upstairs."

Simon entered, "Ok, sounds good."

"This must be the famous Simon we have heard so much about," Katherine said kindly as she entered the hallway from the living room, followed by Nicholas. They were both covered in a little paint, but not enough to not be polite and greet a guest.

"Hi Mr and Mrs Fields," Simon replied, "nice to meet you." He extended his hand and shook both theirs.

"Call us Nick and Katherine, please," said Nicholas kindly. "Mr and Mrs makes us sound old."

"Fair enough, well, it's nice to meet you. Ellie has told me so much about you both, how are you finding the village?"

Ellie's mum seemed happy with this polite conversation, she smiled between Simon and Ellie.

"It is lovely, everyone has been so nice and friendly we have settled right in. Most importantly though, Ellie has settled in and has started to make friends, like you Simon."

He blushed slightly.

"Well, it is a friendly village generally, and Ellie is lovely so being her friend is a pleasure."

He smiled at them all, he knew how to play the parent pleasing game.

"Well, we have work to do and you have decorating to do," Ellie stated, keen to move away before it got any more personal or potentially embarrassing for her.

"Well, have fun kids. Welcome Simon make yourself at home," her dad said as he was ushered away by her mother back into the living room.

"Sorry about that," Ellie said to Simon, it was not that bad, but she was still a little embarrassed. "Drink?"

"Can we have tea?"

Ellie never had him down as a tea man, "Of course, best drink there is."

They went into the kitchen, Simon admiring the house as he went. "Lovely, really nice house you have here Ellie."

"It's not mine but thank you. I like it, well, I'm settling in."

She boiled the kettle and got two mugs out. She made the tea, and they went upstairs, Simon following behind as Ellie led him up the two flights of stairs.

"Wow, what a room," Simon exclaimed as he entered Ellie's bedroom, "This is huge and so cool."

Ellie smiled, "Thank you, it was my part of the deal. I agreed to play nice for the move if they gave me this room. I like it, and its mine."

Simon headed over to the window seat, he looked out, "Great view, and a great place to sit I reckon?" he looked down, noticing Ellie's cross stitch on the seat, he picked it up. "You weren't kidding, were you?" he asked turning to face her, holding the design.

"No, I wasn't! I enjoy it so shhhh," she replied harshly, marching over and taking it from him.

"Ok, I wasn't teasing was just saying. It'll look cool when it is done," he defended.

She smiled at him, "Ok, well, I think it's safe to say we know how to press each other buttons. So, shall we work and get this done so we can go and do something fun?"

"Yes, lets," he slung his bag off his shoulder onto the floor, and sat down cross legged to start work in front of him.

Ellie got her books and sat opposite him. "So, what first?"

They started with maths. Ellie and Simon worked well together, they seemed to naturally fit together as a team, complementing each other and filling in gaps in the others knowledge. Between them, including breaks for drinks and the odd snack, they had completed their homework within a couple of hours, after which, they decided to go downstairs for some lunch. Just like homework they worked together making sandwiches and salads for them both. With a side of crisps and cucumber sticks. Taking their feast into the garden, they sat at the table opposite each other.

"So that's what you're making a cross stitch picture of," Simon stated, he was facing the garden stone and had nodded towards it.

"Yeah, we've been trying to figure out what it is, at first we tried to move it, but it goes down too far. Mum decided to make a feature of it, covering it in flowers and stuff. I didn't really like it to start with, mainly because I didn't see the point, but it's growing on me."

"It is a bit odd isn't it, I mean, what does it do?"

"As far as I know, nothing. Never seen a bird on it or anything, it's just a stone. A large grey pointed stone that goes down deep. What garden isn't complete without one of those eh?" Ellie chuckled at this. "Anyway, what's your house like Simon? You don't really talk about your parents much either."

Simon stopped chewing at this, he looked at her. He swallowed, "That's fair. Although it's parent actually. Never met my dad. My mum, Gemma, has raised me on her own. I like our house, it's not as grand as yours but its home. I help around the house, always tried to act as the man of house so to speak, but it's hard. Think that's why I explore and go out so much, makes me feel free, I guess. I love my mum to pieces, and I'd do anything for her. We were both abandoned by the same man, but I don't remember it, so I can't remember what it was like before, make sense?"

Ellie did not know what to say, she felt like an idiot and she had no reply to anything Simon had just said. She had listened to every word and was almost speechless. "I, I don't know what to say. I'm sorry Simon I didn't mean to..."

"You didn't do anything, you just asked a reasonable question," Simon interrupted, politely. "Its fine Ellie, there is nothing to say. I don't know where my dad is, and I don't care. There was a time when I would have, but not anymore." He smiled at her, "Honestly all good. Would you like to come to my house one day?"

"I'd love to," Ellie replied without thinking, almost like a reflex answer, it was true though. "Really I would. I think friends share and help each other, so if there is anything I can do, just ask ok?" She reached over and took his hand on the table, "I may have only known you a short while, but I think you're awesome and I'm beginning to think you could be someone I trust. A lot." This last part was also true, although Ellie had not planned on saying as much so early on in a friendship. To her relief though, Simon agreed.

Squeezing her hand back, "Thanks Ellie, even though the others know this too, it's still hard for me. It's not a secret, but I only tell those I trust. I trust you Eleanor Fields."

"I trust you, Simon Lesley."

They smiled at each other; a mutual silence of support was shared between them.

"Now, eat up. I want to go out."

With that instruction from Ellie, the pair ate. Chatting about other things like the weather, how much of a bookworm Leo was, and how they both thought Annabelle was always smiling. The sort of things friends should chat about, nothing in particular, but in a way that meant so much to them both. After lunch, they cleaned up and briefly said goodbye to Ellie's parents and left the house. It was a lovely late summer day, they walked up to the folly where their friendship had begun, and spend the afternoon watching the world go by. The only thing that Ellie did not share was anything to do with the council, the necklace, or her dreams. That could wait.

As the weeks moved on, they began to take a familiar pattern for Ellie. School Monday to Friday, hanging out with varying members of her friends in the evenings. Then when the weekend came, spending at least half one day with Simon, mostly working but also just spending time together. This had not gone unnoticed by their friends, or indeed Ellie's parents.

"Why are we never invited?" Leo would ask.

"Are we not welcome on the hill of love?" teased Dan. He had become more vocal as the weeks passed by.

"I'd like to hang out as well," Annabelle would say, who of the group, seemed to be the most genuinely hurt.

Ellie's parents had been far less mocking, but had still shown an interest in the relationship between the two.

"He seems to be very fond of you," her mum observed.

"He does spend a lot of time here, but I'm glad you've settled in Ellie," her dad would agree.

The person who teased the most, but also showed the most interest, was Sophie from back in London. "What's he like? Have you kissed him yet? Is he good looking?" Were just some of the questions that had been fired at Ellie. The answers were: lovely, no, and he's ok. In that order.

"I honestly see him as a friend, Soph," Ellie had said. She honestly felt Simon was turning into a close friend.

"Does he know that though?" Sophie had asked.

"Of course, he knows I'm his friend."

"No, I mean does he know he is only a friend? Is he wanting more? Maybe you should find out?" Sophie had challenged.

She had a point, Ellie did not want to hurt Simon, she should find out how he felt and what he wanted.

The weeks rolled by, soon it was mid-October and Halloween decorations had started to appear around the village, shops, and at school. The friendship that had been forged between Ellie and her group of friends was strong, she had settled in with them and they were all working on different projects for school, so they were supporting each other. A true team. If Ellie was honest with herself, she was closest to Simon and Annabelle. Simon was the one she spent the most amount of time with, but Annabelle was the one that she could have proper girly chats with. She would still talk to Sophie now and then, but she could feel her new friendships growing in strength.

The school was hosting a Halloween disco, something they did every year. Everyone would dress up and go along for some food, dancing, and chatting. Ellie was looking forward to this, it would be a good opportunity to let off some steam and relax. She had already chosen her outfit. She would go as a zombie bride, working with her mum she had created her costume and worked out her makeup. An old skirt had been ripped and a top stained and torn. For her makeup she had found a way to make her arms pale and her face look like rotting flesh. She was, without a doubt, extremely excited.

The night of the party came around, it started at seven, and she was being dropped off at seven thirty by her mum. Just after seven, Ellie was putting the finishing touches on her makeup when her mum came into her room.

"Well, don't you look lovely and scary?"

"That doesn't work mum," Ellie retorted. "I'm either beautiful or scary," she said flicking her hair and smirking.

"Well, you are both of those things," she had an odd look in her eye.

"What's up mum?" Ellie asked.

There was a pause where they stared at each other. "Nothing really, just, haven't seen you a lot lately is all. Miss you."

"Miss me? I've been here with you the whole time. We eat together nearly every night and we've been doing loads on the house, what's do you mean?" Ellie wanted to push a little, she felt this was a little harsh.

"I'm not sure Ellie, maybe you're just growing up and I wasn't ready for it. You're still my little girl."

"I am growing up mum, but I'm still me. I still like the same things, we still hang out together, and you'll always be one of my besties," Ellie smiled.

This was mirrored by Katherine.

"What do you think, too much or all good?" Ellie asked as she had finished her makeup. She looked at her mum in the mirror, pouted, pulled a scary face, and giggled.

"Beautifully scary," Katherine chuckled.

"Right, I'm ready then," Ellie stood. As she did, a few bits were knocked off her dressing table onto the floor, including her jewellery box. "Damn it," she exclaimed.

Her mum came over to help, between them they picked up the few bits. Katherine picked up the gold chain, with an 'M' hanging from it. Standing up, she asked, "What's this? I don't recognise it."

Ellie looked.

"It's a necklace, was given to me by, errr, a friend."

She did not know why she lied but felt she could not tell her mum the truth of it coming from someone in the council.

Katherine looked at her, "A friend? A friend bought you jewellery and you didn't show us? That's not like you Ellie?"

Ellie felt her mother's eyes penetrating her, she knew she was heading down a dead end here. "Yes, I just forgot I guess."

"Hmmmmmm, ok. Well, I'm assuming you're wearing it tonight so let me help."

Ellie was stunned into silence and deciding not to talk about it too much or resist, turned and lifted her hair, which she had partly curled and left down in a ragged looking state for her costume. "Thanks mum," she said solemnly.

"You're welcome, but there is no need to hide such lovely things from us."

Ellie's blood boiled, "I'm not hiding anything," she snapped, turning to face her mother who looked shocked at the sudden turn in her daughters' tone. Ellie, realising this, softened her voice, "Sorry, I didn't mean to snap. I wasn't hiding anything; I really did just forget."

"Ok, I believe you," Katherine replied. "Now, let me look at you," she took a step back take her daughter in. "Perfect. Now, let's get you to the ball zombie-rella!"

Driving to the school was much quicker than taking the bus, it only took ten minutes for Ellie and her mum to get there.

"Message me when you want picking up later, ok?"

"Yeah will do, not sure what everyone is doing but will let you know," Ellie replied as she got out of the car.

"Most of all, have fun."

"Will do, love you."

Katherine pulled away. Ellie turned and looked up at the school. It was dark now, schools always felt strange outside of normal hours, Ellie thought. Whilst in the car, she had messages from Leo and Annabelle that everyone was already there, so she started to walk into the school. The party was in the main hall, Ellie made her way towards the thumping music she could hear down the hallway. Once in the hall, she took a moment to take in the surroundings. The hall had been laid out with circular tables at one end, and a space as a dance floor at the other. There was buffet style food set up along the side wall, although that was not open yet. Groups of friends were claiming tables and space for their own, some were already dancing although not that many. Ellie quickly spotted her friends, Leo and Dan were facing her with Simon and Annabelle facing the other way. She headed over to them, as she arrived, they all turned to face her and opened the circle so she could join them.

"Evening," Ellie said, having to shout a little over the music.

"Hi there, zombie girl," Leo replied.

They had all made a real effort, Leo and Dan wearing matching outfits and had come as Frankenstein's monster. Simon had come as a clown, Ellie was not keen on clowns, but had decided to make an exception. Annabelle stood out the most though, she had come as zombie nurse, complete with stethoscope. It was her makeup that really impressed Ellie though, she had really overdone it with her detail and colours.

"Wow you look amazing Annabelle!" Ellie called to her.

"Thanks, so do you. Question, before we all settle in for the evening, Ellie, do you dance? None of these guys do and I need a partner later."

Ellie chuckled, "Yes I do. Are you asking me to dance, Annabelle? Because the night is young, and I'll be keeping my options open," she winked at Annabelle.

"That's fine, I can compete."

"Ladies, ladies. You could always dance with me?" Simon piped up.

"If you're lucky," Ellie and Annabelle said at the same time.

The group laughed at this and moved to a table. The night went smoothly, they chatted, ate, Ellie and Annabelle danced whilst the boys chatted.

"I'm done," Ellie said as she sat down with Annabelle at the table following a rather long dance floor stint.

"Me too! Thanks for keeping me company though."

"Pleasure was all mine Annabelle," Ellie replied.

Whilst Ellie took a big gulp of drink, Simon leant in, "Can we go for a walk somewhere quiet for a bit?"

Ellie nodded; she would be happy to not have her ears pounding for a bit. They both stood and headed away from the table, both choosing to ignore the mocking 'ooooo' sound coming from their friends. They headed out into the corridor and then into a classroom. They sat at the first table, on the corner so they were side on to each other but could still see each other too.

"So, zombie girl," Simon opened with,

Ellie raised her arms in a zombie type way and reached towards him, "Brains…" she said, eyes wide. They giggled. "Yes, clown boy, how are you?"

"I'm good," he replied, looking into her eyes, "I'm really good. I've enjoyed every moment we have shared together. Never thought I'd have a friend like you."

"What do you mean, like me? You have loads of friends out there, four close ones in fact."

"I know, I mean one where I feel I can trust you with anything and everything. I feel like you've become a best friend that I'd do anything for."

"That's sweet, I feel the same way. I don't think I've ever got so close to someone so quickly. I'm just glad I made a real friend so quickly after moving here."

"Good, glad we agree."

There was a moment's silence where Ellie did not know what to say or do next.

Simon continued, "I just want to make sure we are on the same page in the same book."

"Ok, not sure which book that is?" Ellie was comfortable around Simon, but this made her shift in her seat a little.

"I want you to stay my best friend forever. You're a gorgeous girl, and I'm not the only one that knows that around here, you turn heads Ellie. But I want you stay my friend forever, and I don't want to put anything at risk. Know what I mean?"

Ellie thought for a moment, "I think I do, but go on."

Simon shifted in his seat, "We are great together, we have fun, and we get each other. Everyone else knows that and that's why they tease us each time we go anywhere alone. Haven't you noticed the noises and jokes that come our way?"

Ellie nodded.

"Well, I just want to make sure we are on the same page that we are going to be friends, nothing more and certainly never less." He took her hand in his, "I want to love you forever as a friend, my best friend, side by side, and strong as a pair. Are you ok with that?"

Ellie was frozen to the spot; nobody had ever said those words to her before except her parents. She had not expected this. She cared for Simon a lot and certainly agreed that she did not want anything to spoil that for them. They had grown close, it was true that they had been teased a fair bit by their friends for this, but that was not a reason to go a step further with their relationship. Simon as a friend forever sounded good though, the thought of it sent a warm feeling through her veins.

"Ellie, can you say something, please?" Simon pleaded.

Realising that she had not said anything for a good minute or so, Ellie finally spoke.

"Of course I agree and understand Simon. I never thought I would grow to care for and respect someone as much as I do you as quickly as I have. I don't want to put that at risk either. So, friends, best friends, together forever?"

She squeezed Simon's hand as she said this.

"So happy to hear you say that," Simon replied and pulled her into a tight hug.

Ellie responded by squeezing him tightly too, there they sat, just together in the moment.

They pulled away from each other, Ellie leaned back and flicked her hair over her shoulders and as such revealed the necklace for the first time that evening from inside her top. Simon froze on the spot.

Ellie, noticing Simon looking at her chest, clicked her fingers at him, "I'm up here friend!" she snapped at him, in a firm but kind way.

Simon moved his head and eyes up to meet hers.

"Sorry, I wasn't looking, the necklace, it reminds me of something but not sure what. Sorry. Where did you get it?"

The necklace! Ellie thought to herself, she had not wanted to talk about the council, so why was she wearing it in a way that would make it visible?

She thought fast, "It was a welcome to the village gift," was the best she could come up with. She leant forward and offered the chain to him, so he could take a closer look. Reaching out his hand he took the symbol between his fingers to look.

"Is that an 'M'?" he asked staring at the symbol.

"Yes, an 'M' for Mow Cop you see," Ellie replied with a smile. "It was given to me at an," Ellie paused, she was not thinking clearly and had now put her foot into the very conversation she did not want to have, not now.

"At a...?" Simon quizzed, looking at her with his deep coloured eyes.

"A meeting," Ellie replied, she had no choice really. "At the first council meeting my family and I went to."

She looked down, unable to look into his eyes as she said it.

Simon dropped the necklace and leaned away a little in his chair.

"You went to a meeting? After all the warnings we gave you?"

"I didn't have a choice, Simon. My parents made me go. I tried to get out of it, but I couldn't." This was at least partly true Ellie told herself. She looked back up at him. "Simon, I really didn't have a choice, I was going to tell you but was waiting for the right time."

"So, you thought you'd just flaunt it in front of me and wait for me to see and ask? Was that the right time?"

There was anger in his voice now, pain in his eyes, he looked as though Ellie had really hurt him.

"No, I'm sorry, I hadn't meant to wear it, my mum found it and put it on, and I got caught off guard is all. Simon, look at me!"

His eyes had wandered around the room, clearly looking for inspiration. Or an exit. He looked back at her.

"I'm telling you the truth, I love you guys, all of you. I meant everything I just said, and I don't want that to change. What can I do to prove it to you?" Ellie was pleading now, she really did not want to lose any of them, especially Simon.

"Take it off," he said plainly.

"What?"

"The necklace, take it off, right now and throw it. If you do that right now, I'll believe you and keep your secret from the others."

There was a firmness to his voice.

Ellie knew that this was as close to an order or instruction as it was possible to be without being rude.

"Ok, I'll take it off and throw it away."

She reached round her neck and undid the clasp. Standing, Ellie moved over to the classroom bin and dropped it in with a small clang. She quickly moved back over to sit near Simon again.

"There. Gone. I swear to you Simon I don't want anything to do with the council or what they stand for, I was caught out and you know how it is. None of us can overrule our parents really."

She looked at him. Hoping for a sign of softness and release.

Simon breathed out a heavy sigh, looking at Ellie he finally smiled, his eyes softening, and he spoke.

"Thank you, Ellie. I'm sorry that got very dark and serious there, I didn't mean it to. That council scares me is all, and I know how those associated with them get treated, I don't want that for you. I want you to be happy and safe here. I'm on your side, I too meant everything I just said. I will be by your side and this will make it easier, I promise."

Ellie smiled at him, relieved. After the heart to heart they had just had this was a real gear change, she could feel emotion building up inside her. She chuckled, as she did a tear appeared at the corner of her eye.

"Don't cry. Because if you do, I will start too. See!"

To Ellie's amusement, Simon was now starting to have tears appear too. They laughed together and mutually pulled into a hug, they did that a lot Ellie thought. Hugging. They were huggers.

"Well, at least we know we are on the same page! Thank you, Simon, I needed this tonight."

"Me too. You are gorgeous though, even as a zombie. Any guy will be lucky to have you, but they need to get past me first."

Ellie chuckled, "Ok brother," she sniffed into his shoulder.

"Welcome sister."

For a moment, they just stayed that way. They both felt the same. They had gained a sibling, maybe not by blood or family, but by friendship, and that was just as strong and important. Pulling away, Ellie said, "We should get back before more rumours start."

They smiled at each other and walked out of the room, arms linked, as friends. On the same page.

The evening was drawing to a close when they returned, some people had already left, but not their friends. Walking back over to the table, Simon offered to go and get the last round of drinks. Leo, Tyler, and Dan went to help him, leaving Ellie and Annabelle at the table.

"Soooo, you guys were gone a while," Annabelle queried.

"Yeah, we were just talking. Clearing the air," Ellie smiled.

"Hmmmm?" Annabelle was clearly not going to let her off that easy.

"We were agreeing to be on the same page, good friends. No matter what you guys may think or say, just close friends."

Annabelle's expression softened, "Ok, I believe you. It's about time you sorted it out though, we have all been waiting to see what happens. We see the way you look at and talk about each other. We're not stupid you know, but clearly there was something else there so hopefully it is now done?"

Ellie smiled. What did Annabelle mean by something else there? She looked across the room at Simon, he was chatting and laughing with the boys as boys do. He glanced at her and their eyes met. They both smiled at each other.

"Just friends," Ellie stated, blankly.

"Ok I believe you, now, enough about you and Mr Lesley, you have been turning heads since you got here in the summer Ellie. So, who have you got your eye on?"

Ellie looked at her, "What do you mean?"

"Come on Ellie. You're gorgeous, and I know you know you turn heads, so who do you have your eye on?"

"Nobody," this was true, Ellie had not given any thought to boys since arriving in the village and school. "I've been busy getting to know you guys and settling in, no boys on my mind. I've never really paid them much attention anyway, in general I mean. Always looked at it as what will be will be. Know what I mean?"

Annabelle's eyes narrowed.

Deciding to change tact, Ellie responded, "What about you Miss Jones? You're just as, if not more stunning than me, who do you have your eye on?"

Annabelle smiled, "Fair enough. I have my eye on a few, weighing up my options as it were. Keep them keen and intrigued is my motto. Once I know the time and moment is right, I'll make my feelings known."

She flicked her hair, crossed her legs and sat back looking directly at Ellie like a model in a photoshoot. They both smiled.

"Ok drama queen," Ellie giggled. "Let me know if there is any I need to stay away from."

"Oh, you will be the first to know when I make my feelings known, Ellie," Annabelle smiled, with a soft wink.

Ellie smiled back.

For a moment there was a calm between them, a simple but strong connection that was shattered moments later. The boys returned with their drinks, and as a six they sat and chatted until it was home time. Ellie text her mum to come and pick her up, the group got smaller as lifts arrived, Leo was the first go, followed by Dan and Simon. Ellie and Annabelle were waiting at the school entrance when her mum arrived.

"Hey girls," she called from the car, "Good evening?"

"Yes, thanks mum, this is Annabelle by the way."

"Hi Annabelle, nice to meet you. Do you need a lift or is yours on the way?"

"Mine is on the way, in fact, they have just pulled up behind you."

Ellie and Annabelle hugged, as they pulled apart Annabelle kissed Ellie on the cheek and whispered, "I'm glad you and Simon sorted everything, you're cool Ellie, and you fit in with us. Welcome to the school."

Annabelle smiled at her, as she walked away she gently flicked her hair and glanced back at Ellie with a grin.

Ellie was a little taken aback, but she immediately had a small smile appearing on her face and a warm feeling in her heart. A flutter shot through her stomach, taking her by surprise all she could manage in reply was, "Night Annabelle, thank you too."

Without looking back, Annabelle waved.

Ellie got into the car with a huge grin on her face, closed the door and Katherine pulled away to take her home.

CHAPTER 9

The events of the Halloween party lived long in the memories of the students at Redwing High. There were stories and rumours a plenty, and as with any story, the wider it spreads the more extreme it becomes. If some of the things Ellie was hearing were to be believed, she was not only dating Simon, but had also kissed Annabelle, poured alcohol into the school punch, and stolen a trophy from the main hallway. Ellie chuckled to herself at the thought of these, on paper they sounded much more fun but in reality, she was happy with the way the night went. Except for the council chat with Simon, it had been a completely pleasant evening. She had however decided she must tell Simon everything about the council. If he wanted to know, he should, and if he did not then she would not share it. Ellie had decided to talk to him about it the following weekend when they were together.

The weekend came quickly, with the shorter days and longer nights, time seemed to move faster from day to day. The house had changed a lot in the past month or so, the Fields family had put their stamp on it. Each room had been decorated and been given a fresh new look ranging from paint colours to furnishings. Ellie had helped as she promised she would, maybe not as much as her parents would have liked but she did her fare share. Her favourite room, other than her own was the one she was in now, the living room. Her parents had opened it up, allowing in so much natural light they only needed the lights on in the evening. She was sat on the sofa with a cup of tea, reading, when there was a knock at the door.
"I'll get it," Katherine called from the kitchen.

Ellie heard her move down the hallway to the door, she lifted her head and strained to hear what was being said.

"Oh hi, nice to see you again, Beryl."

Ellie sat bolt upright, she had not been to the last couple of meetings, but she still recognised that name, and then the voice that belong to it.

"Hello there Katherine, nice to see you I'm sorry to intrude on your weekend, may I come in?"

"Of course," Ellie heard her mum reply.

She then heard the door close and the sound of two sets of feet down the hallway. Ellie moved quickly and softly to the door to try and listen, it was closed so she could not open it without giving herself away, but she was desperate to hear what was being said. She could just make out the voices.

"Can I offer you a drink? Tea? Coffee? Juice?"

"No thank you, I shan't stay," Ellie could hear the old woman reply. "I'm just here to make sure everything was ok with you and your family."

This was an odd thing to say, Ellie thought.

"Well, that's very kind of you."

Ellie could hear her mother's voice falter, even though she would be thinking this was a kind gesture, something would feel off to her surely?

Katherine continued, "We are all very well thank you; Nick is out at the moment and Ellie is around here somewhere."

"Ahhh I see, you all go your different ways, then?" Beryl replied. "Fair enough. The reason I wanted to see if all was well is that we haven't seen Ellie at a meeting for some time, we wanted to make sure all was ok with your daughter and your family."

What was all this about, Ellie wondered? Were they really that desperate to see her at the meetings?

"Well, Ellie is a teenager, you know how they are. They do their own thing, and we support that. I'm sure she will come to a meeting again soon when she is available."

There was a stern tone to her mother's voice now, Ellie could tell that her mother was not happy about being challenged in this way.

"Indeed, teenagers always wander. Even ones of great importance and prominence can still stray from the path. Be aware Katherine, we have seen many young ones and their families be pulled apart by distance and decisions. The council accepted her and you, they will look after you all, but you must all work with us as well."

There was silence. This was bold, and Ellie was waiting for her mother's reaction and reply. To her delight, it was one of power and sounded more like her mother than anything she had heard in a while.

"Right, ok Beryl. Let's get something straight. We are grateful for how you welcomed us, you have made us feel accepted in our new home and involving us in the council so early is a real honour. Make no mistake though, my family and I are a family, and you do not come into our house and make judgements on me, my husband, or my daughter. She is being raised as we see fit, and I will not have anyone challenge me on that in my own home."

Ellie beamed with pride at this, was her mother finally starting to see through it all?

"Katherine do not misunderstand me, I didn't come here to insult or offend you or your family. I simply came to express concern on behalf of the council that Eleanor not coming to meetings may be problematic in the future. We need consistency, balance, and focus. If young Eleanor cannot give us that, then we will need to prepare for this."

Ellie processed this as best she could. What did that mean? Prepare for what? Their stupid prophecy, what did it have to do with her? She had not been to a meeting in ages.

"Teenagers are unpredictable at the best of times," Katherine replied.

Ellie was still listening at the door.

"Ellie was quiet after her first meeting with you, maybe she felt overwhelmed or intimidated by you all? She is only fifteen you know, surely you need adults on the council to sort out the stuff we have seen. Building plans, bus routes and the like? Why do you need her?"

Silence.

Beryl cleared her throat, "It is simply a matter of wanting and needing the youthful insight of your daughter, nothing more."

"Right, well, I will talk to her when I see her, but I am making no promises here Beryl. If Ellie say's no, then the answer is no."

"I understand, but if the answer is no, then we will all have to deal with the outcome. I will leave you now."

Ellie heard footsteps coming back up the hall, she quickly moved back to her seat, if the door did open, she wanted to keep her earwigging a secret.

"Thank you for coming Beryl."

There was a finality to her mother's voice, Ellie could tell she was not overly happy with what had just gone on.

"Thank you for your time, Katherine."

The door closed, Ellie could hear Beryl's footsteps crossing the gravel driveway, her mother came into the living room and looked at her.

"Well, that was interesting," she said with a puzzled look on her face. "Any idea why they are so desperate for you to attend these meetings? I know you were listening Ellie."

Ellie considered this for a moment, was now the time to tell her mother everything? Would she believe her? Ellie still did not really believe it herself. "No idea, mum. Honestly, the first one that I went to when dad was late was just a boring meeting, there were no other people there my age so don't know what she meant by youthful insight. How did you know I was listening?" Ellie had just clocked this statement from her mother.

Katherine smiled, "Because you are my daughter, I know you better than you will ever admit Ellie. It is strange though isn't it, why they would want you there? I assume you don't have any intentions of attending them?"

"Not really, no. I have other things to be doing. Like exploring, going out with Simon, Annabelle, and the others. They were lovely but it's just not my thing, mum, I'm sorry." This was partly true; she was sorry as she did not wish to cause her family any undue stress or pressure. The bit that was not true was very much around how lovely or otherwise the council were, they scared Ellie.

"Don't be sorry, I understand and agree that it is odd and probably not of much interest to you right now, I will see what

I can find out. There is a meeting in a couple of weeks I think, would you consider coming to that one to try and sort this out?"

"I think that is when Sophie is coming to visit, mum. I can't invite her here and then go to a council meeting, can I?"

"No, I suppose you can't," her mother smiled kindly, "I will see what I can do."

Ellie smiled.

"Oh, and the other reason I knew you were listening… I would have been. There is no way I'd have let your grandma have a conversation like that without me know about it!" Ellie's mum smiled at this, turned and left the room.

Ellie chuckled to herself, looking out of the window she thought of her grandma for a moment. She would have loved it here, crazy cult council aside of course. Ellie came from a family of strong women, women that were determined and would do whatever they needed to do in order to get what they wanted. She intended to carry this tradition on. Ellie loved her father very much, but it was her mother that she aspired to be more like. All this was very odd though, why would they be so desperate to see her?

Simon arrived mid-afternoon, they had arranged to go for a walk around the hill as it was a pleasant day and who knew how long that would last with winter just around the corner. The sky was clear, and although there was a chill in the air, Ellie knew that once they were walking, she would soon warm up, it was annoying like that at this time of year. He had told her that it would be somewhere new that she had not been before, the thought of this sent tingles of excitement down Ellie's spine, new places were always fun. They set off, side by side up the road, but instead of turning right or going straight over, ways they had gone previously, Simon turned left leading Ellie down the footpath a different way.

"You weren't lying were you, I haven't walked down this road before," Ellie teased.

"Give it chance, it's just a way to get to where we are going, if we are lucky, we will see the sunset."

"Oooooo romantic eh? People will talk."

They laughed; indeed they laughed a lot together and they both understood why people talked the way they did, they were very close. Ellie linked arms with him.

"You know, we could have some fun with these stories," she said with a carefree tone.

"What do you mean?"

"Well, if people are talking about us, we could wind them up and make up stories of our own. Did you know I have a birth mark in the shape of a car for example?" she giggled.

Simon smiled at her, "Right, so you want to start a rumour, and the best you can come up with is a birth mark in the shape of a car?"

"It's a start."

"Thanks Ellie, but let's leave the story making to the story tellers, eh? Besides, we would only end up making it worse."

"Ok, only messing. Where are we going anyway?"

"We, Eleanor Fields, are going to a field. Maybe you know it?"

Ellie stopped, dragging Simon to a halt by the arm.

"How dare you suggest that all fields are the same? We are all individual, beautiful, and most of all different Simon Lesley," she stared at him.

He stared back.

Then they both grinned and burst out laughing.

"You doughnut," Simon said in between giggles. "What kind of rubbish was that?"

"It was about as funny as your joke Mr L."

They walked on, Simon led the way around the bends and into a housing estate made up mostly of bungalows, they went through them all right to the back. They walked down a few steps to a little wooden bridge over a stream and into, as Simon had promised, a field. It was a field on a slight incline, as was most of the village. To the left was the field boundary, about fifty meters away at the bottom of the slope. To the right, the incline, Ellie could see right the way up the hill past all the houses to the folly, standing as it did on top of the hill, its single wall jutting out to the right as she looked with its arch showing the blue sky behind. It looked painted from here, too flat rather than real. Simon turned right and started heading up the incline. As they walked Ellie noticed the field was split into two by a broken low wall, it was the sort of wall that is often found in the country or parks, too low to be of any modern use but clearly was once a significant boundary. Halfway along this wall was a tree, a tree that had split in half at some point, it looked like a 'Y' sticking out of the ground, it had nearly lost all its leaves but still looked healthy despite its depletion. Simon sat on a pile of rocks by the tree, facing down the hill, Ellie did the same to sit next to him. It was the first time she had looked down the hill on this walk. Even though she was not even halfway up the hill, she could still see for miles across the expanse below. As at the top of the hill, she could see cars and trains moving around, houses that looked like match boxes from up here, and for miles and miles, fields. Just fields, lakes, and peacefulness, occasionally broken up by a town or settlement, but generally gorgeously peaceful. She moved close to Simon and leant her head on his shoulder.

"Beautiful, thank you for bringing me here."

"You're welcome, this is one of my favourite spots, right here by this tree," he patted the trunk as he said this.

"This really is a gorgeous village, it just keeps amazing me each time I see something new, stunning."

There they sat, in silence, watching the world go by, until Ellie spoke.

"So, how many girls have you brought here then?" she asked teasingly.

"None, you're the first, this will now forevermore be my friendship spot. Our friendship spot."

"I like the sound of that," Ellie replied in a warm tone. "I do have something I want to ask you though."

"Shoot."

"I know you don't like the council, and in truth neither do I really, and I know we sorted out the whole necklace thing, but, do you want to know what actually happened in the meeting?"

Simon shifted slightly, Ellie lifted her head off his shoulder.

"You can say no, and I will never bring it up again, but I wondered if you would like to know first-hand from me, someone you trust, what actually happened?"

There was silence, just the wind in the tree and the sound of the world passing by.

"Honestly Ellie, I think I would. I promise it won't go any further, but yes, it would be good to know what actually happened," he smiled.

Ellie smiled and relaxed, exhaling, "So glad to hear you say that, I've not told anybody, and it's been killing me. Are you sat comfortably?"

He nodded.

"Ok, here goes."

Ellie told him everything, how she had been there on her own, that the council had introduced themselves individually, that they all had staffs, that she had been welcomed and accepted right down to the piece of paper that listed the rules. She even went as far as when her dad arrived, and it all switched back to a normal meeting about bus routes. Finally, she covered off Beryl's visit to the house, and the confrontation with her mum.

Simon sat and listened, in silence, not interrupting but allowing Ellie to get it all off her chest. She could tell that he was listening and processing it, but it was not until she had got to the end that he spoke, with a look of bewilderment and wonder on his face.

"Right. So, errrr," he paused, "Right. This is the first time I think I have been speechless."

He rustled in his pocket, took out a packet of sweets, opened them and took a handful. He offered the packet to Ellie; she took one and looked at him.

"Ok, I know that's a lot to take in, but I really need you to say something, anything."

"Yes, sorry, I'm just trying to process all this," he paused. Looking away from Ellie out across the view, then back to her again. "How have you kept this to yourself for so long? I mean seriously, how?"

"Well, it's not exactly an easy story to tell is it? Who would believe me? Mum and dad wouldn't I don't think, you and the others were so anti-council I couldn't bring it up casually over lunch, could I?" Ellie felt a little confused at this, was he telling her off for not sharing sooner?

"I know Ellie, I know. It just must have been so hard for you though. So, wow, I have some questions. Ok, the staff thing, do you still have it? The paper, did you throw it away? How did you manage to remember everything?"

"Yes, it's in our garage, mum and dad take it each time they go. Yes, it's in a notepad which is also how I've remembered everything, I wrote it all down. But in truth, I'd remember all that without writing it down. It's scary if nothing else, Simon."

"It is that I agree!" he took another sweet, "And then I had a go at you during the dance, the last thing you needed. I'm sorry, Ellie."

"It's ok, you didn't know, and in some ways, it helped me start to shift some of it, I wasn't sure I could tell anyone until now."

"I can understand that."

The sun had nearly fully set now, Ellie had not appreciated how long she had been telling the story until she realised how dark it was getting.

"So, one of the council came to your house to moan about you not going anymore? What's that about do you think?"

"No idea, I was only listening from the other room, mum spoke to Beryl in the kitchen. She wasn't there long, but long enough to make mum feel uncomfortable which takes some doing I can tell you."

"But it was clear they wanted you? You going to go back?"

"Not if I can help it I won't, I don't want anything to do with them, Simon."

Ellie felt a certain level of satisfaction at this statement, it felt final to have decided like that and to say it out loud felt good. As she said it, even though it made her feel positive and empowered, she got the distinct feeling in the pit of her stomach that someone other than Simon had heard her say it. As if there were ears or microphones in the tree and rocks near where they sat. She quickly looked all around her, nothing. Not a soul to be seen.

"What's up?" Simon asked with a puzzled look on his face.

"Nothing, just felt like we were being watched or something that's all. Guess all this just creeps me out a little or something."

Simon put his arm around her shoulder, "Well, you've brought me into it now too, so if anything bad happens to you, it will probably happen to me as well. So, thanks," he said with a cheeky grin.

"You're welcome, least you'll be the first to know if something does happen though eh?"

Simon smiled, "True. Still can't believe all that crazy cult stuff, I know people joke about it, myself included, but to think that there is a group that actually believe it all. Having meetings, giving out staffs and weird pieces of paper, it's all insane."

"You don't need to tell me that! Speaking of which, Sophie is coming to visit soon, and I'd like to keep this from her. In fact, from everybody!"

"Don't worry, I won't tell. Besides, not sure who would believe you, us, anyway. That's probably why it is such a secret."

Ellie nodded in agreement. It was getting cold as well as dark now, the sun had well and truly set, and the only light was now coming from the feint orange glow in the sky. She shivered.

"We better start heading back, it will be dark soon."

They stood, and walked back across the field to the road to head home. Ellie felt as though a weight had been lifted from her shoulders, she had told him, and he had not freaked out, he was a good friend after all. She took his arm after they had crossed the bridge and they walked back to Ellie's.

CHAPTER 10

The next week went by smoothly, Ellie really did feel elated after telling Simon everything about the council. Everything seemed easier, she could relax at school, around friends, everything was simply better for her. Everything that is, except for conversations with her mum and dad. The council had made a point to them both again, for reasons that they could not understand, that if Ellie was not going to attended then this would cause problems. Her parents had laughed it off initially, but the sheer volume of references was starting to annoy them.

"What would you like me to do?" Ellie would ask. "I don't want to go anymore, and I don't see why it's so important to them that I do."

She really felt that she could not tell her parents the truth, and even if she did, they would not believe her. There had been conversations previously in her life around telling tales and stories for attention. That was a different situation though, this was real and if it were not handled correctly could turn into a bad situation indeed. Her parents were not really pushing her too much on it, which Ellie was grateful for. They had taken a view that it was odd behaviour on the part of the council, but nothing to worry about. Ellie had decided that the clear village air had clearly caused something to change for her mum and dad, back home they would never have been so relaxed. Ellie had started to prepare for Sophie's arrival. They had arranged for her to come up and spend two nights with the family, see the sights, and say hello to new friends and generally hang out with Ellie again. Friday evening came, Ellie and her dad set off to pick up Sophie who was due into the nearest station at around eight. The first part of the journey was conducted in silence, finally broken by Nicholas.

"So, what do you girls have planned for the weekend then?" he asked.

"We are going walking tomorrow morning, then meeting up with Simon and Annabelle in town for a spot of lunch and chatting, maybe even shopping. Then she is having dinner with us tomorrow then she heads back on Sunday. Busy but simple."

Ellie braced herself, she knew that her father already knew most of this plan, she had a feeling that this was a way in to talk about something else.

"Sounds good. I know you have missed her, although you seem close to your new friends?"

"I am, but Sophie will always hold a special place in my heart." This was true, whilst she was annoying at times to say the least, Sophie had always been there for Ellie and would probably be there for evermore. There was a pause, Ellie waited, almost holding her breath with anticipation.

"Will you be telling her everything about your time here? The school? Your friends? The folly? The council and what they have been saying about you?"

There it is, Ellie thought to herself.

"Yes dad, I will be telling her everything, except how the weirdo locals want me at their meetings to discuss who knows what!"

There was a harshness to her voice that she did not necessarily mean, but she wanted to make the point all the same.

"Ok, was just asking. They are odd, but they seem very keen to have you involved is all. I know your mother has spoken to you, and I am not trying to go over it again or make anything difficult, I just want you to know that we are on your side. I understand if you don't wish to tell her everything though, that could be weird."

He squeezed his daughter's knee.

She took his hand, "I know dad, I know. Now concentrate on driving," she smirked.

The latter part of the trip was conducted debating the music choices, and the age-old topic of who should control the audio choice in a car; the driver or the passenger. They arrived at the station at ten to eight, Ellie got out of the car leaving her dad to keep the engine running and crossed the road to wait for Sophie by the exit.

Just after eight, there was a loud scream of, "Ellie!"

Ellie turned towards the direction of the voice. There was Sophie, bag over her shoulder looking travel weary and sleepy, but still with the same beaming smile.

"Soph!"

Ellie moved towards her and when they met, they gave each other a crushing hug.

"Good to see you! How was the train?"

"Ok, lots of loud people, so you know me. I put my tunes on and drown them out with my singing! Dying for a soft chair though, had to stand for the last hour or so."

"Ok, well, let's get home then."

Ellie took Sophie's bag, linked arms and led her across the road to where her dad was waiting in the car.

The return journey was spent with Ellie and Sophie catching up, so much so that Nicholas was almost just a chauffeur, other than saying hello he had not been able to get a word in. Once they made it home, the four of them sat at the kitchen table chatting and catching up. Sophie had always been welcome and involved with the Fields family, and they wanted her to feel at home. After a short while, Ellie and Sophie went upstairs to sort out the room for the sleepover.

"Wow what a room," Sophie exclaimed as she entered Ellie's bedroom. "Seeing it over video just doesn't do it justice!" She walked over to the window seat, "What a view. Let me guess, you stitch here, yes?"

There was a mocking tone to her voice as she said this. Sophie had always teased Ellie for her hobby, but only in the loving way that friends do.

"Yes, and read, and study too you know! Now stop stalling and help me with this air bed."

Sophie was sleeping on an airbed on the floor at the foot of Ellie's bed. Given they had their own bathroom up there, this was the simplest thing to do. The girls worked together and made the bed, by the time they had done this, got into their pyjamas, and settled down, it was nearly eleven thirty.

"So, we have a long day tomorrow, can we save the late-night girly talk until then?" Ellie asked, Sophie had a habit of wanting to talk all night.

"Yes, absolutely," was the surprising reply from Sophie, Ellie's face was clearly showing shock. "No need to look like that, Ellie! I've had a long week; I'm looking forward to tomorrow and I need to be at my best."

"At your best?" Ellie enquired.

"For Simon and your friends. Need to make a good impression," she winked.

"I don't want to know, just be nice. Goodnight."

"Night Ellie."

Ellie turned out the light and they went to sleep.

The next day, after showing Sophie around the village to many moans of too much walking, the pair were on their way into town to meet up with Simon and Annabelle. The four had agreed on meeting for a coffee to chat and would then see where the day took them. Ellie and Sophie were the first to arrive, they ordered their drinks and sat down at a table.

"So, anything final I need to know before they get here?" Sophie asked.

"What do you mean? They are perfectly normal lovely people you know."

"So, Simon is your new bestie, and Annabelle is your new what, fashion guru? Sounding board? You're new chatterbox?" Ellie knew that she was joking, at least partly anyway. "Yes, I am closest to Simon, but Annabelle is lovely too. They all are, shame you can only meet the two really, everyone else was busy."

"I'm ok with just meeting two, means I can focus and really get to know them."

"Fair enough."

They passed the time idly chatting about this and that, until Ellie spotted Simon and Annabelle about to walk in the door.

"Here they are," she waved, Annabelle responded with a small wave and Simon beamed a smile over at them.

Annabelle approached the table whilst Simon went to the counter.

"Hi," she smiled to them both, "I'm Annabelle nice to meet you Sophie."

"You too," Sophie replied, standing and bringing Annabelle into a warm hug, "Heard you were a hugger?" she smirked.

"Always," she took the seat next to Sophie and continued, "Did you have a good journey up?"

"Yes thanks, wasn't too bad, it was worth it though. Worth it to see Ellie again and her new house and village and stuff, so yeah, all good! Have you come far today?"

"Similar to yourselves really, we are all quite close together."

Simon arrived after this, carrying a tray with two drinks and four cookies.

"A treat for us all, kind of felt the lovely ladies deserved a nice cookie," he smiled at the group, "Sophie, nice to meet you, I'm..."

"Simon, I know," Sophie interrupted. "I've heard all about you, Mr. Don't be pulling any tricks with sweets on me, understand?" she smiled.

Simon flushed a light shade of pink, he took a seat next to Ellie, facing Sophie, "So, what do we chat about first?"

The four of them chatted over a couple of hours, two drinks, one cookie, and cake each. Covering everything from friends and school, to hobbies and interests. After finishing their drinks, they moved towards the shopping area, not for anything in particular, just to spend some time together. As the day moved on, Ellie noticed a pattern occurring, yes, all four of them were together, but within that there was a divide. Not a nasty divide or a confrontational one, but whenever they would walk two by two it was always the same pairs. Or when sat at tables it would be the same formation. Sophie had attached herself to Simon, and Ellie was with Annabelle. This split seemed to be working though, everyone was happy and relaxed. There were conversations across all four of them as well, so it was not an issue. She was enjoying chatting with Annabelle, they had chatted at school and over messages, but this was the first time she had properly chatted with her. Ellie began to realise just how much she had in common with

Annabelle, how much they could laugh about together, share in, and enjoy. She was going to be one of her best friends as well. So much so, that Ellie snuck away from the group to ring home.

"Mum," she whispered, not wanting the others to hear, "Can Simon and Annabelle come to for dinner as well tonight? Is that ok?"

"Of course," was her mother's reply.

Ellie quickly returned to the group to tell them the good news, and of course ask if they wanted to come.

The answer was a resounding 'yes' from both Simon and Annabelle. With that, they decided to head home and chat some more there, before, during, and after dinner.

The journey was a simple one, they had decided to catch the bus back which would take longer than getting picked up, but felt it would be simpler. They sat on the back row of the bus and chatted, Ellie could not remember the last time she had spoken so much and so freely with a group before. She was sat by the window and turned her attention to the passing fields and trees. She caught a glimpse of the folly on the hill, set against a dark grey sky. The sort of grey that seemed to suck the colour and life out of the world as if it was pure darkness. What made this even stranger, is when she looked out of the other window, away from the hill, the sky was much lighter. It was as if the sky was changing directly over the hill. As if it were a focal point for a storm.

"Storms always start up there," Annabelle said, breaking Ellie out of her trance. "They always seem to start above the hill and push out to the surrounding areas. It's cool. It's as though the sky opens up above that hill and weather just falls through the gap."

"Do we get many storms?"

"Not in the summer, they normally happen in late autumn and winter. Big, loud, and with rain drops so big they bounce off the floor."

Annabelle's excitement at the potential of a storm amused Ellie. "Why so happy about a storm? Surely that's bad weather isn't it?"

"Well, only if you want to be dry. I like the sounds and the way it feels after. As though pressure gets lifted. Which of course is what is happening during a storm, I remember that from science last year."

She smiled, seemingly pleased with herself for remembering this fact.

"Right ok. Well, if the colour of that is anything to go by, this could be a real big one."

Annabelle smiled an excited smile. Ellie did not feel the same level of excitement, she could not help feeling that there was a connection between the weather, the hill, the folly, and some of the nonsense spouted by the council. Or was she imagining it and making connections where there were none? Was her imagination running wild? She had always been told her mind ran away with her. She needed to stop overthinking and be in the moment. It was only a storm after all. She resolved to ignore it, turning away from the window of the bus, she turned back towards the group and joined back in the conversations.

Dinner was chilli. The same recipe that Ellie and her father had made not so long ago after moving in. Katherine joined Annabelle, Simon, and Sophie to sit and watch from the kitchen table as Ellie and Nicholas worked. During dinner, Katherine and Nicholas chatted with the four friends as if they had all known each other for years, even though this was the first time that Sophie had visited here, and Annabelle had visited for dinner ever. Nicholas and Katherine had met Annabelle before, but not long enough to really get to know her. Sophie they knew from London, so everyone was getting along nicely. After dinner, Annabelle and Simon offered to clean up and sort out the dishwasher, Ellie and Sophie sorted pudding. They had bought a cake whilst they were out in town much to the amusement of Ellie's mum and dad.

"No need and you know I am trying to eat healthy," Katherine had mused, but on the sight of the chocolate cake dripping with sauce, her resistance was broken. "Ok, only a small piece though."

They ate cake, then the four friends moved into Ellie's bedroom to finish off their day. It was around eight now, and they had arranged a lift for ten, Simon was being dropped off by Annabelle's parents. They made themselves comfy in Ellie's room, Ellie on the end of her bed with Annabelle, Sophie sat on the floor and Simon in front of window seat on the floor, leaning on the bench. They were throwing a tennis ball to each other that Annabelle had found in the corner of Ellie's room. The only light was coming from the main bedroom light and two lamps. There was nothing coming through the window as the darkness of the impending storm had fully set in now.

"So, what a day eh?" Simon began. "Been lovely to finally meet you Sophie and get to know you, you're cool."

"Why yes I am, thank you Simon," Sophie replied, giving him a cheeky smile as she did so.

"For me, it has just been lovely to spend time together and mix my worlds," Ellie replied.

"That's quite profound for you Ellie," Simon retorted, "didn't realise you had that kind of language in you," he cheekily winked at her.

"Harsh," Ellie snapped.

She knew he was joking but still felt the need to respond. Rather than throwing the ball to him, she threw it at him. Hard. So hard in fact that when he moved to the side to dodge the ball, it hit the bench and broke a panel off the front. It split and fell off, revealing a dark hole where there had once been white painted wood.

"Oh well done, Simon," Annabelle chastised.

"Me? Ellie threw the ball!" he defended, "I just moved."

"Well, as a gentleman, I think you should take the blame," Sophie chimed in, "Ellie, what do you think?"

Ellie did not reply. She had done nothing but stare at the newly created hole. She had never realised that the bench was hollow, why was it hollow? Was there something in there? She could just make out the blackness of the hole and was sure there was something in there.

"Hello??" Annabelle called, trying to get her attention.

Ellie ignored her, and instead got off the bed and moved across the room. Simon moved out of her way, a concerned look on his face, he did not know what to expect from her. She knelt and peered inside the hole.

"There is something in here," she said plainly.

"What do you mean?" Sophie asked, a far sterner tone to her voice than she intended.

"I mean," Ellie said, now reaching inside the bench, "I didn't know this was hollow, and, I think," she rummaged around, "There is something in here."

As she finished this sentence, she pulled hard. A bit more wood came off as she did so, because the metal tin that she was now holding was too big to fit through the original smaller hole. She turned, crossed her legs and placed the tin on her lap, staring at it. The other three moved closer to see it clearer. Ellie stared at the tin, she was fixated on the lid, she looked at Simon, and he had the same focused look to his eyes. On top of the tin, scratched into it crudely as if done by a nail or screw, was the symbol of the council. A circle with a capital 'M' in, the same as the window, the staff, and the necklace.

"That's weird, it matches your window," Annabelle said simply.

Ellie looked at Simon, imploring him with her eyes to not say anything, they needed to act as surprised as the others. He either got the message or was already thinking along those lines.

"Yeah, that's a bit odd isn't it, maybe the person who put it there really like that window?" he asked, giving Ellie a knowing look.

Relief, he had the same thoughts that she had.

"Yes, freaky," Ellie said shakily, opening the tin as she said so. The lid clipped off with a small ping, revealing its contents to the group.

"What's in there?" Annabelle asked, clearly excited by the discovery.

Ellie removed the items one by one, calling each one out as she did.

"A necklace with the same symbol on, a compass, what looks like a small hand-held telescope, and some pieces of paper."

She laid out the necklace which she internally noted matched the one that Simon had asked her to throw away, next to that the telescope and compass. She began to unfold the paper. There were multiple pages, all of which looked like they had come from the same notepad, lined pages with holes down the left where they had been pulled out of the coiled bindings. They were covered in handwritten scrawls, legible, but either written in a hurry or by someone who did not write on paper a lot.

"What do they say?" Sophie asked. She had picked up the telescope and was turning it over in her fingers, she held it up to her eye, "Avast ye land lovers," she said in a mock pirate voice. The group giggled, it seemed to lift the sudden tension that was settling over them all.

"This is just a small telescope, nothing too exciting I don't think," Sophie stated.

"Yeah, come on Ellie, what do they say?" Annabelle joined in.

"They are not in any kind of order, they appear to be notes or random thoughts scribbled down," Ellie explained.

"Just read them!" Annabelle demanded.

"Ok," Ellie cleared her throat, calmed her nerves and started to read the notes aloud.

I do not understand. They say they want to help, and that they want to protect, but they do not act on the clear information I have given them. The notes that we have found and the instructions they gave are clear. We must have the obelisks in place at the right time, most importantly, the owners of these obelisks must be focused, true, and prepared to act for the council.

Ellie paused and looked up. They were all staring at her, hanging on her every word. She continued.

The first group got it partly right, but in doing so got it partly wrong. The girl may not be completely lost. They did seal the gate and create the locks and keys, but they did not think about protecting from future breaches. There is always a risk, as soon as an obelisk is weakened or broken, as soon as someone does not believe and protect, we run the risk of it all falling apart.

Ellie put the first page down, nobody moved, and everyone was focused on her. The second page did not follow on.

I have realised the location of the obelisks and the reason, but they do not believe me. We must ensure the alignment is true.

Ellie showed them the page as that was all that was written on it, but below was a faded pencil drawing, a circle with three dots around the bottom edge and nothing else. She put that page down as well for all to see. The third page had a different tone again, but more writing than the second.

They have forced me out, not because I did not believe, but because I tried to convince them to change. They do not see the bigger picture, they do not realise the true responsibility we have to the world, and they view it as something to not take seriously. Tonight, I am going to the place. The place where it all began, it is the first full moon of winter and I believe that what I am going to do will work. I believe this will allow me to prove once and for all that we have a greater responsibility, a greater power to work with and support. I will show them how wrong they are.

"Well, this is getting curious isn't it?" Simon mused as Ellie picked up the final piece of paper.
She began again.

Now I see clearly. Now I understand. Now I know what is required of me to fix the world. Now I will begin my work. Now the council and the world will know what I am capable of. They will see. They will all see. I am free once more and nothing can stop me.

Ellie looked up, the faces greeting her were furrowed with concern and stunned silence. "That took a turn didn't it?" she asked, lowering the last piece of paper to the floor. "Reading it sounded like they were written by different people, even though the handwriting looks the same."
"Reading it sounded like different people? Hearing it sounded worse. That was vile to listen to," said Sophie. A look of fear on her face, she had put the telescope away now, and had recoiled from the group a little. She was clearly scared.
"It's clearly the ramblings of someone who had lost their marbles," Annabelle said, there was a tone to her voice though that suggested she was not entirely confident in what she was saying.
Ellie looked at Simon, he looked how she felt. Sick. Whilst

there was nothing to suggest that this could all be real, the pile of things that could not be related was stacking up. She kept her cool.

"Well, they were clearly obsessed with something, doesn't mean he or she, was or wasn't crazy though. I'm glad you were all here when I found it, would not have liked reading that alone."

"Yeah, we are really glad we were here to be as traumatised as you are," Sophie replied in a sarcastic tone. "What happened to a nice, chilled evening of chatting?"

Ellie said nothing. She was distracted by the sound of the rain outside; it was coming down in what sounded like buckets.

Annabelle, Simon, and Sophie took it in turns to examine the telescope, compass, and papers. The whole time Ellie stared out of the window, looking at the rain trickle down it, running down the lead 'M' that was keeping her gaze. What did it all mean? Was something going to happen now? Had the council chosen her for whatever this person was writing about? Did they know about all this? Should she tell them, or anybody? These were just some of the questions bouncing round in Ellie's mind when Simon took her hand and spoke.

"You ok Ellie?" he asked, a concerned tone to his voice. "You've gone white as a sheet!"

She looked down at his hand, then up at his face. She stared at him for a moment, looking into his deep caring eyes. She shivered.

"Yes, sorry, I'm fine. Just a lot to process is all. Easy to get carried away isn't it?" she looked around the room at the others. They all had similar expressions. Their faces projected calm, their eyes wide with a mixture of fear, excitement, and confusion.

"It is a little creepy, you had no idea it was here? Nothing mentioned to your mum or dad or anything?" Annabelle asked softly.

"Not that I know of, how would anyone know? It took us breaking the bench to find it. Not like I'd stumble across it is it?"

Annabelle nodded in agreement.

"Well, why don't we put it all away, take our minds off it and then we can discuss another time, when it's not dark, raining, and even more creepy?" Annabelle was clearly keen to move on, as she looked at Ellie there was almost a begging look in her eyes. She took Ellie's other hand and squeezed it, "Please." "Ok, we can do that. It will still be here tomorrow." Ellie gathered up the contents, placed them into the box and snapped the lid back on. Placing it behind her, near the newly created hole, she turned back to the others, "Now what?"

They really tried to get the relaxed vibe back, the chatting and laughing that had been with them all day. Though, none of them could relax, there was an edge and a tone to everything they all said. A tone of nervousness. Ellie kept glancing over at the box, as if expecting it to have moved or something. Of course, it never did. She noticed the others doing the same thing though, that made her feel better.

The time came for Annabelle and Simon to go, everyone went downstairs to say goodbye, the four hugged, shared words of farewell and catching up soon. Ellie was pleased that they were all able to put on a real brave face for her parents, she did not need them getting involved. Ellie and Sophie went straight to bed, hardly saying anything to each other. After about fifteen minutes, Ellie was snuggled under her duvet with the light off, listening to the sound of the rain on the window. Should I be scared? No. She concluded to herself. I rejected the council; they can't force me. Unlike those notes they didn't reject me, I rejected them. It will all be fine. She closed her eyes and tried to sleep.

Ellie fell quite quickly into a deep sleep, dreamless, calming, and exactly what she needed.

Bang. Ellie woke with a start, the rumble of thunder from above had woken her immediately. The sound of the rain on the window combined with the thunder was deafening. She looked down at the foot of the bed, Sophie had been woken as well. The two stared at each other for a moment. There was a sudden bolt of light through the window, creating a silhouette of the 'M' on the curtains. This was quickly followed by another loud bang.

"How'd you feel about storms Soph?"

"Not great," came the reply through the darkness.

"I'm going to look."

Ellie moved out of bed and across the room to the window seat. As she pulled back the curtains there was another bolt of lightning. Depending on if you like storms or not, this was either perfect or terrible timing. Ellie looked out. The sky was completely black, other than when it was ripped apart by lightning. The rain was hammering down on the window and roof, making a constant drumming noise. She looked up in the direction of where the folly should be. Nothing. It was too dark. Ellie had never seen the sky so absent of colour before. Then, there was a huge bolt of light that looked like it came from the folly itself. For a moment, the structure was lit up, revealing its shape against the dark clouds behind. Ellie jumped back, the bolt of light seemed to be heading towards their house, towards the window directly at her. She closed her eyes, more through instinct than anything else. There was a loud bang, and then nothing. The light went out as quickly as it had arrived. Moving back to the window, she saw the folly had gone again. Through the rain and continuing lightning and thunder, Ellie could see nothing. She looked up, in the pockets of light made by the storm, she was sure she could see a face, twisted into an evil looking smile in the clouds above the hill. Then, from one flash to the next, it was gone. After closing the curtains again, she turned to face Sophie, "Just a storm," she decided not to talk about the face she may or may not have seen. "Nothing to worry about."

With that, she walked back across to the bed, climbed in and wrapped herself in the quilt again. Ellie pushed the image of the evil looking smile from her mind as best she could and drifted into a dark, dreamless sleep.

The next morning Sophie woke Ellie with a shake. "Ellie, Ellie! Your dad has been shouting you, he wants to show us something in the garden."

"What, what time is it?" Ellie replied groggily.

"Nearly ten, come on!" she moved towards the stairs, clearly wanting to move.

"Ok, I'm coming."

Ellie got out of bed, threw her dressing gown on, and crossed the room behind Sophie.

Moments later, they were heading outside, Ellie's parents standing facing away from the house towards where the stone was, but it was hidden from Ellie's view by their position.

"Finally, did the storm wake you in the night? Must have done! Look at this mess," Nicholas said.

Ellie looked. She could see leaves over the floor, broken fences, fallen branches, and damaged plants. Nothing worth waking her up for though. Until her parents moved apart, creating a gap between them. Ellie's mouth dropped open. She could now see the stone, the solid stone that could not be moved or changed. The stone, which had now cracked, with a piece off the top resting in the soil on the ground below. She looked at Sophie, who was also standing with her mouth open in shock. "What kind of storm can crack stone?" she asked.

Nobody said a word.

CHAPTER 11

"I have no idea," Nicholas eventually commented. "I have never seen anything like this, storm damage of course, but not a solid stone. Especially one that we couldn't even move or make a dent on weeks ago."

The four of them were just standing looking at the damage in their garden. Back in London, they had never had to deal with such damage, up here on an exposed hill though meant their garden was all but ruined.

"Well, at least we know what we are doing today," Kathrine commented. She turned to face Ellie and Sophie, "Will you be able to help us, girls?"

Sophie, who was always eager to be in everyone's good books replied before Ellie could say anything. "Yes of course, I can put the things I went walking in yesterday on."

Ellie agreed, although not as enthusiastically as Sophie, "Yes, we will, can we just get some food first?"

She did not know why, but she was suddenly very hungry.

"Of course, help yourselves and get sorted, then we can allocate the jobs," Ellie's mum replied, an organisational tone to her voice.

The two girls turned and went back into the house, within half an hour they had changed, eaten, and were ready to go with the clean-up task at hand. The morning was spent cleaning, organising, and moving. Everything from potted plants to the shed itself had experienced damage. Fortunately, most of it was superficial, nothing too significant other than one fence panel that would require a trip to a shop to replace. Within a couple of hours, they had cleaned up most of the mess, Katherine and Nicholas had gone to get a fence panel via the tip to get rid of the many bags of rubbish they had filled. Ellie and Sophie were cleaning up the last little bit of the flower bed by the stone when Sophie picked up the broken piece from the ground.

"So, what is this stone thing then?" she asked, turning the stone piece over in her hands. "It doesn't seem very special, but your dad seemed a little peeved by it?"

"We all are," Ellie replied, not lifting her head up as she continued to clear out bits of stone and sticks from the soil. "We have no idea what it is, it was here when we moved in. We tried to dig it out, all sorts, but it wouldn't shift. So, mum turned it into a feature, put these nice plants around it and now this," she stopped, sat back on her heels and looked at the stone. "I mean, what is it? It's not a bird table, sundial, or statue. It's not even a table. It's just a rock. A stupid, grey rock!" Ellie hit it with her palm, immediately regretting this course of action as the stinging pain of doing so shot up her arm.

Sophie sniggered, "That'll teach you. Rock or otherwise, it's here to stay," she looked up at the stone, turning the broken piece in her hands as she did so. "I wonder if this bit fits back on."

Standing up, Sophie looked at the piece in her hands and then the top of the rock. After a few moments of twisting and turning the piece in her hands, Sophie lined up the cracks and lowered the piece onto the stone.

"It fits!" she cheered, as if solving a complex puzzle.

"Well done Soph, you managed to fit two pieces of stone together," Ellie replied sarcastically. She slow clapped to drive home her thoughts on the matter, "Let go, see what happens." Sophie did so, and immediately the stone fell again back to the floor. "Well obviously, I said it fits not that I had stuck it there," she bent and picked up the piece again. "What shall we do with it?"

Ellie reached out her hand to take the piece, Sophie handed it over. Ellie had felt the stone before, she had run her palms over it. This piece though felt different, yes it was broken, but it felt like a different surface in her hands now. The stone had felt solid, strong, uneven but gentle. This piece felt rough and harsh in her palm, as if it were truly broken and fragmented.

She stared at it, turning it over in her hands as she did so. Still as therapeutic as when she touched the stone before, but with a level of intrigue now. She felt as though she had questions to ask but did not know what they were or who to ask about them.

"Hello?" Sophie's voice came ringing through Ellie's ears. She took her eyes away from the piece of stone in her hand and looked at Sophie.

"Yes?"

"Yes? YES! I've been trying to get your attention for the last few minutes, you've been staring at that thing muttering under your breath. So quiet I could hardly hear it, it was just mumbles as far as I could tell. You just kept turning it over in your hands, mumbling to yourself as you did. What's wrong with you?"

There was a look of real fear on Sophie's face as she looked at her friend, she had never seen that in her before.

"Sorry, I was just, daydreaming I guess."

Ellie did not know what had just happened, she was not aware of muttering anything, nor was she aware that it had been a significant amount of time. She handed the piece back to Sophie. "Here, you take it and put it somewhere in the shed, will let mum and dad decide later on what to do with it."

Sophie took the stone but did not take her eyes off Ellie, "Ok, but that was freaky Ellie, please don't do that again."

Ellie smiled, "I won't. I promise. I'm sorry it scared you."

"Ok, anyway, the reason I was shouting you is your doorbell is ringing! Wasn't sure if I should get it or not?"

"No, that's fine I'll go. You put that in the shed, finish off here, and I'll go to the door. Deal?"

"Deal," Sophie seemed to be relaxing now.

"Again, sorry!"

Ellie walked away, back into the house glancing over her shoulder. Sophie was just following her with her eyes. As she turned away, she smiled to herself, it was an attempt to get her mind away from the stone. The smile stayed with her until she opened the front door. As she looked up at the person standing there the smile faded. She was looking up at Douglas, the leader of the council. This was the first time Ellie had seen Douglas since the only council meeting she had been to. He looked as stern as he had on that night, his eyes already penetrating through her as they met each other's gaze. There was a moment's pause, then Ellie spoke.

"Hi, Douglas is it?" she said, attempting to sound casual and laid back about seeing him.

"You know very well that is my name," he replied, the stern tone that Ellie remembered coming through loud and clear. "It has been a while since we have seen you, I thought you understood the importance of attending the meetings?"

"My parents have been coming, haven't they? They have been helping with garden fences and bus routes I believe?" Ellie replied. She did not really know which way to take this conversation, what did he want?

"Yes, well, they have been helping with the more trivial matters, but our need is one of greater importance, as you well know." He stared at her, his gaze held hers and she felt as though she could not look away.

"Do I? All I saw was a load of rubbish, and if it was so important, why didn't you talk to my parents about it as well? Why just me?"

"Because you alone were chosen, you alone fit the needs of the challenge that lies before us. Though, I fear it may now be too late."

"Too late for what?" Ellie enquired harshly. "I am not coming back, and whatever it is you needed me to do, you will have to find someone else."

He looked at her, tilting his head to one side.

"The young never understand until it is too late. This is why he chooses the ones he does; they must prove themselves. He always chooses the ones with the most to learn," he smiled at Ellie.

"He?"

"The Man. Did you not take anything in?"

Ellie glared at him.

"Anyway child, I am here to speak with your parents in an attempt to reason with them. I also wanted to see if the damage the storm did is the same here as at the other council houses."

He leaned round to peer through the hallway, Ellie closed the door slightly to restrict his view.

"They are not here, it's just my friend and I, and we have been cleaning up the garden."

"Aha, so you did get some damage?"

"Yes, to the garden. Nothing major though."

Ellie did not understand this course of questioning but was happy to go along with it for now.

"I see. Pot plants overturned, rubbish everywhere, that sort of thing?" he enquired.

"Yes, plus a broken fence panel."

"Anything else broken?" he looked down at her, an expression of concern on his face.

Ellie thought quickly.

"Ellie, are you still chatting or are you coming to help?" Sophie's voice called from behind.

Ellie could hear her footsteps coming down the hall.

"Ellie? You still at the door?"

"Yes, she is," called Douglas over Ellie's head.

Ellie stared at him in disbelief.

Sophie arrived at the doorway, "Hi, I'm Sophie," she said, offering her hand to Douglas.

He took it and shook with a kind smile; his demeanour had completely changed in a second. "Nice to meet you Sophie, are you one of Eleanor's friends?" he looked from one girl to the other.

"Yes, from London. And you are?"

"Forgive me, I'm Douglas, leader of the council that Eleanor here and her parents attend," he bowed slightly.

Sophie smiled, "Nice to meet you, are you coming in?"

"No," Ellie interrupted.

They both looked at her.

Ellie looked at Sophie, she needed to say something without giving too much away, "I just think we still have lots to clean up and Douglas said he wanted to see mum and dad, who aren't here."

"Indeed," Douglas replied, the girls looked at him. "The main purpose of my visit was to speak with Nicholas and Katherine, I just wanted to check that all was ok, see if there was any

damage. I can see that it is fine, and you do not wish me to bother you any longer," he looked at Ellie, staring at her with his deep penetrating eyes. "As you say, Ellie, everything is fine yes?"
"Yes."
"The only thing that was damaged was a fence and some rock thing, why would you be interested in that?" Sophie stated. As soon as she had, the mood changed once again.
Ellie looked at her sharply, as did Douglas with interest, his eyes widening.
"What rock thing, Sophie?"
Sophie looked at Ellie, clearly regretting her last statement, "Nothing, just some gravel stuff that got blown all over the garden."
"That's not what you said, you said rock, Sophie," he looked at Ellie, who met his gaze, defiance on her face. "Eleanor, listen to me and I will leave. If the rock that Sophie mentioned is what I think it is, then we, all of us, are in danger. The protection is growing weak because of your reluctance to accept what is your destiny. We tried to involve you, we tried to help. We needed you and soon you will need us. If I am right, then there is a worse storm coming than what we had last night." He reached out to put his arms on Ellie's shoulders, she let him, he bent down so his eyes were level with hers. "Please Eleanor, I implore you, you must take action, you must work with us, you must do what is right."
Ellie looked at him. For the first time, she saw him as a frightened old man. What could possibly be scaring him so much? She decided to appease him for now.
"Ok, I will talk to mum and dad and then see what they say, ok Douglas? But you need to leave now."
He smiled, released her shoulders and stood. "Ok, thank you Ellie, sorry, Eleanor. I will leave you now."
With that, he turned and walked back up the drive and away from the house.
Ellie closed the door and looked at Sophie. What was she going to say to get out of this one? As it turns out, nothing. Ellie did not need to say anything, Sophie did it for her.
"Well, he is clearly a fruit bat," and she burst out laughing.

"What was he going on about?"

Hardly believing her luck that she had sidestepped yet another moment where people could start to be drawn in, Ellie nervously laughed along with Sophie.

"I know. He's just a crazy old man."

The two girls headed back down the hallway to the garden, stopping off to get some juice on their way. Sophie had clearly relaxed, fully under the impression that Ellie felt the same way, Douglas was a crazy old man. Ellie felt differently though. For the first time, she was starting to question herself about all the goings on. The sheer volume of coincidences was starting to stack up, she would need to start logging these. She decided that later that night she would get out her notepad, the one she had used to record the council meeting notes and start to write all this down. From the weird goings on to the stuff they found in her room. All of it.

About an hour later, Ellie's parents returned not only with a fence panel but with lunch too. The girls helped Nicholas put the panel back whilst Katherine prepared lunch, a collection of meats, cheese, and salad. Soon after, they had fixed the fence and were all sat around the kitchen table eating, discussing the mornings events.

"Well, that was a busy morning we did not expect," Nicholas exclaimed.

"Indeed, who knew putting up a fence would be so difficult," Katherine teased. Nicholas and the two girls had made a bit of a mountain out of a molehill with that. "There was a lot of back and forth, too far now too high, and so on from you all," she chuckled. "Looked like it would have been easier to put it in upside down."

The four of them laughed. The atmosphere was good, positive, until the arrival of Douglas came up.

"The only odd thing was that guy, Douglas, who came to find you both," Ellie said. She did not want to talk about this but knew that if she did not Sophie would, so decided it would be easier to keep it under control if she did it first. "He said he came to find you, to see if everything was ok and to see if there was any damage."

Both her parents looked at her, Katherine spoke first, "What did you say? More to the point what did he say?"

Ellie and Sophie looked at each other, Ellie continued, "He started off ok, he mentioned how he was doing the rounds as lots of people had damage, he said he wanted to make sure everything was ok and that nothing was broken. Then Sophie mentioned the stone, which is in the shed by the way, and he completely changed. He suddenly looked, scared. He gave me some speech about how I needed to think about my destiny, and that they needed me as there was a worse storm coming."

She looked at Sophie, who added some more details.

"Yeah, he suddenly went all serious and 'the world is ending' sort of thing. Something about destiny and that they needed Ellie to help them, and that she had not joined them properly and that was leading to weakened protections around the village. Whatever that means. We put it down to him just being crazy and laughed it off."

Sophie and Ellie laughed at this, for a moment, Nicholas and Katherine did not.

They both had concerned looks on their faces, both looking between Sophie and Ellie, and back again. Finally, both sets of eyes settled on Ellie, she knew what her parents were thinking. They did not believe in the supernatural or unusual, but they did believe in their baby girl being scared, upset, and being used in ways that nobody should go through.

"Its fine," she said, in attempt to settle their nerves. "He is just a crazy old man, we don't seriously believe any of their rubbish, do we?"

"No of course not," her dad replied almost immediately.

"No, we don't. But we do believe in people making you uncomfortable Ellie. We don't like the idea of you being put under pressure, we think that is very unfair."

"He said it was my destiny. Don't see how."

"Exactly. We are from London and new here, how could it possibly be your destiny?"

Ellie looked at her mother, she was right, it could not be.

"I know. Weird is all. Can we talk about something other than the crazy guy telling me I need to save the world? I have enough trouble with maths homework never mind that as well."

There was a moment's pause, then they moved on.

"Other than crazy old men, have you had a good weekend Sophie?" Nicholas asked.

"Yes, thank you. Your new home is gorgeous, and the village is beautiful. Although I'm not used to all this space, fresh air, and walking. Far too healthy for me," this lifted the mood immediately. "And it was good to meet some of Ellie's new friends, Simon and Annabelle are awesome."

"Yes, we are fond of them too," Nicholas replied. "Ellie has settled in well and has been instrumental in making this move as easy as it has been. You are welcome anytime Sophie."

He smiled at her.

Sophie smiled back and flushed a light shade of pink. Ellie noticed this and had not forgotten the many times Sophie had made a comment about her father's looks.

The afternoon ticked on, and soon it was time for Sophie to go to the station to catch her train home. Katherine took the girls, when they arrived Ellie got out of the car with Sophie, they crossed the road to the station to say goodbye there.

"Miss you Ellie."

"Miss you too Soph."

"You will be careful won't you, I know it's probably all rubbish, but that guy was creepy and then there is the stuff in your room which I notice you didn't tell your mum and dad about?"

"I know. I couldn't. And yes, I will be careful, I promise. Simon knows, and he will look after me, I'll tell him about Douglas sometime this week."

"I bet he will look after you," Sophie winked and giggled.

"Oh, stop it, he is just a good friend that's all, he always will be, never more or less than that. I told you, I've never given much thought to boys."

"I know Ellie, I know."

They smiled at each other.

"I better go, train will be here soon."

They hugged.

"Ok, travel safe, keep in touch and I will see you soon ok."

"You too, bye Ellie."

They hugged again, then Sophie turned and walked through the gate to the station. Ellie turned and headed back to the car where her mother was waiting.

"All ok?" she asked.

"Yeah, just saying bye again is all," Ellie smiled at her mother, "Been a long weekend."

"Yes, well, let's get you home then."

The journey home was a simple one, with very few words exchanged between them. When they got home, Ellie made a cup of tea and went upstairs. She wanted to start writing in her notepad. Once in her room, she got set up at her makeup table. Notepad in the middle, the tin from under the bench to the left, pen in hand, and cup of tea to the right. Ellie took a sip of tea, where to start, she thought to herself. After reading her original notes about the council and electing to start with the contents of the tin, she started to make notes in her notepad. Making detailed references to the telescope, covering off its metal trim and wooden casing and that despite clearly being old, it seemed to be in good condition. Although, it did not seem to magnify anything, it was as if the lenses in the telescope were only plain glass and had no zoom capability at all. Odd. Moving onto the compass she noted that the needle was working and always faced north, but the dial was locked in place at a certain angle. This meant the compass could not be used properly as it could not be used to find a baring other than the one it was locked to, again, very odd. Then there were the notes themselves, Ellie read them all again, remembering the chills and shivers that ran up her spine the first time. What had they meant by some of the language? What information had they found that nobody wanted to listen to? What was the first group that got it wrong, what was *it*? Then there was the language change, almost immediately the language shifted to be more aggressive and targeted, as if the frustration were burnt into the page by the ink. After reading all the notes several times over, Ellie moved on to recording the events of the weekend. What had Douglas meant? Comparing the notes to her own experience of the council did not quite fit somehow. The person writing them had described being kicked out and ignored, Ellie felt the exact opposite; they would not let her leave. Ellie also noted down the weird weather over the weekend, the storm, the bolts of light, the face in the sky, and the broken stone. The only thing she could not record was where the broken piece was now. Other than in the shed, she did not know where Sophie had put it. By this point, Ellie had filled nearly half of her notepad, she began to realise that coupled with the research she did in the hotel all those months ago, she had spent quite a lot of time researching this village, its council, and its folly on the hill. She sat back and exhaled. Glancing at the clock she realised it was now nearly half past ten. Odd that nobody had been to see me or say goodnight, she thought. No matter, means I can do what I want to do, Ellie concluded. Leaving her notepad open to a blank page on the table, she put the items back into the tin and decided to get ready for bed. Shortly after, Ellie was in her pyjamas under her duvet, she glanced over at the table where all the stuff was one last time, "I will figure you out," she said to herself out loud. With that, she turned out her lamp, and rolled over to sleep.

"Eleanor," a deep voice called; it was soothing but firm all at once. "Eleanor, I know you can hear me. It is time for you to understand and learn."
She knew she was asleep and dreaming but it was the sort of dream where she could not get herself out of it.
"Eleanor, you are asleep, but this is not a dream. I am real. This is real. This is me talking to you the only way I can. Eleanor, hear me."
Dreams don't talk to me, Ellie thought. It felt real enough to keep her locked into it though, it seemed the only option was to go along with the dream, move through it and see what happened. After all, it was only a dream, Ellie decided. She opened her eyes and sat up. This was definitely a dream. Her room had no ceiling or walls, or at least, the normal ones had gone. They had been replaced with clouds of purple smoke, thick and wispy that moved as she looked at them. The same way steam moves above a freshly brewed cup of tea. Looking around, she could see her makeup table, complete with the

tin of junk, the notepad, and finished mug of tea. Her wardrobe was there too, with her school uniform hanging on it ready for the next day. The window was also still visible, a circle of white light standing out against the purple smoke walls.

"Ok, so this is new," Ellie said out loud.

"Not to me it isn't," the deep voice said, "To me this has been eternity, an eternity of nothing but smoke and ash."

Ellie looked around, trying to locate the source of the voice.

"Where are you? Who are you?"

"I am everywhere and nowhere. Locked in time by your ancestors to be imprisoned forever. Until such a time that things begin to change, and I can work to be free once more. You, Eleanor, you are the key to what happens next."

"Ok, I'm a little bored of being told what I am. Who are you, why can't I see you?"

The light in the window grew brighter, creating a shaft of pure white light into the room. Ellie had to shield her eyes, as it began to dim, a figure became visible to her. The light faded back to its original level. A man had appeared in the room. Thin, skeleton like where his skin was so tight against his bones. Wearing a long cloak over his shoulders, long white hair hanging down his back. His eyes were narrow, more like black slits of no light than a normal colour. His lips curled into a crude smile.

"I am," he said in the same deep tone, "The Man Of Mow."

CHAPTER 12

Ellie stared at him, the movement of the purple walls behind him made it look like he was sliding down some sort of chimney, with purple smoke billowing behind him.

"The Man Of Mow? As in, the one that the rocks are named after on the hill, the guy that people tell stories about?"

"Yes, I am."

"Right. So, I'm talking to what, a ghost?" Ellie knew she was dreaming, and would wake up at any moment, so she did not mind being brave and bold.

"A spirit. The enchantments keeping me locked away mean I can take a form like this and communicate with a chosen few, but only when things are aligned."

"What things? Aligned how?"

"All in good time, but first, I have much to show you. Get up, get your compass, and follow me."

"Compass?"

"From the tin," the figure pointed, as he did, the tin popped open.

Ellie did not move. "I don't want to, as far as I can tell, everything happened the way it should. And how do you know about the tin and what is in it?"

He looked at her. Even though his eyes were not visible, Ellie knew that he was glaring with rage.

"I have been with you since the storm last night, I have been watching. I got close enough to you when the bolt of light travelled in through your window, don't you remember that?" he smiled a twisted smile.

Ellie was in shock, unable to speak.

"Now, I said, move!"

The word 'move' echoed around the room, sending vibrations through Ellie where she sat on the bed.

Then, without realising how, she was in front of the table holding the compass. Astonished, she turned to face the figure, who had also moved and was now right in front of Ellie.

"We can do this the nice way, or the not so nice way Eleanor, I do not mind which."

Ellie was stunned. Even though she was sure this was a dream, she was scared. "I, I don't understand? Why are you so angry with me?"

He glared at her, his none eyes penetrating through her, far worse than Douglas' ever did.

"I am angry with all of you. All those who opposed and imprisoned me. But now, I can be free, and I can correct the wrongs and bring balance. They misunderstood. They were supposed to build what they built, yes, but not for me. It was only meant to be for him."

Ellie tried to take this in, "Him? Who is they? What did they build?"

"Poor girl. So misinformed and lost, I am here to correct that. Give you the knowledge you have been seeking, fill in the gaps as it were. I am here, to show you the light and in so doing free myself from eternal torment." He looked at her, his features softening, "Take my hand and I will show you, I will show you the full story of this hill and what has led us to this point, to you."

He offered his hand.

Ellie hesitated; this was so strange. She kept telling herself it was only a dream and therefore it could not hurt her. Unlike any other dream though, she could not shake herself out of it or wake herself up. Ellie realised that she had no choice, she reached out and took his hand.

All at once, everything changed. The purple smoke started to spiral down, gathering underneath where they stood as if they were at the centre of a plug hole for the room. She felt a pinch at her ankles, looking down, she saw that they had started to turn too. They were twisting around his, linking together like ice cream swirls. Then her legs, waist, and her entire body until eventually she felt like she was being squeezed through a pipe with him. Then, darkness.

Bang. Ellie was blinded by a purple light. She was standing opposite the figure once more. Their surroundings, no longer her bedroom, were being shaped out of the purple smoke, it was billowing out from where they stood, reversing the plug hole feeling from moments earlier. Ellie blinked, allowing her eyes a second to adjust before trying to take in what was now taking shape around her. Her room had gone. They were standing in a field, no, a small patch of land on the side of a hill. There was darkness, unlike her room she could not see any purple smoke walls. Infinite darkness. Trees were taking shape, hedges, and gravel paths, nothing that she recognised though.

"Do you know where we are, Eleanor?" he asked.

"No, no idea. How did we get here though?"

"This is a memory, my memory. I am telling you the story of the hill remember. This is what happened on a fateful night many years ago."

"So, I'm in your mind?"

Fear was starting to take over Ellie now, she did not feel good about where this was going.

"Not really, I am projecting my mind into you, so you can see what I see and remember. This is the night where it all begins, Eleanor. This is the night when the world turned against me for trying to help. This is the night where I was betrayed."

"Ok, ok. I get it," Ellie interrupted, "You're angry. I get that. But I don't see what any of this has to do with me?"

"You will see, tonight you will learn all that you need to know. But first, you need to know what led to this point," he gestured around him. "This is the hill that you know to be Mow Cop, the hill that is the focal point for energy and a connection between your world and the beyond. I am a spirit from the beyond. As with many worlds and realms, there are those that are good and those that are bad."

"Which are you then?" Ellie asked, feeling this was a key question.

He smiled, at least, as much as he could in his current form, "I am a spirit that wants to protect and preserve what is right between the worlds."

Ellie was not sure if this was an answer or not but decided to let it slide for the time being.

He continued, "No, I am not from your world, but I do want to protect it. I became aware of someone trying to penetrate your world from mine, they wanted to exploit it for their own gain. Your world is a physical one, air, earth, water, fire, all exist here in physical form. Mine is a world of spirit and vapour. We exist in a way that means we can only see, we cannot smell, touch, or taste. We have no concept of hot or cold, no connection to our surroundings. This man that I speak of, believed he could change that. He wanted to enter your world to absorb its energy, he wanted to take the life energy that flows through all on your planet, every animal, plant, and human would have the energy sucked from it. He would draw this into our world, believing that doing so would allow ours to exist in a physical way. In short, he wanted to extinguish life in your world to allow ours to thrive."

Ellie was trying to take all this in. It all sounded so farfetched, like something she had seen on TV or read somewhere.

"I can see you doubt me and the story I tell? Think Eleanor, think of your time in your world. Has nothing ever happened that you could not explain? Feel like time repeated itself? Feel that you have had same identical experience more than once? Dreams so real that you can't tell them apart from reality? Ever imagined something that came to pass in some way?"

Ellie considered this for a moment, "Yes, I suppose I have experienced all those things. But that doesn't prove anything."

"Are you sure about that?"

He raised his hands, creating a sphere in each, one took the shape of Earth, Ellie recognised the continents and the mix of blue and green. The other was all in purple, she could just about make out shapes on its surface, but it was all different shades of purple.

"Our world is a copy of yours, except that it does not physically exist," he brought his hands together, allowing the spheres to merge, the purple surrounding the Earth. "It has different rules, different ways of working but it is the same in desire, and it wants to survive. Most in our world are happy with their existence, we can create anything we can imagine, but we can only ever look at it. We are unable to touch or experience it for real. Our energy comes from the sun, same as yours. We use it differently; we use it as a way of pulling in spiritual energy. The things I just described, are when our presence is noticed by those on the physical side. We draw on your energy, experiences, imaginations, and creations to use in our world. The man of which I speak, wanted to open a portal that would allow us to pull all the energy out of your world in one go. In theory, our worlds would merge, but most believed it would mean the end of your world and without yours to support us, eventually ours would end too."

He lowered his hands, the spheres pulled apart and vanished. Ellie stared at him, "Right. Ok, let's say I believe you, about the whole parallel dimension thing, I am still waiting to find out what it all actually means and what it has to do with me."

He lowered his head, "As I said, those answers will come tonight. I wanted to stop this from happening. I wanted to stop him from his plan."

"Who is he?" Ellie was growing frustrated at getting vague or very little information out of this conversation.

"We do not have names. The only reason I am known as the Man Of Mow is from your world. In our world we simply know each other by passing our, what you would call, hands, through each other. We do not shout names or identify in the same way as you. We just 'know' who each other are."

Ellie looked at him. She was concerned that he seemed satisfied that this answer was enough. It was not.

"Ok, I need something here. What do you mean? If you see your mate John walking, floating, down the street are you telling me you can't shout him?"

"I could send energy to get his attention, a signal as it were, but not a name, no."

"Right," Ellie commented. This seemed to be as close as she was going to get as an answer. "Can we give him a name? For the purpose of my information gathering this evening?" she thought that she may as well try to get as much as possible.

"Yes, you said John. Let's say John is his name."

"Right. Got it. So, John the bad guy wants to take over our

world by absorbing its energy into your spiritual world. Thus, turning ours to darkness and yours to, what he believes, would be a better world? Your name is the Man Of Mow, and you tried to stop him? Is that right?"

"Eloquently summarised, Eleanor. Yes. That is correct."

"Phew. How did you try to stop him?"

"That is what happens tonight. For an age I had tried to find a way to warn your world, find a way through to someone that would listen to me and help me prevent John's plans."

He seemed happy with this, as if Ellie should thank or applaud him for helping. Or maybe it was for remembering John, she was not sure.

"I had been working to find a weak spot between worlds, a place I could get a message through. I found this hill," he gestured around them both. "This place, due to its unique structure of being a peak which stands alone, meant it was possible to pass through from our world to yours. So, I did. I reached out to people to try and warn them, none heeded my words until tonight. The village Shaman, Abijah, read my symbols and meaning. He saw what I left for him in the stars, trees, and fire embers. He had seen what would become and had decided to act. The memory you are standing in right now, is the night that he acted. Along with other members of his village, they all acted upon my warnings to protect your world. Tonight Eleanor, you will witness the very beginning of our story."

He moved to be by her side, Ellie followed him with her eyes, there was something that she did not quite trust about him.

Noticing this, the figure raised his hand to point, "There, the evenings events are about to begin."

Ellie looked. Then, created out of the smoke, a figure appeared. Shuffling his way along the path, he had dark hair and looked very frail and weak. Despite his apparent age and weakness, he had a determined look on his face. He moved past Ellie and the Man, they turned and followed him up the path. Ellie realised she was holding her breath.

"They cannot see or hear us, Eleanor," he said in her ear. "This is just a memory of what once was."

Ellie exhaled, "No idea why I was holding my breath. Hang on, they?" she asked, realising the key word in his last sentence. She looked round the figure in front of them, ahead were a group of three people crowded around a fire.

They followed Abijah up the hill. When they got there the Man and Ellie found spaces around the fire to listen to the conversation between the three figures.

"Where is Elizabeth?" Abijah asked.

"What is going on?" Ellie asked the Man.

"This is the first meeting of the first council, Abijah is the one who listened to me and tried to help. He is the one that set everything up this evening, got the group together, got them thinking and working. Around the fire we have Philippa, Isabella, and Thomas, all members of the village that are in high standing. They have met here to deal with the evil that Abijah has been telling them about. At this point, they have already created the keys, and will soon have need for the lock as well."

Ellie turned to look at him, "Keys?" she asked.

"You will see, but now, Elizabeth is coming to join us, the last member of this first council."

At the sound of a crack, the four figures turned and looked straight at Ellie. She gasped. Then realising they were not looking at her, they were looking through her, she turned to see what they were looking at. A woman with long dark hair and tired looking skin was walking towards them, Ellie noticed immediately that she was carrying something close to her chest.

"You are very jumpy," Elizabeth exclaimed, as she walked up the hill to the group.

Elizabeth passed through Ellie, for a moment she felt as though she would disappear, but she was soon able to turn to face the circle once more, moving slightly to her left to see around the new member to the group. The bundle had been placed on the floor and Ellie realised it was a baby, wrapped in a bundle of cloths and rags. Looking up, Ellie noted that the group were looking at the baby but had all recoiled from it as if it were dangerous.

"So," Abijah began, "we all know why we are here?"

Everyone nodded.

He continued, "We have all prepared our totems and left them in the precise agreed location in our huts?"

"Totems?" Ellie asked.

"Totems, keys, obelisks, they are all different names for the same thing. The same five stones that stand strong from this moment until your time, until the moment one cracked."

Ellie's eyes lit up. She turned to face the Man, "You mean, the stone in our garden? The one we couldn't do anything with is part of this," she gestured in front of her. "These people created those stones, tonight?"

"They created them in the build up to tonight, yes, and placed them at specific points around the hill. All following my instruction, through Abijah, I was able to direct the group to create the keys and lock."

"Where is the lock?" Ellie asked.

"Soon. Soon," he replied, "But for now, look."

Ellie turned. The woman who she now knew as Elizabeth was walking up the hill, baby in arms. Looking around Ellie realised the folly was not there yet. It was just an empty hill.

"What is she doing?" she asked.

"She is placing the child at the point where our worlds meet, at the exact point in space. She, the child that is, must be lined up perfectly for this to work. The idea is they are creating a barrier between the worlds, a prison space. They are going to trap, John as you called him, in that space so he is unable to cause any more damage to either world. I gave Abijah the tools he needed, I gave him the information and he followed it perfectly."

"So where is John now? Is he here?"

"He is with the child, he attached himself, soul for soul, to the baby. He needed to grow with the child until they became strong enough, then he would take over and carry out his plan. What the group are doing here is removing him from the child, forcing him back into the space between worlds that they have created."

"Right," Ellie nodded. "So, they are forcing his spirit out of the baby, and into a sort of prison between your world and mine? The keys, the stones, they keep him secure?"

"Yes, along with the lock they keep him in that secure place.

Unfortunately, this didn't go exactly to plan," he gestured up the hill. "The child has been placed as per instructions, head to the north, but I made a grave mistake," he lowered his head. Ellie wanted to ask what the mistake was but decided to watch and ask questions later. The woman had returned now and was being comforted by the others around the fire. All except Abijah who was looking up at the sky. For a few moments, nothing happened. Looking around, Ellie could see that the people who had actually experienced this night for real were equally as puzzled by this. They all looked nervous, uneasy, as if waiting for something big to happen.

Elizabeth took a couple of steps forward, "Why is nothing happening?" she asked.

Ellie was confused, she too was expecting something to happen. With the way that the Man had gone on about this evening, the plan, keys, and locks, she expected something. Then she noticed Abijah. He had not moved but was the only one looking up. She followed his gaze. The stars had gone, the sky was completely black. Ellie squinted, trying to pierce the darkness with her eyes. Then, suddenly, she saw it, or rather, saw him. A figure, with an appearance like that of the Man that she was with right now. He was floating, silently, as if made of smoke and cloud himself towards the crest of the hill. Above him, clouds had appeared, deep purple clouds starting to twist into a spiral with its centre directly above the peak of the hill. Ellie could not turn her eyes away from the floating figure, it appeared to have gone unnoticed by the group around the fire. That is the man responsible for what is about to happen, that is the man that everyone is trying to stop, Ellie thought to herself.

"You are correct," the Man's voice spoke.

She turned to face him.

"Yes, I can hear your thoughts Eleanor, and you are right. That is the person everyone wants to stop."

Still shocked by this, and aware that she should probably be careful as much as she could about what she thought now, Ellie turned back towards the peak of the hill. She adjusted her focus, the ghost like figure was nearly at the peak now, as was Elizabeth. As she looked, she heard Abijah shout.

"Wait! You're too close! Something is about to happ..."

As Ellie watched, the sky seemed to be ripped apart by a bolt of light, it tore down to the hilltop and hit where the child lay, sending Elizabeth tumbling down the hill. As Ellie and the Man were just observing, they were not affected by the force of the impact. Looking around, Ellie could see the group all on their backs, looking up at the sky. Trees were sent sprawling, grass and bushes pushed outwards in a circle with the child at its centre. Glancing up at the sky, Ellie could see the spirals of cloud that she had noticed moments earlier were spinning faster and faster, still twisting round as if the peak of the hill were pulling them in. There was another bright bolt of light, this time, it was reflected out five times, one beam heading straight for Ellie. On impulse, she ducked, then remembering where she was, she stood up and looked down the beam of light. It headed away from the peak, scorching everything in its path until it hit a barrier. Looking around, Ellie could see a purple tinted sphere had appeared around the top of the hill, it looked as though it was containing all the destruction, and nothing was getting through it.

"The sphere has been created by the keys, the stones," the Man explained to her, clearly reading her thoughts again. "The process is being contained and they will force it as closely as they can to the centre, there," he pointed up the hill to where the child lay.

Rocks were appearing around Ellie, and indeed all over the hill now, it was changing, evolving underneath their feet. It felt as though the entire hill would explode with energy. The five beams of light retreated to the centre; Ellie strained her eyes to see what was going on at the top of the hill. At the moment the beams hit the centre, she saw a hand reach out from the bundle that until now, had the child in it. For the next few seconds, everything seemed to be in slow motion. Ellie was sure that this was just for her and in real time this would have been unnoticeable. As the light began to lift back up towards the sky, the bundle of rags that the baby was wrapped up in was lifted off the ground, the hand still sticking out holding the ghost like figure next to it. The bundle unravelled, revealing not a baby, not even a human, but another ghost like figure, another spirit like the Man and the one that it had grabbed hold of. The two figures, now grappling with each other were being pulled up towards the sky, being pulled towards the very centre of the spirals of clouds. The light grew brighter, everyone except Ellie and the man shielded their eyes. She could see the figures getting closer to the clouds, the beam of light following them up like a shining golden rope. Then, darkness. The figures had gone, the light had vanished. All that was left in the sky was a face of contorted pain made up of clouds and purple smoke. Seconds later, the purple bubble around them vanished, so did the clouds and smoke, returning the sky to its former star filled state. Ellie looked around at the devastation, as the group of observers picked themselves up, she noted new rocks, broken trees and bushes, scorched grass, and burnt fences. The energy had destroyed the hilltop. The group, led by Abijah, headed up the peak to where the child, or spirit, had been.

"What was that?" asked Ellie.

"The baby, or at least, what appeared to be a baby, was John. The spirit that he grabbed, the one you saw him grappling with as he was sent through his gateway, was me. I had visited to ensure that my plan would work, I wanted to make sure that his evil would be captured and contained. I got too close, he grabbed me and used all his remaining energy to trap me and keep me in there with him. The face you saw in the clouds, was my own."

Ellie's mouth dropped open, "You mean, you got trapped in there as well, for all this time?" she could not help but feel a certain amount of sympathy for him.

"Yes. It is a small price to pay to ensure the safety of our worlds," he lowered his head once more, "I needed to be sure this would work, Eleanor. I had to know."

"I understand," this was a lie, but she did not know what else to say. "What happened next?"

"I was only able to view from afar, I was not able to move around or listen to the conversations."

He gestured with his hands; the moment he did time seemed to speed up. The weather moved fast overhead, night turned into day and then night again in seconds over and over. Ellie looked; in front of her eyes the folly was being built. It looked like a time lapse video, watching something that clearly took months but reviewed in seconds. Every now and then she would notice a face she recognised from the night around the fire, Abijah, Elizabeth, and the others. The whole village seemed to be helping build the folly. Then, the Man gestured once more, and the image froze.

"The folly was completed later that year, Eleanor. This is it, brand new, its tower standing proud, the wall strong and its purpose fulfilled. This, Eleanor, this is the lock. The lock that would keep John and I hidden away. This, supported by the five keys, would keep us imprisoned. Held strong by a magic that would be firm forever more, for as long as everyone believes in it."

Ellie walked up the peak to the folly. It looked new, because it was, but it was clear that it was the same basic structure that she had explored for real with Simon. The tower had no roof, the windows had no glass, and the wall with its arch was just that. A single wall with an arch.

"How? How does this work?" she asked.

"It's actually quite simple."

She turned and glared at him.

"I mean If you ignore the fact it's a magical lock to a mystical world. The tower acts as the focal point for the energy, it is directly where the scene you just saw took place. The light beams you saw are only visible when huge amounts of energy are being passed through, however the folly is always getting a beam of energy focused through the tower. The five windows around its walls are directly in line with the five obelisks, one of which is in your garden. As long as the five obelisks are in place and intact, the energy is kept in the folly, focused by the tower and pushed up into the portal's entrance. Keeping John, and myself, securely trapped."

"So, the folly is the lock, and the rocks are the keys? But because one has broken, you were able to escape? Does that mean John has as well?"

"Yes. If you look at the compass you brought with you, and line up the needle, you will see that the other arrow points directly from this spot to the obelisk at your house. The person who lived there before worked many parts of this story out."

Ellie checked; he was right. The compass did seem to point towards her own house, or at least, where it would be in the future.

"Though, we have not fully escaped, we can only make small trips at certain times, and I needed to wait for the storm to hit the hill. The extra energy last night allowed me to get through. Now though, I do not know about John's where-abouts, or his next move. I believe he is still trapped, but I am trying to find out. My plan, overall, worked. It did act as a trap and it did hold firm. But I did not consider that belief may not hold, that one day something may happen that meant the lock and keys would not be strong enough."

Ellie processed this, "Are you saying, that because I stopped going to the meetings, because I stopped believing, our obelisk broke, meaning the lock has started to fail?"

"Simply put, yes."

"But my parents have been going to the meetings, why me? Why don't they get told all this?"

"Because, Eleanor, you are the first born of your line to not have any siblings in the timeline. You are the first in your long line of family history to be an only child, with no promise of siblings. Am I right?"

Ellie was frozen to the spot. She had no idea how he knew this, but he did. She was an only child and would only ever be an only child. Her parents had told her before that they did not want nor did they plan to have any more children. They loved her, and she was all they ever needed. She thought hard, her dad was an only child too, her mother had a sister. Her mother's dad had a sister. She pondered, thinking hard.

"I, I can't think of a family member on my mums' side that did not have a sibling."

"I know."

"But I don't know my entire family history! Surely there would be someone that didn't in her family line somewhere?"

"There is, or rather, there was, one child born that did not have a sibling."

"See! So, what are you talking about? Why me? Why now?"

"Because," he said in the softest voice he could, "that child was born a long time ago, but did not live long enough to have an impact." He looked at her, his colourless eyes boring into her.

"Tell me!" Ellie shouted, tears forming at the corner of her eyes now. "Who was it, and why me?"

"The child's name," he said, "was Joanna. And you just saw her be taken into the portal with me."

Ellie collapsed to her knees, all the energy and life seemed to have been sucked out of her. Had she just seen her ancestor die? Or at least get sucked into a portal to another world. "That was my great, great, great, great grandma or something? How is that even possible? If she didn't live long enough to have children, how can she be my ancestor?"

"This is where it gets confusing."

She glared at him though her tears.

"When those events unfolded, yes, the child was taken up into the portal with us, but she didn't appear in there. We do not know where she went. Her spirit did not show itself and the body was not left behind. However, what we have not seen tonight is that when Elizabeth returned to her dwelling that night, there was another child waiting for her. A child with the same birth marks as Joanna, a baby girl. Because the only people that knew what had happened up here were the council, they all agreed that Elizabeth should raise her as Joanna as if that evening never happened. It is that Joanna that became your ancestor. John chose Joanna because of her being an only child. He knew that she would be easier to manipulate on her own."

"Why did the second child appear?"

"That I do not know, that was not accounted for in my calculations and creations. All I know is that the plan worked, the plan worked except that two spirits got trapped instead of one, and one child was lost only to be replaced by another."

Ellie stood up, wiping the tears from her face she looked at the man squarely in the eyes.

"Ok, what do you need me to do?"

He smiled at her, "Eleanor, we need to fix it and trap John for good."

"Right, so we need to restore the obelisk and then that's done yeah? Is that it?"

"In theory, but in practice I fear that will not be enough. The damage is done, the lack of belief has cracked the foundations of that key. This in turn increased the pressure on the other keys which have also cracked, although not as badly."

"So, what do we do?"

"We need to destroy the lock, with John still in it. I believe that if we destroy it, he will have no way to even attempt to escape. Think of a room with no doors to prize open."

"You want me to destroy the folly, how exactly do I do that?"

"We need to recreate the conditions from the night you just witnessed, we need to get John to attach to you in the same way he did Joanna then get you to the top of the hill during a full moon of winter. The combination of his energy and yours, mixed with the power running through the folly still should be enough to destroy the gateway and pull him through."

"And take me with it, you want me to sacrifice myself?" Ellie had pieced this together herself very quickly.

"Eleanor, it will be for the greater good. It is much to ask, but it is you or the billions in your world. He must be stopped."

"Sorry, no. there must be another way, there must be."

He looked at her, "I will try to find another way, but please remember, you may not have a choice. You were chosen, you were destined to be this person and to live in this village. You were chosen for the council, you carry the symbol of the Man Of Mow, my symbol."

"Yes, that's a point. How did that necklace get into my pocket?"

He smiled a knowing smile, "Do you remember this event?"

He gestured with his hands again. The folly and the hill dissolved around her into purple vapour and was replaced by a city street.

Ellie looked around, and quickly recognised it as the street where she used to live in London. Turning, she saw herself walking up the road looking at the sky. "Is this the last night I saw my friends in London?"

"Yes, can you remember what happened?"

Ellie thought then exclaimed, "That guy! He bumped into me."

"Yes, look."

Ellie looked; the scene had frozen at the moment she brushed past him. She walked over to herself and looked at her pocket. As she brushed past him, he had slipped the necklace into her pocket, she had not noticed because she had been so scared that she had ran home and threw the jacket into a bag. "I didn't wear that jacket until…" she paused.

"Until the first night you went to the council meeting, yes. That man is Douglas' nephew, he is used when the council need to reach out without revealing themselves. They knew who you were before you arrived, they knew you would be the one to help. They have tracked the lineage through time, since that first council. They have tracked the births and deaths of the families, right the way down to you. The council members have changed, but their job has not. They knew they may not be there when this happened, but they still created the documents, the notes, and made the preparations. It was always you, Eleanor. Always."

This was too much. She had taken in too much information, too much of a burden. She just wanted a quiet normal life, she wanted to hang out with her friends, laugh, joke, grow up, and make mistakes like everyone should be able to. "It's not fair," was all she could say.

"I know, but it is your destiny," as he said this, with a wave of his hand, the London street started to dissolve into vapour around them. "I have told you all I can for now, it is nearly time for you to get up."

Ellie looked at him, she had forgotten that this was a dream. "You expect me to go back to normal after this?"

"Yes. You must carry on as normal, we must allow John to find you and we must destroy the lock. You need his energy, at the right moment, to pull him up and away before it is destroyed. Remember, you need to be in the right place, at the right time."

"How do I make him attach to me?"

"You must continue to not believe, he must think he can win you over, let him believe he can win."

"Will you be there to help?"

"As much as I can, but I must keep a distance otherwise he

will suspect. You know what is needed, you know the plan, and you must get to the folly, with John, at a full moon of winter."

"Hang on, I can't remember all this."

"You don't have to; you have been writing this whole time."

And with a bang, he and the purple vapour were gone.

Ellie blinked. She was sat at her table, with the compass in one hand and a pen in the other. Looking down at the note-pad, she saw she had written down everything. The last line sent a chill down her spine:

It is up to me, to save the world.

CHAPTER 13

For a little while, Ellie did nothing. She did not move or speak; all she did was stare at her notepad. At that one line. Eventually, she lowered her pen, put the compass down, and stood up. It was six AM, she would need to be ready for school soon. She went to the bathroom, splashed some water on her face and looked in the mirror. She did not see what she expected to see, she thought she would see a tired looking face, one filled with fear, concern, and worry. Maybe she would even see something to remind her of the night's events, would she see the Man looking over her shoulder? But no, all Ellie saw looking back at her, was her own face. Her blue eyes wide, her blonde hair in the same ponytail she had put it in last night, and her face looking surprisingly refreshed. Maybe she had slept well? Maybe the dream had helped her drift into a deep sleep that had refreshed her for the day ahead? Turning off the tap, drying her face and hands she went back into the bedroom. Looking at the table she had a realisation; dreams do not make you write things down. She walked over to the table with determination, picked up the notepad, and stormed over to the window seat. Flinging open the curtains she looked up at the folly, still there, standing proud on the hill. Exhaling with something like rage, Ellie sat at the seat and began to flick through her notepad. It was all there, an almost perfect copy of what she had seen and heard last night. Everything from the compass to the ritual on the hill all those centuries ago, the child, her ancestor, the street in London, all of it was there. She had even drawn a diagram, showing what looked like the folly in the middle with five dots around it, presumably the stones. It had a caption under it:

Five keys and a lock, we must destroy the lock.

Ellie kept skim reading the notepad, flicking furiously in hope to find something to prove that this was all crazy. Nothing. Everything she saw pointed towards this being a physical copy of what she had hoped was only something in her head. Clearly not. She lowered the notepad to her lap and stared out the window. Not at anything in particular, but just at the world. How was she going to get through this one? Ellie concluded that she needed help, she needed to share this with someone. There was only one choice at this stage, Simon. Ellie decided that she would take the notepad with her to school, talk to Simon, and if he agreed allow him to read it. This decision made Ellie feel confident, it even relaxed her a little, the beginnings of a plan no matter how small, was always a reason to be cheerful. She moved off the bench seat, slipped the notepad into her school bag and started to get ready. After showering and getting dressed, Ellie was downstairs eating breakfast when her dad came into the kitchen.

"Morning Ellie, recovered after your long weekend?" he asked cheerily.

"Yes, thanks dad. Was a good weekend, all set for another week of hard learning," she saluted in a comedic way.

"Very funny. I hope you do learn lots, you have your future ahead of you, young lady," he walked over, kissed his daughter on the head and the headed for the door. "Got to go, love you long time, Ellie Bear."

"Love you too dad," she called after him, then looked down at her cereal, "Now more than ever," she muttered to herself.

Ellie got to the bus stop first and was waiting eagerly for Simon when she saw him wandering up the hill to meet her.

"Hey smelly Ellie," he called when he was not too far away.

"Morning serious Simon," she replied.

They hugged and smiled.

"So, did you guys have much storm damage?" he asked.

Ellie realised that with everything that had gone on with Sophie and the garden yesterday, she had not spoken to him since Saturday night when they found the tin. "Yes, the garden was trashed! What about you?"

"Yeah, mainly non-important stuff though, flower beds that sort of thing. Nothing I couldn't fix."

"We had to swap a fence panel; it was a right sight. Dad, Sophie, and I battling a piece of wood into place," she laughed.

Simon looked at her, "What's up? I can see something in your eyes?"

She decided to act quickly, Simon knew about the tin, so she would use that to get going into the detail of the notepad. "Simon, I need your help. You remember the tin, yeah?"

"How can I forget, we did well to keep straight faces I think, did you talk to Sophie about it? I mean that was…"

"Shhhh!" she cut across him.

He looked shocked.

"Sorry, I just need to tell you and ask you something before we have other sets of ears around is all."

He frowned, "Ok, go on. I'm listening."

"So, that night there was the storm yeah? And the next day we all had damage? Except we also had a damaged stone. That big rock you've seen in the garden?"

"Wow, really. A broken stone? How did you keep that quiet for so long?" he replied sarcastically.

Ellie punched him on the top of the arm.

"Ow!" he shouted.

"Just listen. Well, as we were clearing the garden Douglas came to visit and gave me the whole speech about needing my help again bla bla bla. I gave him an answer to shut him up and make him go away."

Simon nodded, seemingly scared to speak now.

"Anyway, last night I had what I'm going to say was a dream. A dream when I saw the past, I saw the folly be built, I saw a ritual on the hill, I saw a man give me the necklace, the one we threw away. I saw all of it."

"All of it. You mean, the stuff that the rumours go on about?"

"Yes."

"Stuff that nobody has ever spoken to you about before?"

"Some of it was new, yes."

"Ok, I'm interested, keep going."

Ellie frowned at him, "I can go off people you know, be nice," she smirked, at the same time pulling her bag round and reaching inside for the notepad.

He smiled back, "Go on."

"Yes, I saw loads of stuff, and I thought it was just a dream until this morning, when I found this," she held up the notepad.

"A notepad?" he asked, raising his eyebrows.

"Yes, my notepad. The same one that I had written in before, about the council, the tin box, all of it."

Simon looked puzzled, "Ok, waiting for the bombshell to drop."

She smiled, "It's now full of everything I thought I dreamed. All of it," she flicked through the pages to show him. "It has got detailed notes, drawings, and loads of stuff that I thought I had dreamt about last night in there. It explains all of it from angles that I would never have known unless the dream was, well, real." She looked at him, trying to read his response. Nothing. She slapped her hands down against her sides, "Say something Simon!"

He snapped out of whatever trance her was in, "Sorry Ellie, I was trying to process it all. Wow. Ok. Right." He seemed to be gathering his thoughts. "So, you're saying that you wrote down the dream you had, whilst you were in the dream, in perfect detail? So now you have a written record of what was going on and potentially what all the craziness means?"

"Simply put, yes. I woke up sat at my table, pen in hand over the last page," she turned to it and turned it around to show him, pointing at the last line.

Simon peered at the page, then his eyes widened, "Really? That serious?"

"Out of context it seems crazy, actually with context it's crazy but without it is even worse I grant you. It's all in there Simon. You're the first person I've told and the only one I feel I can really trust."

Simon stared at her.

"Will you help me?"

"Save the world?" he asked, a look of fear spreading across his face. "That's a bit much don't you think?"

"Yes it is, I'm not really sure on that, but will you please read this, process it, and let me know what you think I should do?" Ellie was pleading now, and she knew it.

Simon looked at her with a sympathetic smile, "Ok, I'll read it. I won't tell anyone, obviously, but yes, I will read it and let you know what I think. It is creepy though Ellie."

Ellie went to give him the notepad.

"No, don't give it to me yet, I don't want it at school as I can't read it there. Can I come around tonight and read it? A home-work visit?"

Ellie beamed at him, "Yes, yes, yes. Absolutely. Thank you, Simon." She leapt forward and gave him a big hug and a kiss on the cheek, "Thank you so much."

"I haven't done anything yet."

"Exactly. You didn't laugh, mock, or tease me, you just said yes. That's why I love you as I do Simon Lesley," she pulled back.

"You love me?" he asked.

"Yes, as a friend silly! Love doesn't just mean the other thing you know. When will boys learn this?" she smiled and put the notepad back in her bag.

He smiled back, "I understand. Love you too Ellie."

A few moments later, the bus arrived. They boarded and moved onto other less sensitive topics on their way to school.

The Monday morning at school was a normal one, Ellie was relaxed and calm considering her predicament. She was sat at a table during lunchtime with her friends, looking round at them all she began to realise how lucky she was to have met and be accepted by them. Tyler did nothing but talk sports, he had got Ellie into the girls' football team. Dan and Leo were reliable for homework help and anything related to technical stuff. She had spoken to them many a time about her phone and laptop, not to mention homework. Simon was her best friend that she trusted with anything. Then there was Anna-belle. Annabelle with her long dark hair and gorgeous happy face. Ellie found herself staring at Annabelle, fixated on her smile. Anabelle turned to face Ellie and smiled. Ellie smiled back but was drawn into her brown eyes.

"What are you staring at?" Annabelle asked quizzically, looking at Ellie.

Ellie blushed, "Sorry was just daydreaming." Ellie was not sure why she had been staring at Annabelle so intently, something had clearly caught her eye, but she did not know what it was.

Annabelle raised an eyebrow, "Hmmmmm ok! Well, stop it," she smirked.

Ellie realised that even when angry Annabelle looked happy and chirpy. She smiled back, "Will do." Whilst Ellie had been having a good day, she had spent a lot of it daydreaming about the notepad and what Simon would say after reading it. She turned to look out of the window. It was a grey overcast day, but otherwise dry.

"We best be getting over to science, Ellie. Simmons won't like us being late," Leo called.

She turned and looked at him, "Yeah guess so, bell will go soon and it's a walk."

She stood and slung her bag over her shoulder. As she did so, one strap slipped, and her bag dropped open spilling some of its contents onto the table and floor.

Cheers from her friends greeted Ellie, who stuck her tongue out in retaliation at them. With a little help from the others, soon her bag was back together, and she left the room with Leo. The bell rang just as they got to science, they were not too worried though as they were by no means the last to arrive. They took their seats and got their stuff out, ready for the class to start. Ellie found the class to be normal, the usual mix of chatting and learning. No experiments today, but lots of theory and textbook reading. One thing that was different, was an increased amount of chatter coming from behind. Ellie and Leo were sat in the middle of the class, with about the same number of tables behind as in front. Ellie was intrigued, what was causing all the giggling and chatting behind her. She glanced over her shoulder, Rochelle, the girl who had been rude from the beginning and indeed had competed with Ellie regularly this term was sitting in the middle of her two friends, Lucy and Mary. They were both very much in the camp of 'whatever Rochelle says, we like, laugh at, or support'. Ellie concluded that they were just being their usual giggly selves and turned back to face the front. Then she overheard Rochelle say something that made her heart skip a beat.

"Five keys and a lock, break them to save the world. What a load of old rubbish."

Ellie turned sharply to look at them, she could not quite see what they were looking at as their bags had been stacked deliberately to hide it. She reached down for her own bag and started to rummage through it quickly. After a few seconds, her fears became more real, the notepad was not there. She looked up again, she was sure they had the notepad, it must have been missed when she dropped her stuff in the canteen earlier.

"What you got there Rochelle?" she asked.

In the moment Ellie had decided that being upfront and forceful was probably the best approach. Forgetting who she was dealing with, this may not have been the best move. Rochelle, Lucy, and Mary all looked up at once.

"What's it to you, Eleanor?" Rochelle replied, backed up by the sneers on the faces of Lucy and Mary.

"It's clearly giving you a giggle, thought you may want to share with us all," Ellie replied, thinking quickly but not clearly or indeed at her best.

Rochelle stared at her, clearly trying to weigh up her options, "None of your business," was the stern reply.

Ellie flashed scarlet with rage, "Rochelle, I don't think what you're looking at is yours, I think you should hand it in or find out who it belongs to." Ellie spoke through gritted teeth; she had now resigned herself to the fact that Rochelle would know it was hers.

Rochelle smiled, "I think I already know whose it is," she winked at Ellie. "I wonder what it is worth to you, Ellie Bear?" The three girls roared with laughter.

Ellie stood up without thinking, fists clenched at her sides, "Give. It. Back."

"OOOO Somebody didn't know they had lost this did they, how long have you been working on your novel, Ellie Bear?"

"Stop calling me that! You only know that from reading that thing anyway!"

"Exactly," Rochelle replied, calmly. "I've enjoyed reading this since I found it earlier, even though it is poor even by your standards."

Ellie went to move forwards, but before she could, Mrs Simmons had appeared at her shoulder.

"What exactly are you doing Eleanor? Standing up and turning away from me. I have been trying to get your attention for far too long, what is going on here."

Rochelle spoke before Ellie could, in her sweetest possible voice, "She was trying to take my notepad from me, Mrs Simmons," smirking at Ellie as she said it.

Ellie stepped forward, "That's not true and you know it, Rochelle! It's my notepad and I want it back."

Mrs Simmons had positioned herself between the two girls, "Well, I don't care who's it is, it is distracting my lesson. So, here is what will happen next. Rochelle, put the notepad away, if I see it again, I will confiscate it, I am well aware that you have been reading it all lesson. Eleanor, you will sit down, face the front and ignore Rochelle for the remainder of this class..."

"But," Ellie tried to interrupt.

"No buts. Just do it. Or it will be detention for both of you."

Rochelle, grinning, sat down and slid the notepad into her bag. Ellie, glaring, turned and sat down.

"Now then," Mrs Simmons said, "Shall we get back to photosynthesis? If I hear a peep out of either of you, detention!" With that, she walked back to the front of the class.

"What was that about?" Leo whispered to Ellie.

"Nothing, just my sort of diary thing is all. Must have fell out my bag and she's got it," Flicking her head back towards Rochelle.

"We will sort it," he smiled.

Ellie smiled back, knowing internally that this was a problem. She needed the book back but also did not want it being spread around. Rochelle would not give it up easily, she needed a plan.

After science had finished, when the class was packing up, Ellie turned to face Rochelle. She had clearly been expecting this, and her reply stunned Ellie into silence.

"Listen, Eleanor, I don't want your book. I am however enjoying watching you want it. So, how's about we make a deal. A bet."

This was not what Ellie was expecting, but with little options available to her she replied, "Go on."

Rochelle grinned, clearly enjoying the power she currently had over Ellie. "I challenge you to a basketball shootout, everyone knows you're the star on the football field, but what about basketball?" the grin on Rochelle's face turned to a sneer.

"Ok, you're on," Ellie replied. "Best of five? Winner gets the book?"

"Best of five. If you win, you get the book and I swear I will not mention it again. But, if I win, I get the book and will share it as widely as I can. Wonder if you will still be little miss popular then?"

Ellie could feel rage building inside her, "Fine," was all she could manage.

Rochelle smiled, "See you after school then, on the main court, I'll bring the ball."

With that, she left flanked by Lucy and Mary.

Ellie turned, snatched up her own bag and stormed out of the room.

The rest of the afternoon was a blur, all Ellie could think about was the challenge laid down by Rochelle. Normally she would feel confident, but the pressure and anger of what would happen if she got this wrong was affecting her. The end of school could not come soon enough. Between them, Leo and Ellie had told the others. What did surprise Ellie, is how much support she got from all the others even though they did not know what this was really about. They thought it was all over a diary, Ellie could not help but wonder to herself who would get so wound up about a diary but that was a thought for another day. The bell rang, signalling the end of the day. Ellie left the school building and headed over to the main court where she could see that Rochelle was already there. Along with Lucy and Mary, all of whom looked happy with what was about to happen. Ellie was pleased that all four of her friends were able to come too, they would not be able to do much, but their support was appreciated. She gave her bag to Annabelle to hold and stepped forward.

"Ok, Rochelle. I'm here. Let's get this over with."

"Well, where is the competitive fun spirit Eleanor?" she sneered.

"This is no time for fun, Rochelle, you know full well that I just want my notepad back!"

"I do, Eleanor, I do," she smiled. Then after a second of silence, "Ok, shall we get going then? Best of five, that is, whoever scores the most out of five wins. In the event of a tie, sudden death. Agreed?"

"Yes. Who goes first?"

"Why, I do of course. It is my game after all."

"Get on with it then," Ellie took a step to the side as she said this.

The group shifted, Rochelle moving to the free throw line, Leo and Lucy standing either side of the hoop to return the ball. The others all formed a semi-circle around the throwing line, meaning there was a nice audience for the person doing the throwing.

Rochelle bounced the ball, then took aim. Straight into the basket.

"All net," she shouted to cheers from Lucy and Mary.

Leo grabbed the ball and threw it to Ellie, "Come on Ellie!" he shouted.

The others clapped and gave words of encouragement.

Ellie bounced the ball. Took aim, threw, in off the backboard. Yes! she cheered to herself internally. There were cheers from her friends.

Rochelle took the ball, took aim and threw. Again, straight in to cheers from her friends.

The event was turning into a mini cheering match as well as shooting competition.

Ellie collected the ball, took aim, threw, and missed. The ball hit the edge of the ring and bounced back straight into Rochelle's hands who roared with laughter.

"Two - one to me with three to throw," she gloated, stepping up to the line.

Ellie turned away; she was angry with herself as she knew she could do this. She stared at the floor, hands on her hips. She heard cheers from behind, surely this was three - one? Turning, she realised it was not. The cheers were coming from her friends, Rochelle had missed. Ellie felt uplifted, focused, and driven once more. Leo threw her the ball, she caught it and stepped up to the line, without bouncing the ball she went straight for the throw and it hit nothing but net. "I think that's two - two isn't it?" she asked, a small smile crossing her face as she saw Rochelle's face drop.

Rochelle took the ball from Lucy, anger across her face now. She looked at Ellie, sneered, and then focused on the hoop once more. Bounced the ball, straight in. she smiled at Ellie, "Advantage is mine still," flicking her hair with arrogance.

Ellie stepped up, focused.

As she went to throw the ball Lucy shouted "BANG" at the top of her voice.

The sudden interruption caused Ellie's hands to slip, meaning the ball did not get the elevation it needed. It fell short of the hoop and missed. This though caused the already simmering pot to boil over.

"You are a cheating bunch of losers," Simon shouted, advancing on Lucy. "You couldn't take a fair one on one, could you?" Lucy, clearly pleased with herself retorted, "What you gonna do Simon? You going to hit little old me defending your girlfriend?"

"She is not my girlfriend!" he shouted and clenched his fists.

"Simon, leave it," Ellie shouted. Whilst she loved the support, she did not want a fight breaking out. "It's not over yet," she finished off, glaring at Rochelle.

"You banking on me missing, are you? Let's see shall we."

Everyone settled down, back into a viewing mode. Simon, still red from his anger, stood right by Lucy, clearly readying for whatever may happen next.

Rochelle, steadying herself, bounced the ball once more. She went to throw. Simon, Annabelle, and Leo all shouted "BANG" at the same time.

Rochelle did not release the ball, "Nice try," she gloated and then threw. As soon as it left her hands she turned to Ellie, looking right at her and not the ball or hoop. "I hope you enjoy reading your diary online later," she glared at Ellie with a smirk.

Ellie did not respond; she was too busy watching the ball. Which to her delight, had not gone in. She smiled, fully aware that Rochelle did not know what was going on behind her.

"Well, I will read it, but not online I'm afraid Rochelle. It didn't go in, it's three - two to you, and I still have one shot left."

Rochelle whirled around, "What?"

"It didn't go in, Roch," Mary said sheepishly.

"Why didn't you tell me?" she demanded. "You have made me look like an idiot now."

"You do that easily yourself," Annabelle commented, much to Ellie's delight.

"Shut it you," Rochelle snapped.

Annabelle stepped forward squaring up to Rochelle, "Why? What you going to do?"

Rochelle backed off a little at this, Annabelle was taller and clearly not afraid to stand up to her if she needed to.

"Anyway, you missed. It's my turn. I miss, you win, I score, sudden death. Now, shall we agree no more silly interruptions Rochelle?" Ellie asked, trying to get a little calmer, though in truth the way Annabelle stood up for her sent a few flutters through her stomach.

Turning to face Ellie, Rochelle agreed, "Ok, yes. Everyone shut up now."

She stomped away to watch.

Ellie stepped forward, picked up the ball. She bounced it, taking aim. Nothing but net.

"Three - three then, sudden death it is," she said, smiling at Rochelle.

Ellie was still nervous, the pressure was on, but seeing Rochelle's concern helped her relax a little.

"Fine," Rochelle snapped, picking up the ball and stepping forwards. After a moments delay, she threw. Missed. Ellie and her friends cheered with glee, Simon punching the air.

"Come on Ellie, one more you got this!" he shouted.

Rochelle, clearly angry at herself, stormed to the side, "You still have to score, Eleanor!"

"I know," Ellie replied calmly. She stepped forward, bounced the ball and took aim. For a brief moment, she could see nothing but the basket and hoop, she poured all her energy and focus into it, willing it in. She released the ball, taking a deep breath and holding it, she closed her eyes unable to watch. For a moment there was nothing, then, the noise was deafening. Dan and Annabelle screamed and ran over to Ellie, wrapping her in a big group hug. Simon jeered in front of Lucy and Leo did the same to Mary. Ellie broke away from the huddle, breathed a sigh of relief and walked over to Rochelle, who was crouched to her knees on the floor.

"Good game Rochelle, good game," she offered her hand to help her up.

Rochelle slapped it away and stood, putting her face right into Ellie's and snarled, "You just wait, you just wait. I've had enough of your little miss perfect attitude and I'm going to wipe that smile off your face one day you show off little…"

But she was cut short. She was cut short by Annabelle who had moved round, pushed Ellie to one side and shoved Rochelle to the floor. Rochelle went tumbling backwards, Lucy and Mary tried to get through, but Simon and Leo were containing them. Rochelle lifted herself up onto her elbows, a look of shock on her face.

"You will never wipe the smile off of anyone's face, Rochelle," Annabelle said through gritted teeth. "Now hand over the diary."

Rochelle picked herself up, still showing signs of anger across her face. She took a step forward, "Who do you think you are, Annabelle?"

Annabelle squared her shoulders, drawing herself up to her full height apparently preparing to fight. "I'm just me, and you're just you. You lost, fair and square, now hand it over," she offered her hand.

Rochelle glared, "Fine! But this is not over, all of you, especially you and you," pointing at Annabelle and Ellie, "This is not over." She stormed over to her bag, pulled out the notepad and threw it to Ellie. "There, enjoy writing your precious diary."

Ellie caught it, "Thanks," Was all she could say. She was still staring at Annabelle; she had never seen her so pumped up and physical before.

The three girls glared at each other, then Rochelle gathered her things and stormed away. Lucy and Mary following close behind. For a moment, Ellie just stared after them, almost making sure they kept walking, then the five that were left all gathered together in a mini group hug celebration.

"Thank you all," Ellie said through tears and sniffles of joy, "I couldn't have done that without your help."

"We didn't do anything," Leo said, "Well, Annabelle did, never seen you be so tough before."

"Well, now you know to watch your step don't you," she winked at him. "I'm tougher than I look and when I see someone I care about being bullied, I'll step in."

She turned slightly and smiled at Ellie.

"Thanks Annabelle. Thanks to you all! You have no idea how important this book is right now."

"We don't need to know, if it is important to you, it is important to us," said Dan, reassuringly.

The group stayed together for a short while, but soon they all needed to head to the buses to get home. As usual, Simon and Ellie were the last ones on the bus, alone, they finally had a chance to discuss the diary and the day they had.

"So, that wasn't bad for a Monday was it?" Simon asked cheerily.

"You're telling me! Never been so stressed about something not school related. You still ok to come over and read it?"

"You're kidding right? After what we just went through today, damn right I want to read that thing."

They chuckled together.

They were home before Ellie's parents, they made cups of tea and headed upstairs to her room.

"Ok," Ellie began, "I want a shower, so how about you read the book whilst I do that, then we can discuss after? Is that ok?"

"You're going to shower whilst I'm here? Will your dad be ok with that?"

Ellie looked at him, "It's a shower, I'll take my clothes in there and get changed in there, don't worry little boy. You won't see anything scary," she smiled at him sweetly.

"Ok, if you're sure."

"I'm sure," she smiled. "I'll lock the door if it makes you feel better."

With a grin, she turned, grabbed some jeans and a top out of her drawers and went into the bathroom, leaving Simon sat on the window seat with the notepad. Ellie showered, it felt good to wash away the worry of the day. Shortly after, she was out of the shower and dressed, she opened the door to the bathroom and walked into the bedroom. Simon was there sat on the window seat where she had left him.

He turned to look at her, "Hey not so smelly Ellie, nice hair."

She smiled, "It's wet dummy, I leave it to dry naturally," she flicked her hair, "See, model looks," she smirked and pouted.

"If you say so," he laughed back at her.

"So, did you read it?" she walked over and sat opposite him on the seat.

"Yes, I read it."

Ellie nodded, "And? You're killing me here!"

"It's deep, Ellie. Really deep. I don't really know what to make of it, I mean, it can't be true but yet it all fits together so neatly that it couldn't be not true either. Know what I mean?"

"Yes, Simon, I do. You do know it is my head that this is all spinning around in, yes?"

"I know it is," he took her hand, "Truth is Ellie, I don't know what to tell you. It's crazy. The only thing I can say is that I think you need to tell your mum and dad. They need to know why the council is putting pressure on you, they need to know what may or may not be going on in your head. You never know, they may be able to help."

His eyes looked concerned, there was a deep meaning behind his words.

"What is it Simon, tell me. I've never seen you like this, there is something more going on here."

He looked on the verge of tears. "Ellie, even though this is happening to you, you are so lucky to have your mum and dad around to help. I see the way you are with them; they love you, and they would do anything for you. My mum loves me, but

I only have my mum, we would fight it together, but three is better than two don't you think?"

Ellie was stunned, "I didn't mean for this to affect you so much Simon. I'm sorry, for what it's worth I think you and your mum would be able to tackle anything."

"We would," he interrupted. "I'm not making this about me, Ellie. I just mean you should take advantage of the family you have to help you. I will still be there, right by your side to help. After today, I'm sure the others would be too, Annabelle especially."

Ellie smiled, the mention of Annabelle sending a warm feeling through her body and causing her pulse to quicken slightly. "That's good advice, thank you Simon. I will talk to mum and dad, maybe the others soon, I may need your help for that last part though."

"Whatever you need, I'm here," he put his other hand on top of their already paired hands.

"I know, thank you," she looked into his eyes, "There is something else though isn't there? What is it?"

He looked at her, looking deep into her eyes, Ellie could feel him looking into her soul.

"Ellie, I don't want to lose you. I've only just got a friend like you; I don't want to lose that. Short version, I'm scared."

A tear formed at the corner of his eye.

Ellie squeezed his hand, "Simon, believe me, I'm scared to. I thought I was moving here to a better life, a quiet life. I met you and the others and thought I was set, now all this. Even if it is not true it is a massive thing to process and deal with. But I am going to do what I can, I'm not going anywhere. The only reason I can even contemplate dealing with this is because of the support and love that you give me." She smiled, "Now, shall we try and be happy?"

"Only if you promise to save the world," he chuckled through the tears.

"Promise," she laughed. They pulled each other into a hug.

They stayed that way for a minute or so, in silence, just together. "You do realise that I've shared more with you than I ever have with my friends back in London?" Ellie said as they pulled apart.

"That's good, right?"

Ellie laughed, "Yes that's very good! Now, shall we do some actual work?"

She took the notepad, headed over to the desk and put it with the tin along with the other bits and pieces.

They studied for a couple of hours; Simon was asked about staying for dinner by Nicholas when he got home but he politely declined. The reason given that his mother was already cooking for him, the real reason was to allow Ellie the opportunity to talk to her mum and dad about the notepad, the dreams, everything. Just before dinner, Simon left, Ellie said goodbye at the door and he whispered, "Good luck," in her ear as they hugged. Ellie headed into the kitchen where her mum was cooking.

"What's for dinner?" she asked.

"Curry, homemade of course," came the reply. "How was school?"

"Good thanks, was a long day but a good one," Ellie smiled. "Lots going on."

"That's good to hear, set the table for me, would you? Nearly ready."

Ellie started to set the table, getting the placemats, cutlery, and drinks all set. She welcomed the distraction, even though she was happy to talk to her mum and dad, the idea of doing so was making her incredibly nervous. Despite her nerves, Ellie waited until they had all eaten and were chatting after to bring up the issue at hand.

"I need to talk to you about something," Ellie had been debating internally how best to open this conversation, this was the best she could come up with.

Her mum and dad stopped and stared at her.

"Sure Ellie, what's up?" Katherine replied kindly.

"I need to talk to you about the council."

CHAPTER 14

The air in the room seemed to solidify, as if that moment in time was locked forever. The mention of the council from Ellie had seemingly caused her mum and dad to freeze where they were.

"The council? I thought you were ok with all that? What's going on?" her dad asked.

Ellie took a deep breath, "A lot has gone on, a lot that is strange that I don't fully understand but it is starting to build up. I'm scared."

She looked down at her hands.

"Tell us what's wrong, Ellie, talk to us," her mother said, reaching over to take her hand. "Just tell us what it is, and we will make it work, right Nick?" she looked at her husband.

"Yes, we tell each everything in this family, go on Ellie, tell us." All the focus was now on Ellie, her parents were looking at her ready to listen and help. Ellie took another deep breath, "The council isn't what you think it is. The meetings you go to are not the same as the one I have been to nor what they actually are. They are like a cult or something," Ellie looked away, she could not believe what she was saying. "They believe they are protectors; they believe they are here to guard us against another world. Or at least that's what they believe," she looked at her parents, they were both simply staring. Pushing on, Ellie continued, "At the first meeting I went to, the only meeting I went to, they explained how I fit into their plan. I was chosen as the fifth member, they introduced themselves to me and what their roles were in the council."

"Ok, this is sounding very strange Eleanor, why didn't you tell us about this before? Why now?" Nicholas asked.

"I'm building to that dad," Ellie said softly, she felt like she could cry at any moment. "The meeting that I went to, the one you arrived late at, do you remember what happened?"

Nicholas looked puzzled, "Not sure I'm following. I was late, yes, they gave me an agenda we went through it. Standard local council stuff as indeed it has been ever since. Why? What are you building up here lovely?" he leant forwards, concern etched over his face.

Ellie looked at him, staring into his eyes, "You missed out on what I can only describe as an initiation ceremony. Before you got there, they explained about the staffs on the floor, they were shaped like the folly by the way. They explained about the Man Of Mow and that they are his council today like the ones before them. How belief was needed and that I, as the representative of this family, needed to believe and buy into it." Ellie looked at her mother, "That's why they have been so keen for me to go back. They want me, not you. They need the young generation to keep the council going, needing my belief and support to succeed."

"Succeed at what?" Katherine asked.

Ellie paused, there was only one thing for it, "Defending the world," she braced herself for the responses.

"Defending the world?" came the first reply, from her dad. "You need to expand on that Ellie, how can a group of five normal people in a village hall defend the world?"

"They believe they are working for the Man Of Mow, they believe that if they work together they can keep us safe."

Ellie could see both her parents holding back laughs, she did not blame them.

"How did they explain all this to you?" Katherine asked.

"At the time they gave me this," Ellie pulled the piece of paper from her pocket, the one that council had given to her with the rules on, and slid it over the table to her, "That is the rules, so they say, of the council."

Her parents unfolded the paper and read it together. Once they had finished, they looked at each other, then at their daughter. Ellie tried to read their expressions, work out what was coming next, what did come next she was not prepared for.

"Ellie, this is the same agenda I was given," her father said, turning the page over and sliding it back to her.

Ellie, confused and angry, snatched at it. He was right. This paper had changed, all it had on it was the agenda they had gone through after he had arrived in that meeting. She looked up, "I swear this was different, it had weird rules on and explained how I was now a part of it all and what I needed to do. They must have swapped it back on me, I never checked after leaving the hall," her parents' faces were still concerned, but Ellie knew she was losing them, she knew she needed to convince them now. "There's more though," she exclaimed.

"Ok, we are listening," Nicholas said, his voice still calm but there was a new tone there now, a sort of tone that suggested he was starting to lose patience.

"Let me just go get some things from my room," Ellie stood and left. Running up the stairs, she was thankful for the distraction, the ability to get away from the penetrating eyes of her parents. She quickly grabbed the tin and ran back downstairs again. When she got back, her parents had not moved, they both focused on the tin in her hand.

"You know the bench window seat in my room? Well, the other day we were playing catch and it got a bit broken."

"What? When, how, by who?" her dad exclaimed. All support removed from his voice now. "So, you mean to tell me, that as well as being a part of a so-called cult which by the way is sounding very farfetched right now, you have also damaged your room and not told us?" he was clearly angry at this, interpreting Ellie's actions as deceit.

"Dad, please I'm sorry but please let me finish. I promise it is all true and I'm sorry about the bench, I'll fix it but please let me finish," Ellie implored. She sat, placing the tin in front of her. "I'm scared, I feel alone I need your help. Please."

"Let her finish Nick," Katherine stated, putting her hand on her husbands, "Go on Ellie."

Ellie smiled a small smile and continued, "The bench got broken, and inside it we found this," she opened the tin. "The tin was holding some paper notes, a compass, and a telescope thing," she placed the itmes on the table, "Read those then I will explain this," she slid the paper notes to her parents, whilst indicating her own notepad as what was next.

Her parents read the notes, passing them between each other back and forth. Ellie waited.

When they had both read all the pages, Katherine spoke first, "Ok Ellie, carry on."

Ellie relaxed a little, then continued, "I don't know what the telescope thing is for, but have an idea about the compass. Even though it is locked into place, it has a specific use for this house alone. The stone in our garden, the one that we couldn't move but got broken by the storm, the compass points directly at it from the top of the hill by the folly." She paused, waiting to see if there were any questions, there were none so she proceeded. "The other night, I had what I'm calling a dream. A dream where someone spoke to me, the Man, supposedly," she looked away again, embarrassed to be telling this part of the story. "He told me that the folly is actually a lock, that there are five stones that are the keys, and they are keeping our world safe. He told me the story of why the folly exists, he told me about the first council and our ancestor. Most of all, he told me why it is happening to me," she looked back at her parents, they had turned ghostly white.

"This was a dream though, yes Eleanor?" Katherine asked.

"Yes, I think. But what makes me doubt that is this," she picked up the notepad. "When I woke up, I wasn't in bed, I was sat at my table having finished writing in this. It is a record of everything from the council but also from that dream. Have you ever heard of anyone writing down their dream in detail as it was happening?" she slid the book to them. "Read that, it will tell you everything then I can carry on."

Her parents picked up the book and started to read, clearly fixated by what they were being told, unable to make up their mind. Ellie stood and went to make a drink; she needed a cup of tea. Whilst the kettle was boiling, she took stock of the situation, other than the bench seat there had been no negative or angry reactions, but they had not offered much support yet either. Would they even believe what she was telling them? The kettle boiled, and Ellie finished making her tea, once done she walked back over to the table.

"How far have you got?" she asked tentatively.

"I'm done," Katherine replied, "Dad is nearly there."

She was giving nothing away, and clearly wanted to wait until they had both read it before discussing it with her daughter. Ellie waited, looking at her father for any sign of his current thought or mood.

After a minute or so more, he spoke, "Done, that's a lot to take in isn't it?" he asked to the room in general.

"Well, do you believe any of it?" Ellie asked hopefully.

Her parents looked at each other, clearly neither wanted to speak first. After a moment, Katherine spoke, "It's a lot to take in Ellie, I mean, it all sounds very farfetched doesn't it? That they have chosen you because of some distant relation from hundreds of years ago? That because you don't believe the stones are cracking, stones that act as keys apparently as well? You have to admit, it is all a bit crazy."

Ellie nodded, she agreed, it did. "Yes, it does. But it's so crazy together that I'm starting to believe it, if that makes sense? As if individually the pieces are crazy, but putting them together means they make sense somehow." Ellie looked at her dad, "What do you think, dad? You've been very quiet."

Nicholas furrowed his brow, scrunched his hands together and then looked up at Ellie, a look of frustration on his face.

"Honestly, Eleanor, I don't believe a word of it. I think this is more fanciful than some of the stuff we watch on TV, and I honestly don't know why we are discussing it."

Ellie looked at her mother, who in turn was looking at her husband, both women showing the same look of disbelief.

"Are you suggesting she has made all of this up, Nick? Because that's a bit harsh at this stage don't you think?"

"I don't know what to think. All I do know is Eleanor has changed, a lot, since we moved here. I am not sure I entirely like it either."

"Wow," Ellie said, in shock. "Nothing like speaking your mind eh dad? Why would I make this up?" Ellie accepted that this was all farfetched and strange, but she had not been expecting this reaction. A reaction of anger, contempt, and frustration. Confusion, yes, but not this.

"I'm afraid I agree with Ellie at this stage, Nick. Why would she make this up?"

"Well, that's hardly surprising is it? The two of you teaming up against me, that's the way it always goes isn't it. Outnumbering me constantly, making sure you get your own way."

"Ok, where is this coming from? I feel like there is more at play here," Katherine replied.

Nicholas shrugged, "Well, I'm outnumbered here clearly, so we might as well just go along with whatever you say Katherine, as per usual. It's your fault we are all here anyway, your fault that this, whatever this is, is happening to Eleanor. Your fault that she is changing and going out more. Everything is your fault."

Ellie was stunned, she had never heard her father speak like this before, neither it would seem had her mother.

"What are you going on about, Nick? Where is all this coming from? It's not my fault that it made sense to follow my career instead of yours."

This was getting serious now, Ellie felt this was more important than her issues, "Maybe I should go? We can talk about this later, perhaps?"

"I think that is a good idea Eleanor, I want to have a word with your father in private," Katherine replied, a cold icy tone to her voice.

Ellie did not need to be told twice, she quickly gathered up her notepad, the tin, and its contents and left the room straight upstairs. Historically she would try to listen in on the conversation, but she had no plans to do that tonight. As soon as she was upstairs, she rang Simon to tell him what had happened. After a very brief conversation, Simon was busy at the time, Ellie was sat on her bench seat stitching, she needed to do something to take her mind off what was going on. What could she do now? From downstairs, she could hear raised voices from her mum and dad, but nothing that she could make out. She looked down at her creation, the picture of the stone was taking shape now. Ellie had started to add a round border to the design, making it into something that could be hung on the wall. It was getting late, despite what was going on downstairs, she knew it was time to go to bed.

Shortly after, Ellie was settled into bed, with the noise from downstairs still ongoing she put some music on to drown it out. After a short while, she was in a deep sleep, and the dreams came once again but in a new way, completely different to that which she had experienced before. Ellie found herself by the folly, alone, but it was not the folly that she had seen with her own eyes. It was intact, the same as the one the Man had shown her before. She looked around, the sun was shining, and she could see for miles. She knew this was in the past though, there were no large houses, just some stone huts here and there, no traffic moving that she could see. She walked down the peak of the hill, there was nobody around although she was not sure if they would be able to interact with her anyway. After walking down the hill a little way, to where she thought the car park would be, she found herself on a dirt track that had clearly only ever had carts dragged along it. Ellie walked. The village seemed empty, there was nobody around anywhere. She looked through hut windows, peered over hedges and fences, nothing. Nobody.

"Hello," she called more in hope than belief. Nothing. Just the sound of the breeze in the trees. Ellie kept walking down the hill, she did not really know where she was going, with no modern point of reference she did not really know where to go. Down seemed like a good idea though, so down she went. She walked down roads and paths, passed homes, workshops, and a church. Not a soul. After a while, she came to a spot that looked like a good place to rest. She sat against a rock, sticking out of the ground in such a way that it was an almost perfect post to lean on. Ellie sat catching her breath, looking up at the folly on the hill. It did look grand, its tower intact, and the clear blue sky behind it. Ellie was puzzled though, if this was a dream, what was it about? Where was the meaning? She sighed.

"Not giving up already are you Eleanor?" a soft voice came from behind her.

Ellie stood and whirled around, finding herself face to face with someone she had not met before.

"Who are you?" she asked, as politely as she could.

The figure was spirit like, the same as the Man in her previous encounter of this type but this one felt different, it felt cleaner, purer. The figure appeared to have the same ghost like form, floating a few inches above the ground. The face was the same too, rounded with small colourless eyes.

"My name is not important, or at least, it is not as important as that which I have to say. Would you listen more or less if you knew my name?" his voice was soft, almost kind.

Ellie pondered this, "How do I know that what you have to say is of value if I do not know where it is coming from?"

The figure nodded, "I am someone you can trust, I am someone who wants to help you, and I am someone that can help you." He paused, "But I can only do these things if you wish me to. If giving me a name helps you, then you may choose one for me."

"You want me to give you a name?"

"Names are formalities, and if what needs to happen does not happen, then names like everything else will be far less important. If it helps you to listen to me, then yes, you may give me a name."

This was baffling to Ellie, but she seemingly had no choice, especially if this was the reason she was here.

"Ok, well, I have already met one person this way and you are not them, but we did talk about another and we called him John, is John ok?"

For a moment, there was silence, just the sound of the light breeze in the trees, then the figure spoke.

"If John is what you choose, then John it is. Though I fear that it may be too late if I am not the first to speak to you." He drifted towards Ellie, "Am I not the first spirit you have come to face? Does it not surprise you that this is possible?"

"After the things I've seen, it will take a lot to surprise me. No, you are not the first, could you not have come and spoken to me together?"

The figure chuckled, "Yes it would have been easier wouldn't it. But we do not see things the same way, we have different goals, one is destruction, one is protection. One of darkness, one of light."

"Which are you then? I have been given a spiel about saving

the world, and was told what I needed to do, what makes your version different?"

"My version, as you say, is different because I will not tell you what to do, I will only tell you what I believe needs to happen. Will you listen to me?"

Ellie considered, "Ok, I'll listen to you, then I will decide who I want to help, if either of you."

"Very good, but I am sure I can guess what you have been told, maybe I will later, we shall see. Do you know where you are Eleanor?"

"Mow Cop of course."

"Yes, but do you know where on Mow Cop specifically?"

"No, I don't recognise any of this, where is everybody?"

"There is nobody else here, just me and you, for what I need to share does not need anyone else. Do you recognise this?" he gestured to the stone Ellie had been leaning on.

"It's a stone, sticking out of the ground," Ellie said factually.

"Yes, but what if it looked like this?" he gestured with his hand, immediately the rock cracked, and a piece fell to the floor silently.

Ellie's eyes widened, "Is that the stone from our garden?"

He nodded, "Yes it is, this is the location of your garden and house a long time before. If you had your compass, you could reverse the needle and it would point straight to the folly," he gestured behind Ellie.

"Ok, you have my attention, continue," she said calmly.

"Very well. You are aware that this is one of five keys and the folly is the one lock keeping your world safe from something from my world, yes?"

Ellie nodded.

"Given this, I assume you are also aware of the way our world works and that keeping them separate is the only way to keep them both surviving? Merging them would be catastrophic for both?"

"Yes, I was shown the worlds coexisting and it was explained to me how someone wants to steal the energy from here and put it into your world."

"Good, then I can get straight to the point," with a wave of his hand, the sky turned dark as night, the only things left visible to Ellie were the folly and the rock. "I want to show you the energy flow between the folly, our world, your world, the stones, and the prison between them."

With another wave, a purple beam of light came down from the sky into the folly, lighting it up from within. The light then came down towards Ellie and to the stone by her side. It seemed to absorb the energy and vibrate slightly when doing so.

"The light from above is the entry point from our world, the beam itself is the prison between our worlds, held tight and slim by the folly tower. Once in the tower the energy is split and cascaded down to the stones, follow?"

Ellie nodded, fixated by the purple light. She could make out some of the other four beams heading down to the other stones on the hill.

"The stones are placed in specific places, but also hold the energy here," a sphere appeared around the folly, covering the top of the hill. Ellie could still see the folly, but through a purple haze of energy. "The energy is contained around the top of the hill; this acts as the barrier keeping the prison secure. I am calling it a prison, do you know what I mean by this?"

Ellie looked at him, almost insulted, "Yes I know what a prison is," she replied indignantly.

"Good, well, the prison is the cylinder beaming out of the top of the folly tower." As he said this, the purple light that was the cylinder glowed brighter, as if it was being selected on a computer screen. "It works by using the energy from both our worlds to stay strong, it must have both or it will fail. Do you know what, or rather who, is in the prison?"

Ellie went to reply, then stopped herself. How could she answer that? Logically, if the two spirits she had met were on opposing sides then one of them knew more about the prison and its occupants than the other. "All I know is it is someone who wanted to steal the energy from our world for yours, they wanted to make yours a physical world rather just, is it mist?"

"Yes, mist is fine. It is a good description, and you are correct with the person in the prison as well. They do want to take your worlds energy to make ours a physical world. Or at least this is what they wanted to try to do."

"What is this energy? Can you tell me?"

"I can show you."

With a wave of his hand the darkness disappeared as quickly as it had arrived, showing all the green trees and hedges, the blue sky and the wind all came back into focus.

"The energy we use flows through your world like water, it is created and nurtured here, everywhere."

As he finished this last sentence, a yellow haze appeared all around Ellie. It was flowing in the breeze, spurting out of flowers and trees. At the nearby stream it was bubbling up and flowing into the sky. Even from Ellie herself, there was a yellow dust coming from her breath as she exhaled.

"The yellow mist shows you the energy, it is invisible to all in your world but not us, it channels up through weak points between worlds, like above the folly, look."

He pointed. Ellie looked up, the purple beam of light from the tower was still visible but all around it the yellow haze was being pulled up to where the purple met the sky, an invisible hole. It looked as if someone had a giant vacuum and had attached it to the other side of the sky to suck up the dust.

"It's beautiful," she observed.

"Yes, yes, it is. Once it arrives in our world it transforms, it becomes as visible as the mist you see me made from. The person in that prison believed that if he could suck it all through at once our world could become solid like yours. He is mistaken. It may work, but without a constant flow it would soon disappear, and if it were all gone from your world, where would we get it from? This would mean the end of our world as well as yours."

Ellie stared at him, "So, the energy is needed by you, but not by us, so why can't you just take what you need?"

"I agree. It has worked for centuries without incident, as with any civilisation though, there is always someone who wants more. Always someone hungry for power."

The images changed again, back to darkness with the purple energy flowing between the stones, the folly, and the sky.

"The prison is held firm by the stones, they focus the energy as they were designed to. They are, or were, keeping two spirits contained in that prison."

Ellie looked round sharply, "Two? So, one that wants to destroy our world and one that, what?" she was playing dumb here and treading very carefully but it seemed like the best thing to do.

He turned to face her, "Yes, two spirits. One that was correctly imprisoned, one that was not. Releasing one however would release the other, they are bound together so tight that it would not be possible to control. The prison is too strong, with the stones intact that is. The flow you see here is with all stones secure, let me show you what it is like now."

He waved his hand once more, the stone piece fell to the floor, and the purple light stopped flowing from the stone.

Looking up at the folly, Ellie could see that the shaft of light above the tower was no longer solid and bright but was pulsating, from bright to dim. The other beams were still visible, but it was clearly weakened.

"Without all five stones intact, the energy flow is not constant enough. It leaves gaps, the more stones that fail, the bigger the gaps. In these gaps the prisoners are able to reach your world, one of these will want to carry out their plan still."

Ellie stepped back, "Is this why I have seen two of you? At different points? Why you say that you don't see this the same way? You are one of them, aren't you?" Fear was creeping into her voice now. The realisation that one of the two people that had spoken to her this way was evil, and one was good, scared Ellie to her very core. "How do I know which you are?"

He turned to face her, "You do not. I can only tell you what I know and what I believe to be true. You, and you alone Eleanor, can work out which is the right path."

"So, what do you want me to do then?"

"I want you to do what you think is right. I believe the world should continue as it always has, I believe the two souls should remain incarcerated above that folly forever."

"You want me to fix the stones? The exact opposite of what I was told before. You want me to believe and fix the stones to keep the prison as it is?"

"I do not believe that will work. I believe that the stones are now damaged beyond repair. I do not think you will be able to fix the stones. I believe that which is broken can only be fixed by that which is also broken and then repaired."

"What then? Is that it, game over?"

He moved towards her, his face inches away.

"No, the game is not over, Eleanor. I believe that if we encourage the spirits, both of us, to the folly, we can close the prison for good, we can seal it with your energy."

"My energy?"

"Yes, if planned and positioned correctly, I believe your energy will be enough."

"Why mine?"

"Because it was your ancestor's energy that created it, you know the legend of your family I presume?"

"The only child thing? Yeah, it came up."

"Well, that should be enough to close the prison and trap both souls for eternity."

"Taking me with it?" anger was creeping into Ellie's voice now.

He paused, "That I do not know, but I do know that the evil is already spreading. Haven't you noticed anything strange happening? People out of character for example?"

Ellie's eyes widened, "Yes, my dad tonight!"

"Was he showing signs of anger for no good reason?"

"Yes!" she exclaimed.

"This is the energy being removed from your world, starting with those closest to the broken stones. You need to get away from that stone Ellie, you need to get away from it, fix it if you can but do not dwell on that for too long. Then at the full moon, you must get those spirits to the folly. Do you understand?"

Speechless, all Ellie could do was nod.

"Good. Then my message here is delivered and done, I must go. Before I do, I want you to ponder this. The stones are positioned in a certain way, around the folly. I was never able to prove it, but, changing the configuration of the person, the folly, and the stones should seal the gate to the prison. Your energy combined with that shift should work."

"Wait, what? How come you suddenly know that? Why should I trust you?"

"I do not demand anything of you, I do not intend to guide you, I simply mean to tell you what I know for you to make the right choice. That is your choice as this is mine."

"You're making no sense! Just tell me, are you the one who wants to create or destroy?"

He turned to face the folly, "We would both give the same answer to that question child, you must find another question for the answer you seek. Until then, goodbye."

"No, wait!"

But it was too late. He had vanished, and the world around her was draining out of sight as if the colour had been turned off, and then the lights.

Moments later, Ellie was sat at her desk once more, pen in one hand over her notepad again. This time, rather than a note telling her to save the world, it simply said:

Only I can choose who to believe, and what to do next.

CHAPTER 15

Ellie did not know what to say, think, or do. She had been given too much information in too little time to be able to process. The realisation that she did not know who was who in terms of good and bad did not help much. There was so much that she needed answers to, but to start with, Ellie wanted to know what had happened last night between her mum and dad. She got up from her desk and went downstairs, still in her pyjamas she crossed the landing, no sign of anyone. Down the last set of stairs, checked the living room, nobody, and then finally the kitchen. Nothing. Not a sign that anyone had been there that morning. Ellie frowned and turned to leave, as she did so she noticed a piece of paper on the worktop. Crossing over to it, she picked it up and read:

Ellie, your father and I love you very much, but things were said last night that cannot be unsaid. I'm sorry that I wasn't there this morning, but I want you to know that we both love you. I will be home later, and we will have a chat over cake (I will get some).

Have a good day, try not to worry too much, we will sort everything.

Love you, mum x

That's not like her at all, Ellie thought to herself, she has never left a note like that before, the only notes I get are pick up milk! Ellie folded the note and left it on the table, looking at the clock she realised she needed to be at the bus stop in fifteen minutes. She ran upstairs, got ready, and was out the door in record time, in her haste briefly forgetting everything that was going on. As she walked up the road to the bus stop the memory of it all came flooding back. How was she supposed to decide now? What was she to do? As she turned the corner, Simon waved and beamed at her.

"Morning, so, how did it go?" he asked with a smile, clearly hoping for some positive news.

"It was not what you would have expected or guessed," Ellie replied. "I never actually got far through the notepad before mum and dad had a row with each other, I went to bed, had another overnight visitor, then when I woke up there is a note from mum saying she loves me."

All that came out in one breath.

"Oh, so, errrr, they didn't offer to help or give any kind of insight then?" he asked.

"No, not really. Was useless and has clearly added to troubles that I didn't know were there, then this guy last night."

"Same one? The Man?" he interrupted.

"No, he wouldn't give me his name, made me choose one, I chose John. Basically, he is saying that I need to decide which of them I believe and carry out what I think to be the right thing to do. I haven't brought the notepad, don't want another Rochelle incident, you'll have to come over to read it."

"I can do that, tonight?" the enthusiasm in his voice was evident and clear, as well as reassuring.

"That would be amazing. Do you think we should get a third opinion? Annabelle maybe?"

Ellie had thought about Annabelle a lot, and had said her name without really thinking about it, as she did, she flushed a little red.

"Yeah, maybe. I mean, if you trust her? I know I do but it's your thing. Another view may help I guess."

At that, the bus arrived. Ellie finished this conversation with, "Right, not a word about it today, Rochelle will be on the lookout. I'll talk to Annabelle and see if she can come over tonight as well. Then the three of us can go from there, thanks Simon."

They boarded the bus and it pulled away. Ellie decided to act fast and text Annabelle now to get her thoughts. She wrote:

Morning! Listen, need your help but it is a secret! Can you come to mine tonight, want to show you something and see what you think? Simon will be there too as I could really use your views but please don't say anything to anyone else! See you soon E x

Ellie put her phone away and started to chat to Simon about the day ahead, moments later there was a ping, and Ellie got her phone out and read the message from Annabelle:

Morning El. That message got me excited until I saw Simons name ;) thought it would just be us, anyway, yes absolutely, won't say a word and I will be there tonight no trouble. See you in a min, A x

Ellie smiled, "Annabelle is coming tonight," she said to Simon. He smiled back, "Great, we will crack this Ellie, I promise."

Compared to recent days, this one was very normal. It went by quickly and it was not long before Ellie, Annabelle, and Simon were walking down the road to Ellie's house together.
"So, Simon, do you know what this is all about? Or are you in the dark as well?"
"I know part of it, not all, it's all very odd though, I'll let Ellie tell you."
They walked down the drive and entered the house.
"Right," Ellie said, "Let's go upstairs, I'll set you both up with what I want to show you, you can then read and stuff whilst I make drinks then we can discuss. That ok?"
Annabelle and Simon nodded. The three of them went upstairs into Ellie's room, Annabelle sitting on the window seat and Simon on the floor cross legged.
"Ok, I'm not going to tell you anything Annabelle, I just want you to read something. Then when I come back up, I will fill in the blanks that ok?"
"Ok, this is all a little creepy though," came Annabelle's reply.
"I know, I'm sorry about that," Ellie gave Annabelle the notepad that now had two night's visits in as well as all the other notes she had taken. "Ok, read this," she instructed, flicking through the pages, "When you get to here," she stopped at a page before last night, "Get Simon to read with you, that bit is

new to him too. Make sense?"

They both nodded.

"Good. Thank you," she hugged Annabelle, "Right. Tea." Ellie left to make tea. She had planned this evening in her head all day, she wanted them to read and get up to speed and to the same point before asking lots of questions. This also gave her the chance to process some of the information alone and then talk to them. She took her time making the tea, she wanted to be sure they had read it all before going back upstairs. When she was ready, she headed back upstairs with tea and biscuits. Ellie walked into the room and put the tea tray down on her desk and turned to face the others. Simon had moved to the bench seat to read with Annabelle, they both looked up, Simon had an odd look of confusion on his face. Annabelle's look was more of concern than anything else.

"So?" Ellie asked tentatively.

Without saying a word, Annabelle stood and walked over to Ellie and wrapped her arms around her in a tight hug, "I'm in awe of you, you're so brave Ellie."

Confused, Ellie hugged back and said, "Brave? I haven't done anything."

"You have kept all this bottled up and dealt with it so far, basically alone. That's amazing Ellie." She released the hug and put her hands on her shoulders, looking directly into Ellie's eyes. "You are incredible. Whether or not this is true or turns out to be a load of rubbish it's just amazing that you have kept yourself together. No wonder you were desperate to get that book back from Rochelle. I did wonder, but anyway, we are here, we have your back, what can we do to help?"

Annabelle picked up the tea for Simon and herself, and headed back over to the seat, giving him his drink when she got there. The two of them sat there, smiling looking at Ellie.

It took a moment for Ellie to process what Annabelle had just said. "This is a wind up right? You're waiting to roll on the floor with laughter at me, aren't you?"

"No," Simon said, "We are with you Ellie, and we want to help. So, what do you need?"

Ellie had not expected this, she had expected a reaction of fear or reluctance. Especially after what her own parents had said the night before. "Wow, thank you. That's incredible, I, I don't know what to say."

"You can start by telling us what you want to do next," Annabelle said, an aura of impatience radiating from her.

"Ok, well. For that and for what's next, are we all assuming that this is real? That these things exist, the folly is a supernatural prison, and the stone in my garden is one of five that are keeping it all locked and safe? Most of all that I, me, Eleanor, am supposed to save the world? Are we all saying that?"

There was a moment pause, Simon and Annabelle looked at each other, nodded to each other then looked back at Ellie.

"Yes," Annabelle said confidently.

"Wow ok. You have to admit that all sounds crazy though right?"

"Oh, absolutely insane," Simon agreed.

"Never heard anything so mad in my life," Annabelle added. "But yes, we believe it. So, what's next?"

"I don't know. In truth, I was expecting tonight to be about me convincing you to help me! Never mind anything else."

"Ok," Annabelle said, standing up. "I have an idea. Why don't we make a list of the things we can do, and the things we can't do? Then we can work out which ones to do in which order and go from there? How does that sound? Given it is just us, seems like a good place to start."

Simon and Ellie agreed, Ellie got an A4 pad out of her drawer and opened to a clean page. She drew a line down the middle, on the left wrote *doable* then on the right *not doable*. "Ok, I'm ready."

"Oh no," said Simon, "This is your crazy adventure, you don't get to write it. Give that here," he snatched the pen and pad away. "You talk, I write, Annabelle listens. Ok?"

"Yes boss," Annabelle said, giggling a little.

Despite what they were discussing, this was the first time that Ellie had felt relaxed and normal about the whole thing, this just felt like three friends hanging out and having fun.

"Ok, so, starting with what we can do," Ellie began.

The evening moved on, after a short while they had composed their list and put them in order. For the doable side:

1. Find and restore the broken stone piece.

2. See if Kathrine (mum) will help.

3. See if the council will help (there is a meeting tomorrow night anyway).

4. Convince both spirits that Ellie is on their side (this depends on them reaching out again).

"Are we sure on the fixing the stone thing?" Ellie asked. "Feels like we are saying that we side with Mr Fix It rather than Mr Break It?"

"Well depends on your point of view. Some will say that you can break and then repair, you know, can't make an omelette without any eggshells," Simon offered.

"That's not how the saying goes silly," Annabelle mocked. "But you do have a point. On the other hand, and this is what I believe, everything was ok until it got broken yes? So, it stands to reason that fixing it in the right way may help us doesn't it?"

"Ok, agreed, can we divide and conquer though?" Ellie asked. "How?"

"I'll go and look for the stone piece in the shed, can you two look at a map and try to pinpoint where these stones are in relation to the folly? Both of them mentioned it but didn't really confirm. Assuming that all five are with council members, their addresses are in that notepad."

"Sure, sounds good to me. You go play outside in the dark shed, we stay in here and look at a map. Done!" Simon agreed, cheerily.

"Very gentlemanly of you Simon," Annabelle teased.

"It's fine, I could use the air anyway," Ellie said. Beaming, she left the room.

Ellie hurried down the two flights of stairs, taking some two or three at a time, bolted along the corridor, and out into the garden. She turned the torch on her phone on and moved towards the shed. Since they had lived there, Ellie had spent many a time in the garden, but she noted that things are often creepier at night. Opening the shed door, she looked around quickly, just to be sure she was alone. Moving inside she looked at the shelves, nothing. Moving some pots and tins around, still nothing. Ellie looked on the floor, at the back and front of the shed, behind, and under things. Everywhere. But the stone was nowhere to be seen. She stood and wracked her brains for what Sophie had said about where she had hidden it. She was sure she had said in the shed. Leaving the shed, Ellie decided to call Sophie. She picked up after a couple of rings.

"Hey Ellie! What's new?"

"Hey Soph, going to get straight to it as there is a lot going on, do you remember that piece of stone that broke off whilst you were here?"

"The grey one? Yeah, what about it?"

"Where did you put it? You were putting it in the shed when I was at the door, I can't find it."

"Oh man was hoping you wouldn't notice until it was ready."

Ellie froze on the spot, "What? Until what was ready? What is going on Sophie?" panic setting in her heart.

"Ok, I was trying to do something nice and creative, nowhere near as creative as you but I was trying to be nice."

"Sophie tell me!" Ellie shouted; all pleasantries forgotten now.

"Ok. The stone is here, I brought it home to put in a frame as a gift for you, was going to make it all pretty and send it to you. Kind of as a memory for our first weekend up there is all, lets video call and I'll show you."

Ellie lowered her phone, fear and panic setting in now, she pressed the button to go to video call whilst walking back into the house and upstairs.

"Whilst you're finding it, Annabelle and Simon are here too, we are trying to fix something, sorry for snapping but we need the stone piece."

Ellie had reached her bedroom again now, Simon and Annabelle turned to face her. They were smiling but seeing the look of horror on Ellie's face soon changed that.

"Sophie has the stone piece," she stated to them.

"You say it like I stole something important," came Sophie's voice from the phone.

"It is important," Ellie stated.

"Wow ok, ok! Here it is, look."

The three gathered round the phone to look at the screen to see what Sophie was showing them. Sophie was holding up a white 3D frame, the sort used to display cups and trophies. Inside it, clearly glued to the backing as if it were floating, was the stone piece. It had a ribbon around it with a caption underneath written in calligraphy style writing:

Best friends until the stone fades.

In any other situation, Ellie would have been overwhelmed. Sophie had never been one to show her emotion, or at least not until she orchestrated the photo album earlier that year.

"That's lovely," Annabelle said, "Really sweet. Did you make it yourself?"

"Yes, I practiced that writing for ages to get it just right."

"Can we please focus here?" Ellie interrupted.

Sophie looked hurt; Annabelle surprised.

"Sorry, I really am sorry Sophie it is a lovely gesture and that is the most creative I have ever seen you be; I'm flattered and if I wasn't desperate to have that stone piece here, I would be welling up right now. But we really need it! How quickly can you get it to us?"

"Well, it's not finished yet, but if you're desperate I can post it tomorrow, so it should arrive by Friday? That ok? Do I get to know what this is all about?"

"That would be great, can you do that and let me know as soon as it is posted? Yes, I will tell you everything but right now I need to move onto part two of our plan. Can I message you later?"

"Yeah, I guess. Is everything ok Ellie, I'm worrying now."

"Yes, I'm fine, or at least I will be don't worry. I will fill you in on the details later, ok?"

"Ok, bye then everyone," Sophie put the phone down, leaving the three alone once more.

"Well, that's put a spanner in our plan hasn't it?" Simon stated.

"Only a little, we still have a chance," Annabelle reassured. "Ellie, we want to show you something."

Annabelle gestured to the floor, there was a map there with some markings on. The three sat down around it and Ellie could see it was a map of the village, with the folly at its centre.

"We have been doing some investigating, and well, it is interesting reading."

"I'm listening," Ellie said excitedly, her positivity returning now.

"The folly is here," Annabelle indicated a black spot in the centre of the map. "Your house, here on Fords Lane, is almost perfectly south of the folly, in line with the folly wall. Following?"

"Yeah, I'm there, keep going," Ellie agreed.

Simon joined in, "We plotted the other four council addresses based on your notepad, and, well, look at this."

Simon picked up a pen and marked four other dots on the map, they were all around the folly, slightly further away than the first one marking Ellie's house, but all in a sort of circle shape.

"As you can see," he continued, "They start to," he stopped, looking at Ellie. "Ellie? You ok?"

Her eyes were wide with realisation, "You are geniuses!" she exclaimed. "Stay right there, I think I know what you are about to say but I want to find something first."

"Do you mean this?" Annabelle asked, pointing at the staff in the corner of the room. "Way ahead of you."

"How did you find that?" Ellie asked.

"In the garage, went to get it whilst you were on the phone, now please let me have my moment," Simon pleaded.

Ellie smiled, "Ok, go on."

"Thank you. The dots are in a pattern around the folly. We didn't see it at first, but it forms a perfect circle, as if drawn with a protractor from the folly itself."

Ellie stood and moved towards her cupboards, "I'm listening, keep going."

Simon continued, "Well, we didn't see the pattern at first, until we join the dots together inside the circle."

"Exactly," Ellie shouted, turning. In her hand she had some thread used for stitching. "Sorry Simon, I got excited as I saw the pattern immediately, my stitching hobby that you all tease me about is finally useful."

"According to your book," Annabelle said, "The council introduced themselves in order, putting you at number three yes?"

"They sure did," Ellie confirmed. "So, if we join one to two, then two to three."

"She's got it," Simon shouted, "This is amazing, it actually all starts to fit together."

Ellie broke off some thread, and together over the map they joined the dots. They had already been joined around the edge by a circle, this time they were joining them inside the circle.

"The one to the bottom left, for council member number one," Annabelle said, "Beryl on Church Street, joins to council member number two."

"Kenny," Simon confirmed looking at his notes, "Lives on the lane behind Wood Street."

They joined the two dots with thread.

"That links to my house, council member three here on Fords Lane," Ellie stated, laying down some thread between the dots in the top left and bottom middle on the map.

"Number four is up here," Annabelle said, pointing to a spot in the top right of the circle, "Hannah lives behind the campsite."

They joined Ellie's house to this dot.

"That leaves Douglas," Ellie concluded. Pointing to a spot towards the bottom right of the circle, "He lives here on Sands Road."

The final piece of thread was added. The three sat back and looked at their work, stunned into silence. After a moment, Ellie stood, crossed the room and collected the staff. She walked back across towards the map and knelt, carefully placing the tip of the staff by the side of the map.

"Unless I am mistaken, the pattern we have just made, by joining the council member houses together in number order inside that circle, matches that perfectly."

She pointed at the staff, more specifically, the symbol engraved into the hilt. The 'M' inside a circle. Silence, nobody spoke or moved. They were all processing the same thing, as crazy as all this was, the more they dug into it, the more sense it made.

Finally, Annabelle spoke.

"This is why the council are always so protective about their houses, this is why the members only live in these five buildings. They must be where the stones are. In your notes Ellie, you mention a few times that they were placed there by the people who made all this stuff the first time for a reason, they must have planned it all."

"I guess so," replied Ellie plainly. She was struggling to process the whole thing, "I was kind of hoping that the more we dug into this, the crazier and less convincing it would get, not make it seem more real."

Annabelle and Simon stared at her.

"We know Ellie, we know," he said. "But at least we know we can move onto the next set of ideas though; we are getting somewhere."

"Ok, what's next?" Ellie asked.

"We need to find out if the council will help, and if their stones are intact. When your mum gets home, let's get her to help us. See if she will help and work with us to convince the council to help."

Ellie looked at Simon, then at Annabelle, then back again. They both had looks of hope now, looks that showed faith and belief in her. She felt uplifted by their confidence.

"Ok, that's the next step. So, we talk to mum tonight, the council tomorrow, restore the stone by Friday night then go to the folly that evening for the full moon. Easy yeah? Ok, let's do this," Ellie said defiantly. She was going to do this; she was sure of it. The three tidied up and moved their investigations downstairs to make it easier to explain to Katherine when she got home.

A little while later, Katherine had returned to the astonishing sight of her daughter, Annabelle, and Simon gathered around a map on the kitchen table. A map no less that was covered in pen drawings and post it notes, backed up with written ones and diagrams. Even the staff caught her eye as she demanded to know what was going on. To Annabelle and Simon's credit, they allowed Ellie to explain everything, in full, to her mother with little interruption. They felt that being there for moral support was enough and that contributing would have only made thing worse.

Katherine sat and listened, sipping on a cup of tea that was made for her as her daughter explained everything. Finally, when Ellie had finished, Katherine spoke about it properly for the first time.

"Wow, and I thought what you started to tell us last night was crazy. You really believe that all this is true?" she lifted the staff to inspect the marking on the handle. "You really think it is all connected?"

Ellie looked at Annabelle and Simon, who said nothing, but smiled in encouragement. "Well," Ellie started, "I don't want any of it to be true, I kind of want to find out it is all a dream and that everything is actually normal. But the more we have investigated this, the more it has fitted and made sense. Know what I mean?"

"I do indeed," Katherine agreed, turning to Annabelle and Simon, "What do you two think?"

They looked at each other, as if waiting for the other to speak first.

"We think it is completely crazy," Annabelle said with a smile. "But, we believe in and love Ellie, so if there is even a chance that this is true then we will help her."

Simon nodded, "Yes, what she said," he added with a smile.

Katherine turned back to Ellie, "Ok, let's say I believe you. What's next? What do you need from me?"

Ellie beamed. The fact that her mother was listening and willing to help meant the world to her.

"Well, if we are right, we have until the full moon on Friday to get the stone fixed, get the spirits to the folly and trick them both into thinking I am on their side. Along with that, I need to work out how I am going to split them from me, I don't want to be a sacrifice. As for how you can help, I need the council to help me. Can we go to the meeting tomorrow and try to convince them?"

"Tomorrow, no we can't," Katherine replied.

Ellie, Annabelle, and Simon's faces all turned to shock.

"Why?" Ellie asked.

"Because my dear children," Katherine replied calmly, "The meeting is tonight not tomorrow."

Ellie grinned, "That was cruel mum. Ok, I don't think Annabelle and Simon should come though, they don't know them, and they may react badly to strangers knowing more about them and their ways."

"I agree," Annabelle said, "Mrs Fields."

"Katherine, please," Katherine interrupted, "Or Kath, but not Mrs Fields."

"Sorry, Katherine, can we stay here to carry on planning? Or at least come with you to stay in the car?"

"I think you can stay here, no problem at all I trust you both. If Ellie does that is?" she looked at her daughter.

"I trust them with my life, mum," came the confident reply.

"Very well, you can stay, help yourselves to anything in the kitchen and we will see you soon. Ellie, grab that staff and map, we have a meeting to go to."

CHAPTER 16

Ellie had never seen her mother drive with such urgency, still within the rules and limits of the law, but this was the first time she had felt haste when in the car with her mum. She was not scared but was very aware of how dangerous driving can be.

"Mum, can we slow down a little? The council likes to talk you know, they will still be there later."

"We are doing just fine Ellie; we need to get there quickly so we can convince them to help you."

"About that, why are you so keen to help? I mean, I'm grateful, but you didn't even challenge us on it? Just accepted our thoughts, details, and concerns, and said yes."

Katherine pulled over, "Ok, let's do this quickly now."

Ellie was confused, "Why have you stopped?"

"Because I want to explain this properly Eleanor, and I can't do that whilst driving can I? Now just listen."

Ellie looked at her mother, "Ok, I'm listening."

"The reason I am helping without question, the reason I believe you and am willing to go along with this. The remarkably simple reason, is your father."

Ellie's expression changed to one of confusion.

"The other night your father and I had an argument unlike any we have ever had before, genuinely. Even back to the early days when we would often disagree, never like that. I have been wracking my brain trying to figure out why he would say what he said to you, calling you a liar, why he would turn on me the way he did. I'm guessing he hasn't text you or anything?"

"No, nothing. I mean, I haven't either but no he hasn't spoken to me."

"See even that is odd. You and your father are close, closer than you or I have been I think, and I'm not complaining before you argue with me," she added, seeing Ellie about to jump in. "He started behaving very strangely, very quickly, very out of character."

"I agree mum, but I still don't understand?"

Katherine smiled at her daughter, "Ellie, I love you so much and I am so proud of you. Listening to you explain all this to me, so calmly, in detail, all this crazy stuff made me realise how much you have grown. But there was one thing you said that stuck with me, one thing that convinced me to help. Do you know what it was?"

Ellie shook her head.

"It was when you said that this energy can cause people to act in strange ways, you said that all this stuff can be making us as people act out of character and differently? Well, I think that is what is affecting your father. It fits, it makes sense to me. He has never acted that way before; he has never spoken to me or you like that and certainly never accused us in the way he did. I have to believe that, and if that's the case and working with you all helps fix whatever is going on, then so be it."

Ellie was stunned, she had not even considered that this could be impacting her mum and dad like this.

"Wow, so, you think that the reason he said and did all those things is because of this? Because, of me?"

The realisations were setting in, Ellie was starting to blame herself.

"No Ellie, no," Katherine comforted, she reached across and took her daughter's hand. "None of this is your fault, this is something bigger than all of us, but you have handled this so well and been so brave. You're tougher than I could ever dream to be."

Tears started forming in Ellie's eyes, "I get that from you," she chuckled through the tears.

They were both crying a little now, completely overwhelmed with what they were feeling and thinking.

"Now, shall we go and get those silly people to help us?" Katherine asked, a determined tone to her voice.

"Yes mum, let's do this."

Katherine restarted the engine, and they moved on to the council meeting.

When they arrived, the meeting was already in full swing, in the car they had decided on the plan for getting the council involved. They would enter the room together, Ellie would explain what she knew and had seen, they would go from there to convince them to help. Katherine had made it clear that she was there to support Ellie and would jump in as it was needed but they both felt that the majority of the talking needed to come from Ellie. They entered the room, all four faces turned towards them with a shared look of surprise.

"Eleanor, Katherine, we weren't expecting you," Douglas exclaimed. "We are in the middle of a something important at the moment you see."

"Believe me, this is more important than whatever you are discussing Douglas," Ellie interjected firmly.

"Yes, given the almost stalker like level of attention you have given my daughter, you had better pay attention," Katherine supported.

By this point, they had reached the circle, and were staring down at Douglas.

He blinked.

"Of course, please sit and share," he gestured towards the seat that would belong to position number three. "I am keen to know what could be so important, given the negative attitude we have received from you previously."

"Now is not the time, Douglas, we should listen," Beryl interjected, much to Ellie's surprise.

There was a moment when time seemed to freeze, when Ellie was waiting for reality to catch up and break the silence. It did not happen, so she took it upon herself to do it. She moved forwards and placed her staff on the floor, creating the wall of the folly in the diagram, and then she spoke.

"Firstly, I am here not because of anything you have said or done, but because of things that have happened to me. Things that I have been told and have seen that have shocked me and have made me realise that I need to help and do something." She looked round the group for any kind of re-action, there was none so she continued. "To be clear, if what I am believing to be true is indeed true, then we all have something to worry about. I will need your help as this is bigger than all of us and we need to work together in order to deal with it." There was still nothing but focus and attention from the council members, "I am going to talk about everything in one go, summarising the information I have and the steps I believe we need to take."

"Eleanor, this all sounds marvellous," Hannah interrupted, "But can you begin by explaining where this information has come from? Start there and then we can go through it all, you have our attention."

Ellie did have the attention of the room, she had not noticed until now, but they were all leaning in to listen, showing complete focus on her every word. She looked at her mother who seemed to be sharing her surprise.

"The information is from," she paused, not quite believing what she was about to say. Looking down at her hands, they were clenched on her lap, "It is from the Man," she said. "The Man Of Mow and his companion."

She looked up to see a sea of faces, all showing an expression of shock and awe.

"You mean, he came to you in a vision?" Douglas asked, a soft tone to his voice. "You have seen him? Spoken to him?"

Ellie was puzzled, "Yes, why, haven't all of you?" she asked.

The four looked back and forth to each other, Hannah answered on behalf of the room, "No, we haven't, only the chosen few get this privilege and we have only read about it in the texts that have been passed down to us through this very council."

"Carry on Eleanor, we are listening, we will listen then we will see if we can help," Kenny added.

Ellie took a breath and continued.

"So, you believe that you need to get these spirits to the folly this Friday, and send them back to the space between worlds?" Douglas asked.

Ellie had been speaking for about forty minutes now, and had covered off the dreams, the folly design, and the fact that she was a descendant from the original council. They had been stunned throughout, and generally had let Ellie talk. Only asking questions when they needed some real clarity on something.

"In short, yes," Ellie answered. "I have met two different spirits, one said they were the Man, the other did not. One said repair, one said destroy. I don't know which to believe but they did both agree that I need to get the other up to the folly."

She pointed at the map, she had laid it out during her explanation, pointing out where the councillor houses were as she did so. This had gone down more surprisingly than she had expected, Ellie had thought that they would already know this, but they evidently did not.

"I think if we can convince them to go with me, I can figure out a way to know who to believe, I think we can do it there, and then trap one, or both of them again."

She finally stopped, feeling quite exhausted after her story-telling. Ellie sat back and looked around at the council members, expecting a reaction.

Douglas spoke first.

"Eleanor, you have spoken with maturity and given us an insight into what needs to be done. I see now that the way we conducted ourselves, the way we tried to get you involved in our world whilst was done with good intentions was wrong. For that, I, we, are truly sorry."

Ellie was astounded, she had been expecting anything apart from this, an apology. She did not really know how to respond to it, before she could, Beryl interrupted.

"You see Eleanor, we have been given the same key information down the generations, we have always been prepared for the key person, the generational line to give the right person that could allow this to happen. We are all told to be prepared, but nobody ever knows when it will happen. Now, you have come, and you are the one that can protect or destroy."

"No pressure then," Ellie replied sarcastically.

"We understand child," Beryl attempted to comfort.

"No, you don't understand!" Katherine interjected, much to the surprise of everyone including Ellie. Katherine had been quiet up until this moment, indeed for a time Ellie had forgotten that her mother was there.

"Unless it is you that is going to go up to that folly and put yourself at risk, take on all of this pressure, then you do not understand," she finished.

Ellie could see the surprise on Beryl's face but was also feeling buoyed and uplifted by the support from her mother.

"Forgive me, Katherine. I simply meant that we," she paused, clearly looking for the right words.

Douglas stepped in to help, "We are here to help, and whilst we do not know exactly what your daughter is going through, we do understand and want to help her. We have knowledge, information that will support her and help fill in some blanks perhaps."

"You have more information?" Ellie asked, this had piqued her interest massively.

"We do, you are not the only one to have found things in storage tins in their house, Eleanor. It would seem that information has been passed down for generations. The person who had your house before you, Alistair, thought he had also cracked it but also thought he could take over and force the issue. I believe that is what he is referring to in those notes, the bit about being forced out? We didn't force him out as it were, but we did not agree that he was the saviour. He believed it should fall on the shoulders of those that had the most information and knowledge, we did not. We believed that it could only be done by someone that had been chosen within the rules of the first council and the prophecy."

Ellie raised an eyebrow at this.

"Well, we call it a prophecy, it is more of a guideline," Douglas confirmed, a wry smile on his face. "Surely you can forgive us for not believing in it fully ourselves? Things have never aligned like this before."

Ellie said nothing, she knew that Douglas was right. She had not believed it, and still did not really want to.

"I'll take the silence as a yes," Douglas said, "We chose to believe as it gave us a sense of purpose, it would appear that you have chosen to believe because of the crucial step that we did not get. A visit from them."

"I assume you mean the spirits from the other world?" Ellie asked.

"Of course. Now, we need to work out how all of what you know fits with all of what we know. What is the best way to do that?"

He looked at his fellow council members, clearly looking for inspiration or ideas from them. Nobody spoke, Ellie concluded that they talked a good talk but had never actually planned on using what they knew.

"Ok, I can see you are all really keen to help here, so how's about I start?" Ellie began. "All I need to know, is anything you know about the folly, and anything you can give me on its design and creation, any notes on changes to it over the years, any clue as to how we can do this without me having to, you know, go with them."

Silence. Then Hannah spoke, "There is one thing. The wall, the wall with the arch."

"What about it?"

"I remember reading somewhere, in one of our packs, that the wall was not part of the original design, it was added after the tower was constructed and in place. There were notes and transcripts, they said something about a visit from a spirit that asked them to add the wall to the tower. To allow it to focus its energy in the right way as and when it was needed. I can go home and try to find the notes?"

"Yes, please do," Ellie answered.

Hannah stood and left.

"Well, that's something, that arch is odd, have we got something we can draw on?" Ellie asked the room.

"Yes," Kenny answered, he stood and crossed the room to the storage cupboard and wheeled out a whiteboard. "This is used for some of the evening classes in the hall, we can use it."

"Brilliant," Ellie said excitedly, she stood and crossed to the board and picked up the pen. "So, we know we have the tower on the hill."

She drew, a small mound to show the top of the hill and a rectangle to show the tower, as if looking at it from the side.

"In it, we know there are five windows, each aligned to the stones that we now know are in all of our gardens."

She indicated her map on the floor, with the symbol drawn on it, linking the houses together. As she did this, Ellie realised that again she had the attention of the whole room, they really were focused on her and what she was saying. After adding in the windows to her diagram, she continued.

"We also know that the tower is being used to channel the energy up into the sky," Ellie drew squiggly lines to represent the energy. "Here is where it gets sketchy. Supposedly, our world is creating spiritual energy that is pulled up towards the gap between worlds." She added more lines aiming up towards a point above the folly tower. "Let's call it the prison, is somewhere between the two worlds." Ellie drew a black circle to represent this, "And is where both these spirits should be. Both have told me that if I get the other to this point," she indicated the tower on her diagram, "At the right time. The energy from me will force them into the prison once more."

"If the energy flow is right at the time, as in if the broken stones are working," Kenny added.

"Yes, the stones are a problem. Are yours all intact?" Ellie asked the group.

There were three nodding heads.

"Good, we can check with Hannah when she is back. Assuming the stones are working, and we get the timing right, how do I choose between the spirits? Any ideas? How can I find out who to trust and which to, send away?" Ellie lifted her arms, miming sending something away from her. "Anyone?"

"We can help with that," came a voice from the back of the room.

Standing in the doorway, out of breath and sweating, were Annabelle and Simon.

"How did you get here?" Ellie asked, surprise all over her face. As the two walked towards the group, Annabelle explained, "We borrowed your bikes from the garage, hope that's ok? We are sorry to intrude but we want to help."

Ellie looked at Douglas. His expression was a curious one, it was one of mild distaste, but also a resolute impression of acceptance.

"We wouldn't normally discuss matters like this with non-council members," he said, an icy tone to his voice.

Ellie was about to jump in and say something, as she opened her mouth to do so, he raised his hand, stopping her.

"But, we are aware that circumstances have changed, and that we need to accept that. As well as help from outside. So, please continue, sorry, what were your names?"

"I'm Annabelle, and this is Simon," Annabelle stated, politely. "Anyway, Ellie. We have an idea as to how you can split the spirts."

"I'm listening," Ellie replied excitedly.

"They both look the same yes? They both have the same physical appearance?"

"Yes, identical from what I can remember."

"Right, so the only thing we can use to split them is their words or their actions, yes?"

"I guess."

Simon jumped in excitedly, "We created a game."

Silence fell across the room.

"A game?" Ellie asked, nervousness in her voice now.

"Yes, have you ever heard of the riddle about two doors with two guards, one lies, and one tells the truth?" he asked.

Ellie shook her head, "No Simon, I haven't."

"Anyone else want to help out here?" Simon asked. "No? Ok, let me explain."

He stepped forward and flipped the whiteboard over, so it was blank again, taking the pen he drew two large rectangles on the board next to each other.

"Imagine these are doors, one leading to freedom, one leading to death. Each door has a guard." He drew a stick man next to each door, "One guard has to and will always speak the truth, the other has to and will always lie. You can ask one guard one question. What question can you ask that will allow you to choose the right door?"

He smiled, as if that explained everything. Nothing, everyone just stared at him. Then Annabelle decided to help him out.

"This is a riddle to help deductive reasoning, the question needs to be worded in such a way that you can identify which guard you are asking, truth or lie, and then work out which door is safe."

"Ok, so you're suggesting that I ask the sprits a question, then work out which one they are to focus onto the right one to send back?"

"Yes!" Simon shouted excitedly.

"We need to understand more I think," Katherine said, in a supportive but constructive way.

"Right, let's do it like this," Simon said, and he then pointed to Kenny and Douglas. "Gentleman, could you please go over there, discuss amongst yourselves quietly who will tell the truth and who will lie. Also decide which of these two doors leads to safety and which to death."

He wheeled the whiteboard round to them, Kenny and Douglas looked at each other.

"Please?" Annabelle added, impatiently.

They stood and walked away, then Kenny called back, "You want us to choose which of us will lie and which door is which yes? But not tell you?"

"Yes," Annabelle shouted back.

After a few more seconds, Kenny and Douglas came back and stood at the white board, one at each end.

"Right, before we do this, to confirm, you have agreed that one of you will tell the truth and one will lie, yes?"

They nodded.

"You have also agreed which of these two doors is the one we want?"

They nodded again.

"Perfect, Annabelle, this was your idea, over to you," Simon exclaimed.

Annabelle took a deep breath, clearly aware that everyone was watching her.

"To recap the problem. You are a prisoner in a room with two doors and two guards," she indicated the whiteboard and to Kenny and Douglas. "One of the doors will guide you to freedom and behind the other is a hangman, you don't know which is which." Again, indicating to Kenny and Douglas, "One of the guards always tells the truth and the other always lies. You don't know which one is the truth-teller, or the liar either. You must choose and open one of these doors, but you can only ask a single question to one of the guards. What do you ask so you can pick the door to freedom? Everyone with me?"

"Yeup," Ellie said, she was starting to see the picture but could not quite get the final piece.

Everyone else just nodded, it appeared as though they were simply playing along.

"Good," Annabelle stepped forward. "Then I ask my question to you," pointing at Douglas. "If I asked which door would lead to freedom, which door would the other guard point to?"

Douglas paused, thinking, then he replied, "The other guard would point to this door, the door of freedom."

Annabelle smiled, then pointed at the door by Kenny, "Then I choose that door, and you Douglas are the guard that lies. Am I right?"

Douglas and Kenny looked at each other, "Yes, you are right," Kenney said, astounded.

Annabelle turned and smiled at Simon, then beamed at Ellie. "See? Now all we have to do is change the question slightly to be worded around light and dark, or protection and destruction, and you will know which of the spirits you have spoken to."

"Sorry, how does that work exactly?" Douglas asked politely. "Are we assuming they will answer truthfully as per your game?"

"No, all we need is enough for Ellie to know which is which, I believe that she will then know who to pick at the time. This is just a way to find out which is which."

"How?" He asked, "I just want to understand."

Annabelle smiled, "If you asked the truth-guard, the truth-guard would tell you that the liar-guard would point to the door that leads to death. If you asked the liar-guard, the liar-guard would tell you that the truth-guard would point to the door that leads to death. Therefore, no matter who you ask, the guards tell you which door leads to death, and therefore you can pick the other door. Make sense?"

Annabelle looked around the room, everyone was clearly processing this and working it out.

Ellie was the first to react, "Yes Annabelle, it does make sense! I get it, so all we need to do, is change the wording so that I can ask something like if I were to ask the other spirit if you are the one that wants to protect, what would they say?"

Annabelle and Simon grinned, "Yes, exactly like that Ellie, exactly like that," Simon exclaimed.

Ellie exhaled, "Wow, that's amazing."

She rushed forwards and pulled her two friends into a hug.

"We may actually pull this off," She said as she pulled away.

Their smiles faded, "But we still don't know how to do this without potentially losing you though, do we?" Simon asked solemnly.

"I think I can help with that," came Hannah's voice.

The group turned; she was striding across the room towards them with a real sense of purpose. She was clutching a bundle of old looking papers, when she arrived at the group she went straight to the whiteboard.

"Can we do a diagram of the folly?" she asked.

Beryl smiled and answered first, "Flip it over Hannah."

Hannah did so and revealed Ellie's drawing from earlier.

"Perfect. So, if this is the side on view of the folly, then the wall can go here." She drew on the board, adding in the wall to the right of the tower, complete with arch. It was a very crude diagram, but everyone knew what it was. Hannah took a step back, "Right. I have done some quick reading of all the stuff that was in my house," she began, turning to face the group. "As we thought earlier, the wall was added later, this is why the stones are slightly different. The wall though is interesting, anyone know anything specific about it?"

She looked round the room.

"It is exactly on the north south divide," Annabelle said.

Hannah whipped her head round to face her, "Yes! Exactly, sorry didn't catch your name?"

"Annabelle."

"Well, gold star. Yes, the wall is on a perfect divide of north to south, but also points at council member number three's house." She gestured towards the map on the floor, "Can anyone else recall when the mention of a north to south divide in any of this?"

She scanned the room. Nobody spoke.

"No, well, I can," she turned to Ellie. "Specifically, from the night this all began. Do you remember the instructions that were given to lay the child down on the hill?" She stopped, looking into Ellie's eyes.

Ellie thought, then began thinking out loud, "From the dream, vison, whatever it was I had, I can remember them all being gathered on the hill. They had the baby, Joanna, there." Then it hit her, her eyes grew wide and a smile over her face. "He told her to lay the baby down north to south. He had marked it with stones."

Hannah smiled, the first time Ellie had seen her do so, "Yes Eleanor. The baby was laid north to south as well," she turned away to address the group. "I have gone through the notes and details, I think we have all the pieces here to put together, and that is where the wall comes in." Facing the diagram, she added, "On the first night, the night Joanna was lost, and all of this started, she was placed here." She indicated the bottom of the tower, "lying down with her head to the north and her feet to the south."

"Then why was the wall added?" Simon asked.

"As a way to protect anyone that had to do this again," Katherine added.

Everyone turned to face her, she was holding a scrunched-up piece of paper in her hand. Ellie's mother had kept her word and was allowing them to do the talking, but now she was speaking everyone was listening.

"Looking at these notes, they say that the wall was added to allow someone to be under the arch, this would channel the energy into the tower without the person actually being in it. The reason this wasn't done the first time is the details that were given in the design did not specify a wall. When, is it Abijah I think," she peered at the paper, "first designed it, he did not mention a wall because he had only been told to lay the child at the specific spot, where he built the tower." Katherine approached the board, "If, Ellie got the spirits to the tower, the energy should hold them long enough for her to get to the archway and position herself underneath it. All that, assuming the stones are ok, should be enough to protect her and allow this magic stuff to do what it needs to do." She turned and looked at Ellie, "My baby girl." A tear was forming in her eye.

Ellie stepped forwards and wrapped her arms around her mother, "We can do this," she said.

"Yes, Eleanor," Douglas agreed, "I believe you can. We will be there with you on Friday, we may not be able to do much, but we will be with you every step of the way."

"All of us," Hannah agreed.

Ellie smiled at the group over her mother's shoulder.

"I can't believe it has come to this, all of us together, trying to solve an impossible puzzle, I can't thank you enough, and all we need to do is get the piece back and then do this on Friday." She smiled a nervous smile, "Easy."

"All because you're an only child in the line, talk about luck eh Ellie?" Annabelle added with a chuckle.

"On Friday we will know," Douglas added. "We will know if everything we in the council have known, worked towards, been told and tried to share was true or for nothing. I make this pledge to you all here and now, members and non-members. If this turns out to be false, and the Man Of Mow is nothing more than a story, if nothing happens on this night and the world keeps turning, then the council will be herby disbanded, and we will no longer inflict our message on this village."

"And if it is true?" Simon asked, an amused look on his face.

"Then we will either all burn in which case it doesn't matter, or we will survive. And Eleanor can decide what is best for us to do."

"Wow, even more pressure then," Ellie replied with a nervous smile.

CHAPTER 17

Friday came. The events of the planning meeting in the hall kept going around in Ellie's head. Annabelle and Simon had kept their word, they did not discuss any of it with anyone but were there if Ellie needed them. The main concern though was put to rest when they all got back from school that afternoon. Simon and Annabelle had been given permission to stay over at Ellie's, Katherine had spoken to their parents and arranged it for them under a façade of a party. When the three arrived home, there was a package on the doorstep.

"The stone is here!" Ellie shouted and ran the last few steps to the doorstep. She picked up the package and without any hesitation ripped it open to reveal the stone piece in the frame, exactly how Sophie had shown them. Inside was a note in her handwriting:

Wish I could be there to help you Ellie, I will be in spirit (no pun intended!) love you. Sophie x

After the plan had been made at the council meeting, Ellie had spoke to Sophie and told her everything. She was coming up to see them tomorrow, but that was too late to help tonight. A tear formed at the corner of Ellie's eye. She whispered quietly, "Thank you Soph."

Annabelle hugged her from behind, "Shall we go fix this thing?"

Ellie nodded, opened the door and all three of them hurried through the house into the garden, they gathered round the stone. Ellie carefully opened the frame and pulled the stone out; she did not want to ruin Sophie's handy work if she could help it. She put her left palm on the big stone in the ground and held the piece in her right. Slowly bringing the two together, lining up the broken piece with the top of the larger stone.

"Good luck everyone," she said when the pieces were millimetres apart.

Closer they got, until the small piece was latched onto the big piece. Ellie looked at the others, they had all been expecting some kind of big moment, a bang, a flash, something. Nothing happened.

"Is that it?" Simon asked.

"I don't know," Ellie replied. "Shall I let go?"

The three looked at each other, none of them knew what to say.

"I'm letting go, countdown for me?"

Annabelle and Simon obliged, together they counted, "Three, two, one."

Ellie let go.

With a quick and very devastating thud, the stone piece fell to the floor.

Silence fell across the three friends. Whatever hope and optimism there was, it had gone, as if blown away by the autumn breeze. Ellie dropped to her knees, picked up the stone piece and frantically tried to make it reattach to the larger stone. She tried over and over, each time with more anger and despair.

"Why won't this work?" she shouted, tears of loss forming now, her voice cracking.

Annabelle moved round and took hold of Ellie, who resisted at first, desperate to carry on trying to get the stone attached. Annabelle held her tight, until eventually she dropped the stone piece and squeezed Annabelle.

"We were so close," she sobbed, "So close I actually believed we could do this, Annabelle! I believed."

"We, all did, Ellie. We all believed," Annabelle replied soothingly. "Simon, go and put the kettle on, Ellie, let's calm down, breath, and focus. We have time, we will figure this out, ok. We have come this far, and nothing will stop us now." She pulled away, putting her hands on Ellie's shoulders so she could look into her red puffy eyes. "Still as gorgeous as when you smile," she said with a grin.

Ellie snorted a laugh, enjoying the fluttering feeling in her stomach as Annabelle said this.

"Now, let's go have a drink and talk about this, we must have missed something somewhere."

A short while later, after making some calls, the Fields family kitchen was full. The entire council was there as well as Katherine. They were all gathered around Ellie trying to work out how to fix the stone, they all agreed that without it, it would be difficult to carry out the rest of their plan.

"We have tried everything, and we have all tried too," Hannah finished explaining to Beryl, who was the last to arrive. "Nothing is making the stone stick. It is dark now, so it is not a daylight thing either."

Beryl turned to Ellie, "Eleanor dear, is there anything you can remember?"

"NO," Ellie snapped and interrupted, "There is not, ok Beryl, and know why? Because if I could remember something, I would have done it already, ok?" Ellie stood and stormed out of the room; she could hear mumblings as she left.

"She is just under pressure is all, she didn't mean it," she heard Kenny say.

I did mean it, Ellie thought to herself as she stormed upstairs to her room. Once there she settled on her seat and looked up at the folly. She could just make it out in the moonlight. After a while, her mind wondered, she recalled the first time she sat at this seat, her dad had surprised her and then come to sit on it with her. That visit to a house viewing seemed like a lifetime ago now, so much had happened since then. She remembered visits from friends, calls from London, chatting to her mum and dad on this very seat. All the normal things that she should long for, and now in a matter of hours she was going to try and save the world. "How has it come to this?" she mused out loud.

She sighed, it all hinged on the stone being fixed. Looking up at the folly she took a deep breath and closed her eyes. She focused, determined to do one last sweep of her memory to see if there was something somewhere she had missed. She recalled finding the tin, she imagined holding the compass and the telescope in her hand. Nothing that could help there, although she was curious as to what the telescope was for. Moving on, she re-imagined the first spirit visit, being dragged out of her bed. He made her take the compass, they went to the top of the hill and saw the first council and the fateful first night. Remembering the realisation that she was related and had been tied to this since birth Ellie shivered and quickly moved on. Finally, she went through the last spirit visit in her mind. She remembered the tranquillity of it, walking peacefully down the hill and being shown the colours of the energy flowing. That was of course what this was all about, the energy. He had told her that everything in our world creates the energy needed to support theirs. She remembered the colours, the purple and yellow, how it looked majestic as it flowed from the stone to the folly. In her mind, Ellie could recall the stone, and the broken piece on the floor with the floating figure standing by it. Attempting to remember the conversation, she could hear his voice once more.

"I want you to do what you think is right. I believe the world should continue as it always has, I believe the two souls should remain incarcerated above that folly forever," he had said.

"You want me to fix the stones? The exact opposite of what I was told before? You want me to believe and fix the stones to keep the prison as it is?"

"I do not believe that will work. I believe that the stones are now damaged beyond repair. I do not think you will be able to fix the stones. I believe that which is broken can only be fixed by that which is also broken and then repaired."

Ellie's eyes shot open when she recalled that last line, she said it aloud to herself, "I believe that which is broken can only be fixed by that which is also broken and then repaired. That's it!" she exclaimed, still talking to herself out loud. "The stone can only be fixed by something that has been broken and then repaired, but it must match all this energy stuff that is going around, what could it be?" Then the revelation hit her in the same way the bolt of light had hit the hill all those centuries ago. "Us. It must be repaired by us. Mum, me, and dad. That which is broken means the relationship between us."

She grabbed her phone and started to call her father. As she did so, she ran downstairs. Approaching the kitchen, Ellie lowered the phone and put it on loudspeaker, doing so seemed to quiet down the chatter as the sound of a phone calling a number came down the hallway. As she arrived, she moved into the middle of the room so that everyone was around her. They all stopped and stared at her, before they could ask any questions he answered.

"Ellie, you there? Everything ok? I've been meaning to call but I haven't known what to say."

Ellie looked at her mother, Katherine's look was one of confusion and loss. Then Ellie spoke, her voice broken with tension. "Dad, please, that doesn't matter now. I need you to listen and trust me. Can you do that?"

"Eleanor, if this is about the other night, and the council rubbish then."

"Dad please," Ellie pleaded, "Can you trust me and help your Ellie-Bear?"

Silence.

Then there was a small sound of sniffling from down the phone, her father was clearly tearing up at the thought of his daughter desperate for help.

Then, he replied softly, "What do you need Ellie?"

Ellie breathed a sigh of relief, "I need you to come home, right now and help mum and I fix something, can you do that for me?"

There was a pause, then his soft voice came once more "Yes, will be there as soon as I can. About half an hour, best go so I can get there quickly, see you soon Ellie."

"See you soon, thanks dad, love you."

Ellie put the phone down, Katherine moved quickly over to her and gave her a hug. "What's all this about?" she asked.

"We need all three of us to fix the stone, he said that it could only be fixed by that which was broken and then repaired. I think he meant us; we need to do it together." Ellie smiled at her mother, "I hope I'm right. If not, at least we get to see each other again, eh?"

She grinned. There was a general group feeling of relief, the feeling of despair had lifted and now they waited once more, waiting to see what may happen next.

A little less than half an hour later, the front door opened. Ellie ran from the kitchen with Katherine not far behind to greet her dad at the door. He put his bag down and they embraced in a huge hug. As they parted, Katherine arrived and looked her husband up and down.

"Nicholas, nice to see you, glad you could come."

"Nice to see you too Katherine, I'm sorry about what happened, can we discuss it later, please?"

There was a pleading tone to his voice, as if he knew that he did not have the high ground for this argument.

Katherine crossed her arms, "Yes, we can. But only once you have tried to help all of us."

"All of us?"

"Come on dad, there isn't much time," Ellie said, and led her father by the arm into the kitchen.

When they got there, they were greeted with a warm welcome. Nicholas was clearly taken aback and at a loss as to why there were so many people, most of whom he believed to be crazy, were in their house.

"Ok," Katherine said, "We don't have much time, so Ellie, Nick, and I will go outside alone and see if we can fix this. If we can then you can all go up to the folly and I will stay here with him to explain what is going on. That ok with everyone?"

There were solemn nods all around.

Ellie, her mum, and dad went outside and closed the door behind them. They led Nicholas over to the stone, Ellie picked up the piece from the floor.

"Dad, I promise this will all make sense, but for now I need you to trust us."

He smiled at her, then took his wife's hand, "I do trust you, both of you."

"Ok, I don't really know how to try this, so, here goes. Dad, put your hand on the stone, anywhere will do but keep hold of mums' hand with your other one."

He did so, as he did this, Ellie took her mums hand in her

right, holding the broken piece in her left.

"Now what?" he asked.

"Now, we try this," Ellie replied.

As she did so, she reached out with her left hand, moving the piece closer to the stone in the ground. When she got it within a few inches, it started to buzz, a very gentle but noticeable vibration was moving through the stone in her hand.

"Errrr, can you all feel that?" Ellie asked.

"Yes," came the reply from her parents, this was both comforting and exciting to Ellie all at once.

She kept moving it closer, the vibrations got stronger, until it felt like her whole body was buzzing with energy.

"Keep going Ellie," Katherine encouraged.

All three of them could feel the buzz now and seemed unable to let go of each other's hands. Ellie gave one final push to set the piece on top of the stone. As the pieces touched, a bright yellow light formed along the crack, like it was coming from inside the stone and was being extinguished by the pieces joining together. The light was blinding, they needed to close their eyes to shield them from it. Ellie let go of the piece and with a bang they were sent sprawling backwards across the garden, letting go of each other's hands as they fell. Ellie quickly lifted herself up onto her elbows, looking at the stone she could see the piece had held. The yellow light was still visible through the crack, but the piece was there. She stood; her parents quickly followed suit.

"Everyone ok?" she asked.

"I'm fine," Katherine replied, "Nick?"

"I have no idea what is going on, but yes I'm ok."

Ellie took a step towards the stone. She could hear it buzzing, humming with energy. The yellow light was focused in one area, forming a circle. She moved closer to look, the light had burrowed a hole into the stone, not very deep, but noticeable. She reached out and touched it, as she did the yellow light pulsated and she could feel its energy flowing through her.

"Annabelle, Simon! Need you, quick," she shouted.

The patio door opened, and her two friends emerged, followed by the council members.

"Did you do it?" Annabelle asked, "Did it work?"

"I need to finish it, don't ask me how I know I just do, but I need the telescope. Now." Ellie looked at Annabelle, and as if there was a connection between them Annabelle immediately turned and ran into the house.

After what felt like an eternity of silence, even though it was only a few moments, Annabelle returned with the telescope. She gave it to Ellie and stepped back.

"I've been trying to work out what this was for," she said to the group. "What's the point in a telescope that doesn't zoom or focus? I've just realised, it's not a telescope. It's just a single lens."

She leant forward and slotted one end of the telescope over the newly formed hole on the stone. It was just deep enough to hold the metal tube. As soon as she let go, the yellow light became focused, charged, and seemed to get brighter but in a controlled way that meant they could all see it. Without warning, a surge of light shot out of the telescope lens, heading in a single beam towards the folly. They all followed it with their eyes, once it appeared to reach the structure it faded, and the metal tube fell to the floor. The rock was once again whole. The only difference was that there was now a symbol where the tube had once been. A symbol of an 'M' in a circle.

For a few minutes there was silence. Everyone was simply taking in what had just happened, they had all seen the yellow light. They could all see the feint symbol on the stone, though this was only because they had seen it before. It was too well hidden to see for the first time now. Finally, Ellie spoke.

"Ok. To the folly, this might just actually work you know."

She headed over to her mum and dad, they had separated slightly from the group but were together and that was all that mattered to Ellie right now.

"Mum, dad. I need to do this, my friends will help me, but I need you to stay here and be safe. Dad, mum will explain everything."

Her father pulled her into a hug, "I'm so proud of you, I have no idea what is going on, but I am so proud."

"We both are," Katherine added, joining in on the hug. "I'll tell him everything Ellie, you go save the world. It's what you were born to do."

Ellie chuckled, "Enough with the pressure."

She gave one last squeeze, then pulled away to face the others. There they were, four members of the council, each holding their staff waiting for Ellie. In the middle, Annabelle, and Simon, ready to help. Annabelle was holding Ellie's staff.

"Believe this is yours, Miss Fields," she said handing it over.

Annabelle was also holding the necklace from the tin, Ellie turned and allowed Annabelle to put it round her neck. "Figured you may as well complete the look".

"Thank you," Ellie agreed. Turning to face the group once more, "Right, let's do this, to the folly," Ellie shouted.

With a look over her shoulder at her parents, Ellie led the group out of the garden, through the house, and onto the street. She was leading them to her destiny.

It was a night of typical darkness. The black seemed blacker than black now, walking up these paths with no lights seemed to make the darkness feel thicker somehow, like it was sucking the energy and light away. Ellie led the group up the hill, through the paths and fields until they rounded a corner where the folly came into sharp focus. Here she stopped. Almost immediately the group gathered around her, they had all silently agreed that Ellie was in charge and they would do whatever she needed. She looked at the group around her, she had decided.

"I think we need to split up," she said. The reaction was muted confusion. Nobody directly queried, but there were mutterings of misunderstanding.

"Why Eleanor, why do you think we need to split up?" Douglas asked. He was clearly hurt; of all the council members he had been the most receptive to the change of working with outsiders. The idea of losing that again was clearly troubling him.

"I've been thinking about these," she gestured to her staff. "They haven't been mentioned in any of the notes or anywhere, but they have the same symbol on."

"Yes, we put the symbol on, the symbol of the Man Of Mow,"

Kenny commented.

"Yes, I know. But does nobody else think it is odd that the stones were placed in the positions so that the symbol was created perfectly from the sky, way before they knew they needed a symbol or had the ability to prove it? Maybe it is more than a symbol? I don't know, what do we all think?"

Looking round the group, Ellie could see a mixture of understanding and concern. She had a point, and she knew it.

"Ok, what do you suggest?" Hannah asked.

"You all know where your houses are from the folly yes? Well, I think each staff should be positioned on the line of sight between the folly and the stones, as a guide for the energy to flow through or something. I can't tell you why I think this, I just feel it."

"Very well Eleanor," Beryl confirmed, "We can do that."

"Yes," Douglas added, "We can do that for you."

"We can go between you all to see if all are ok," Simon added, gesturing to himself and Annabelle.

"I want to stay with Ellie," Anabelle said, "She shouldn't have to face this alone."

Ellie looked at Annabelle, her soft features warmed Ellie's heart.

"Right, here is the plan. Douglas, Hannah, Kenny, and Beryl take up your positions around the folly between it and your houses," Ellie instructed firmly. "Annabelle, Simon, stay with me but everyone keep your phones on, if I'm right we only have one chance at this. I need your help, and this feels right to me."

As she finished, she knew she was clutching at straws, she had no right to ask this of so many people. Looking round, she had never felt such a feeling of belonging as she did in that moment.

"Thank you, I love you all," was all she could think of to say in thanks to them.

With words of thanks and good luck, the group split. Kenny and Beryl went to the left, Hannah and Douglas to the right. This left Ellie with Annabelle and Simon, she took a step forward, her two friends followed further up the hill. The three friends walked in a line, side by side as much as the paths would allow. They turned a corner, only the top of the folly was visible over the crest of the hill, but they all knew they were in line with the wall that pointed to Ellie's house. "I need to go on alone now," Ellie said.

Simon and Annabelle looked at each other.

"We want to come with you," Annabelle said, her voice soothing but with a firm undertone.

Ellie looked at her, smiled, and then said, "I know, but I need to do this, and I need you to do something for me." She held out the staff, "I need you to keep this here, held vertically."

Annabelle took it, "What?"

"I meant what I said back there, I believe these need to be kept on the line between the folly and those stones, I can't do that and be up there," she pointed at the folly. "Please, I need you to do this. There is no one else that I would rather trust with this."

"We can do that, can't we Annabelle," Simon commented. "We came to help, and if this is what you need then this is what we will do. Would rather be with you up there but we can hear about it after, when you come back."

He stepped forward and pulled Ellie into a hug, she responded in kind and gave him a squeeze.

"Good luck Simple Simon."

"Good luck Smelly Ellie."

She let go and turned to Annabelle who had tears streaming down her face now.

"I want to look after you Ellie," she said through sobs.

"You are, by doing this for me. Annabelle, you are my rock and I need to know you two have my back down here. Please?"

Annabelle nodded. The two girls hugged, through sobs and tears Annabelle demanded, "You better come back in one piece soon. Otherwise, I'm coming to find you!"

"I promise," she pulled away, smiled at them both and then turned to do the last part of the journey on her own. After a few steps, she looked over her shoulder and called, "Keep that staff vertical on that spot."

"We will," she heard Annabelle call back.

Ellie grinned to herself, It's going to be fine, she told herself, and powered on. The path she was on was the same one she had walked along on her first exploration of the hill and the folly. It was a gravel track with a gradual incline, after going through a small gate she turned to go up a steep part of the hill. As this levelled off, she paused to look up at the folly. Even though it was pitch black she could make out its shape against the dark purple sky, it looked more foreboding at night, the silhouette of the arch did not look anywhere near as innocent now.

"Now or never," she said out loud, and moved on. She was at the base of the final climb now, she climbed up the steps that led to the crest of the hill, there seemed to be more of them tonight. Up she went, three to go, two to go, then the final step. She breathed a sigh of relief, as if this were all that needed to be done tonight. Looking out over the view, she could see cars moving about, a train moved past down below, and houses glowed in the night. It all looked so peaceful.

"Beautiful isn't it?" a soft voice spoke from behind her.

Ellie whirled around. She found herself face to face with two floating spirits, identical in appearance. Immediately she recalled to herself, one with a desire to save, the other to destroy.

"One of the most beautiful things I have ever seen," Ellie replied, she was determined now, focused and driven. There was only one way out of this and that was to remain in control. "Here we are then, the three of us, you each have a different plan, but both need me to carry it out. Anyone want to suggest what should happen next?"

The figures said nothing, floating just above the ground a few meters away from Ellie. They were between her and the folly, she needed to change that and get them both up the peak of the hill and into the folly itself. Ellie looked into the eyes of the figure on the right.

"Which are you then?" she asked. "Are you the Man or John? Do you want to protect or destroy?"

Nothing.

"How can I help either of you if neither of you will tell me who you are?" she demanded.

"Eleanor, we know your resolve and we know that we are asking two different things. As such, we cannot help you, you must do what you must do."

Ellie took a step to her right, to her surprise the spirits floated to their right, her left, at the same time meaning they were still exactly opposite her and the distances were all the same. "I had a feeling you would say something like that," Ellie said, "I mean, you both want help but neither of you is willing to make a decision or take a stand. You are just quite happy letting little old me do all the work aren't you?"

Her confidence was growing now, she could feel it flowing through her veins. She took another sideways step, the same thing happened, they mirrored her movements.

"So, I had to do some thinking of my own didn't I? I needed to work out what was best to do to save my world whilst preserving yours as it is. After all, if we have all survived for so long then why should anything change tonight?" another step, same again.

"You are lying," the figure on the left said, "You have not figured anything out that we have not told you. You only know what we wanted you to know, and because of that you know what you need to do."

Ellie looked at the figure that had said this, whilst taking another step said, "But how will you get what you want if I don't know which one you are?"

Nothing.

"See, I think I figured it out," this was a bluff, but Ellie's confidence was so strong at this stage that she kept going. "You both need me, so, you won't let any harm come to me because without me, you both lose eventually don't you?"

Another step to the right. Ellie looked around, she was almost at the folly now having nearly completely switched the layout around putting herself between it and the spirits. Out of the corner of her eye, she could see something glowing, she focused her eyes, peering into the darkness. She squared her body up to allow herself a moment to look and work out what it was. Even from this distance, it was eventually clear to her. Whilst she was not sure who it was, she knew they were holding a staff. The glow she could see was coming from its handle, it was channelling the yellow energy and making it visible. Ellie grinned slightly, she turned around further, there was another yellow dot, and another. She could not see them all but was certain they were all doing the same thing, glowing with energy. Each staff was helping to focus the stones energy onto the folly, this was her moment, she needed to act and force the issue now. She turned back to face the spirits.

"Ok, well, if neither of you will speak up, then I guess it is down to me and my friends. See, there is something that you didn't count on, something that I figured out moments ago that is going to tip this in my favour. Right now, the energy that you speak of is being channelled and focused, more intense than ever before."

She took a step backwards toward the folly steps, she needed to get as close as possible without alerting them, so she could turn and run when it was needed.

"That energy flows through all of us, even me, you could absorb the energy from me right now couldn't you? Taking my imagination and energy as you did so."

"We could," one of the figures said, they both glided slightly closer.

Ellie took another step back to keep the distance.

"The question is though, who gets that energy? Who wants it, who needs it?"

She was thinking fast now, she was banking on them both rushing at her at once.

"How is the power stronger? What do you mean?" the figure on the right asked, moving closer still.

"My friends are focusing it, they are standing on the sight lines between the folly and the stones, and they are using the staffs of the council to focus that energy. If I am right, that will make it more powerful and focused on a specific point, me. Giving me more energy than either of you."

"You lie!" he stated, frustration entering his voice.

"Maybe. Maybe not, the fact is, who wants to find out last?"

With that she turned and sprinted as fast as she could up the steps. Ellie was focused, she could not afford to look over her shoulder, but nor could she hear movement behind her, the spirits always moved silently. She climbed the steps that ran alongside the wall of the folly towards the gated door.

This was it, the moment of truth, her plan would either succeed or fail in the next few seconds. As she reached the top step, Ellie flung herself to the floor, making herself as small as possible. Once on the ground she turned to look up above her, never had she been so happy to be lying on the wet ground. As she lay there, both spirits glided over her, unable to react in time they flew over her and through the gate into the tower. Ellie had been banking on them chasing her, and it had worked. As soon as they passed through the gate a bright yellow beam of light shot out of the top of the folly tower into the sky. Ellie stood and approached the folly gate, inside the spirits were both facing her, expressionless as always.

"You cannot contain us in here Eleanor, this will not hold for long."

"I know," she replied, "It only needs to hold you long enough for me to figure something out."

They moved towards her, reaching out with an arm each. Ellie took a step back, but as they approached the gate the light grew brighter, when they tried to touch it there was a bang and they recoiled into the centre of the tower. It was containing them for now.

"What, Eleanor, do you need to figure out?" came the angry question from one of them.

Ellie not knowing which, smiled.

"I am going to ask one question, and I want the figure on the right to answer me, that is my right. Understand?"

No reply.

Ellie took a deep breath, "If I were to ask the other spirit if you are the one that wants to protect both worlds, what would they say?"

CHAPTER 18

Ellie waited. She knew time was limited but was also aware that to remain in control of the situation she needed to allow them to respond before saying anything else. Looking through the gate, glowing with energy, she could see both figures floating what would be side by side, looking at her. All she needed was enough time to work out what to do.

"What if we refuse to answer?" came a soft voice from inside the folly tower.

"Then you both lose," Ellie replied defiantly.

"If we lose, you lose," came the mocking voice of one of the trapped spirits.

"Do we though? I'm willing to take the risk. I mean, if I do the wrong thing, we lose, if I do nothing, we might lose. So, I'm ok waiting to see what happens next."

This was another bluff. Ellie knew she needed to do something, but she needed time to calculate and work it out. She turned away from the tower door to think, she had not noticed until now what was going on around her.

The tower was pulsating with light, sending it in waves up into the sky. She could no longer make out the yellow from each staff, but knew they were there as she was sure that without them this would not be working. One thing that did not make sense is how nobody else could see what was going on, the folly looked like a lighthouse. It was shining bright and sending beams of light into the sky.

How is no one seeing this, Ellie thought to herself. Then, she saw it and remembered at the same time. She looked up. As the light was sent up by the folly it was hitting a purple barrier, this was then vibrating down in a sphere to the top of the hill. Ellie was inside the purple bubble she had seen in one of her dream visits, it was shielding the folly from outside eyes containing all the energy and light inside it. Ellie looked around, the sphere was focused on the top part of the hill, the very peak that the folly was sat on, and her friends could not see what was happening as they were outside the barrier. She was alone. She turned and faced the door once more; she had taken a few steps back but could still make out the figures inside. She approached the door.

"So, made up your mind yet? I think we have a few minutes before this all comes crumbling down," Ellie challenged.

She was right. Time had not been kind to the folly, it was not as strong as it once was, and cracks were starting to appear in the stone walls.

"We think you are running out of time, Eleanor. Time is against you and your world. For you have made a grave error in judgement, Eleanor Fields, Imaginari will survive."

"Imaginari? Is that your world?" Ellie replied harshly, "What error in judgement?"

"Yes, it is, Imaginari is our world. You have assumed that we are working against each other, you assumed that because we suggested different views to the same problem, we wanted different things. This is not the case."

Ellie was confused, "But you came to me at different times and spoke in different ways? One of you wanted to destroy, the other wanted to fix? How can you both want the same thing?"

There was concern in her voice now, she began to feel as though the situation was slipping away from her.

The figures moved closer together and forwards towards Ellie.

"Eleanor, your mistake was assuming that either of us wanted to save your world. Indeed, it was founded on the view that you were visited by different spirits."

Ellie's eyes widened slightly in shock, as she looked through the gate, the spirits moved closer together until they started to overlap and merge. First an arm, then a leg and body, finally the head and the other arm until two figures had become one. One spirit.

"One Man Of Mow," Ellie said in a disheartened tone.

"Yes Eleanor, there is only one Man Of Mow, and I am he. You may have trapped me in here for a short time using your staffs and blind luck, but you cannot stop what is inevitable. Repaired or not, the stone was broken long enough for me to form and bend your mind to my will. You have done exactly what I needed you to do, when I am free from here you will take my place. Your sacrifice through this tower will split the prison in two, your energy will not seal it, it will shatter it. Allowing all of your world's energy and imaginations into mine and we will have physical form."

Ellie was stunned. She had been fooled into thinking that one of these spirits was good, when in fact they were not only both the same person, but that they wanted to destroy unreservedly.

"I see the realisation on your face, Eleanor. You know it is true. I have waited for the right person to come, the right person to come and break the pattern. The single child part is true, that was important, but I needed to wait for you to come and start to pull apart the foundation of my prison. You have done that, just in time."

Ellie looked up, "Time. That's it," she looked around, "I just need more time."

"How can you do that? There is no more time, Eleanor."

"There is in your world," Ellie replied defiantly, turning away from the door. She headed towards the arch, paused and turned to face the door. "I'm taking a chance on Imaginari, I bet I'm right."

She looked up at the arch, it was glowing gold and sending waves of energy towards the tower itself. She stepped forwards, under the arch. Ellie felt a static charge flow through her, she looked at her arms. They were glowing too, yellow strands of light were moving from her to the archway to be absorbed into the stone. Ellie moved until she was directly under the arch, the buzzing and energy was strong now, she could feel her whole-body pulsating with it. Her skin was glowing, but it did not hurt, Ellie experienced no discomfort at all, other than fear and nervousness around her newly formed plan. She sat on the floor, it was damp but not cold, and with a look up at the arch she aligned herself directly underneath it, meaning she knew she was going to be lying directly under it. Ellie lay back and looked up, she could see the energy flowing from all around her into the arch and the tower. The energy from her was going into the arch directly, all of this was contained by the purple bubble around the crest of the hill that the folly and Ellie were on. Taking a deep breath, she closed her eyes and focused on the light, the energy, and the gap in the sky.

Silence. There was nothing, Ellie could no longer feel the ground beneath her back nor the wind in her hair. She opened her eyes, the sky was blank, the folly had gone, or at least the arch had from above her head had gone. She sat up and looked around. Nothing, just a feint purple glow lighting up the view. There were no hills, fields, trees, buildings, or anything that Ellie could use to work out where she was. Looking at her own body she was wearing the same clothes, but there was no longer any light coming from her. Standing, she took one more look around. Nothing. It was as if she were standing in a large room, where she could not see the walls or ceiling but still felt contained. In the pit of her stomach Ellie knew she could not move far. Despite this, she took a few cautious steps. The ground felt firm beneath her feet but not as solid as she would have liked, as if walking on sponge.

"Welcome Eleanor," a loud voice said.

Ellie turned, looking everywhere to try and find the source of the voice. Floating opposite her was a figure. Ghost like, just like the spirits she had seen before, but more refined, sharper edges and clearer to see.

"Where am I?" she demanded.

The figure floated towards her, "You are in the space between our worlds."

"Our? So, you're the Man, you're not trapped in the folly?"

"I am the Man yes, but you are slightly wrong with that last part, at the moment we are trapped in the folly. I in the tower held fast by the force of the energy between worlds, you held under the arch, pouring your own energy into the arch and then the tower. This has allowed you to join me, spiritually, and allow us to have this conversation, Eleanor."

Ellie frowned, "So, we are now both in the prison space, between the worlds? The energy is trapping us both?"

He nodded, "Indeed, you catch on quick don't you Eleanor. Bright girl, shame you will soon be lost like I was."

"Lost? How? If I'm controlling this, then why would I be lost with you?"

He chuckled, "My dear girl, you are not controlling this, the energy is. By allowing yourself to be drawn into it, letting it flow through you the same way that the folly was designed to, and you are sacrificing your soul to this prison."

"What?" Ellie asked, alarm creeping into her tone now. "I haven't sacrificed anything."

He glided closer still.

"Eleanor, you still do not understand that this has been my plan all along, your energy is what I needed to break myself completely free from this place. It may not have gone exactly as I had hoped, but you are still here. Completely at my mercy."

He was inches from Ellie's face now, floating so that his head was level with hers. Ellie clenched her fists.

"That will not help you, I'm just a spirit remember. You have lost, you cannot defeat me. Once I have absorbed your energy, as the first sole descendant in a family line I will have the strength to break free properly, destroy the folly and its stones, then begin taking the energy from your world."

Tears formed at the corner of Ellie's eyes, could this really be it? She was wracking her brains for something, anything that she had missed that could help her.

"Trying to think if there is something that can help you?" he mocked. "There isn't. Think about it, you fixed the stone. If it had stayed broken this would have been quicker but it will still happen. Your friends are focusing the energy as well, they are channelling it through each staff. Given that you told them to, and they cannot see the folly crumbling due to the purple sphere they have no reason to move or change tact. You have put me in the tower, yes, I grant you that was not expected but not a significant inconvenience. All I need to do is wait for you to tire and then I will be free."

Ellie's face dropped, "You, you wanted this all along? You wanted me, here in this space so you could escape?"

He nodded, "Yes Eleanor. I wanted you here, you are the only person whose bloodline, imagination, and energy could help me. I have waited and waited, and now my plan is finally coming to fruition. Your world will end!" he was almost snarling at her now.

"So, when you showed me the first council, when the baby Joanna was lost, why did you show me two spirits? You showed me two of you battling in the beam of light?"

"Tricks of the light. I made it appear as though there was another, in truth there was not. I alone floated over the scene; the child was supposed to be a sacrificial energy to break the link between worlds. The plans I gave Abijah and the first council were to build something that would not trap me but would help me harness the energy. I was mistaken in my design. As I got close to see what was happening, the child's soul grabbed hold of me, and we got trapped together. She broke free though, another mistake on my part. She had not been willing; her mother had put her there, but her soul did not want to sacrifice itself. That is why I needed you, someone who could think for themselves."

Ellie stood silently, taking all of this in, processing, thinking. She knew that the longer he kept talking, the more time she would have to think and find a way out.

She asked, "So you needed someone who would willing put themselves in the folly? So, their soul would be drawn up with yours?"

"Correct," he hissed. "By willingly putting yourself in the folly you have given up your protection, you have given over your energy to me and my world, Eleanor. Everything has worked as I intended it to. My first mistake was that the tower should have been built before the stones, this would have solved part of the problem. The second was that the person needed to be willing and to be laying north to south. Do you know why this is important?"

Ellie shook her head, but for the first time in this conversation, she felt a twinge of excitement.

"Because it matches the shape on the ground. With the head

to the north, you are pointing towards the two tips at the top of the letter 'M', thus sending your soul, along with mine through the gate. When it gets there, it will be torn apart and your energy will be absorbed by me, shattering the folly and the stones in one go. Freeing me to rip open the sky and pull all of your world's energy through into my own."

Ellie allowed a small smile to cross her lips, this did not go unnoticed.

"What are you smiling at girl?" he snarled.

"Oh nothing. Out of curiosity, there seems to be a lot of focus on the letter 'M' around here. What would happen if, say the willing person was lying south to north? Facing the bottom of the 'M'?"

He had no expressions, but there was a flicker across his face that suggested he had not considered this.

"It would make no difference; the sacrifice would be the same," he replied, but not as confidently as he had been speaking previously.

Ellie grabbed hold of this and ran with it, "Oh I think it is important," she stated. "Think about it, that letter and symbol shape has been everywhere since the first design. The layout of the stones, the significance of the letter 'M'. I mean, you said yourself that it was all connected and part of your plan, didn't you?"

"Yes, I did, but it would make no difference. You are still giving me your soul; it will still reach the portal door and be torn apart. It will be mine."

Ellie had an idea, it was a long shot, but she had no other choice.

"When are you going to take my energy then?" she asked, a new-found confidence flowing through her.

He moved quickly towards her, "Any minute now," he answered chillingly. "Any moment now I will move through you and then we will both flow towards the portal. Then it will end for you."

"That's it? We just float up there like angels, get it over with will you, I'm bored now!"

Ellie folded her arms, she wanted to bring this to a close and fast.

"Why are you in such a hurry?" he asked, moving closer. "I suppose I can start the process early, this shouldn't hurt, yet."

He moved towards Ellie, closer and closer until he was touching her, his ghost like form moving through her body. Ellie unfolded her arms to defend herself, but it made no difference. She could not feel anything, there was nothing to fend off. It felt as if a cool breeze was blowing against her and nothing more. The Man moved right the way through her and out behind, as he appeared behind Ellie, she collapsed to the floor her eyes closing. Then, moments later it was as though she was floating. Ellie looked around and could see her own body lying on the ground. This was the real ground though; they were back in the real world as she was looking at her own body lying on top of the hill beneath the arch. She looked around, everything was as it was before, the tower was still pulsating energy into the sphere, that was shielding the top of the hill and the arch was pushing her own energy into the tower. Ellie could see the man in the tower, still trapped. She looked down at her own body, she looked asleep, peaceful and calm on the ground and in an instant, she knew what she had to do. Looking at her arms, or at least where they should have been, she could see a ghost like form. She had started to become a spirit like the man, his plan was working. She had an idea though, and now was the time. In her new spirit form she closed her eyes and allowed the energy to flow through her. She felt the arch pull her in, a feeling of evaporating into dust or steam spread through her body. Opening her eyes, Ellie could see as well as feel herself being pulled along the stone of the arch towards the tower. Moments later, she was in the tower, looking down on the Man.

Looking up at her, he began to gloat, "You see Eleanor, you are now becoming one with Imaginari. Together we shall destroy your world."

As he finished this, he began to float up towards her, after a few seconds he was level with Ellie.

"So, let me get this right," Ellie began. "You have allowed me to turn into a spirit because you need my energy, this is going to work because I willingly lay down, so my soul is free to be removed yes?"

"Correct, you can repeat it over and over, but it will not change anything," he confirmed.

"See, I still believe there is something in the symbol. The 'M'. You said before how lying north to south meant that both spirits went up? I think that's the key. When lay north to south the 'M' has two spikes at the top, but if I lay south to north, my head is pointing towards to bottom of the 'M', the single spike. One spike, one soul. And I'll bet my pure soul can survive longer than yours."

Ellie smiled, or at least she thought she did. It was not clear to her if she still had a face at this point. She looked up, and as she did so she began to rise up the tower. Up she went above its peak flowing through the yellow pulsating light. Eventually Ellie reached the tear in the sky just inside the purple barrier, a hole that was filled with a deep darkness. She looked down; he was not far behind.

"You foolish girl, you risk everything on a chance?"

"It isn't a chance, it's logical. But yes, I am risking it."

She reached up with a ghostly hand into the dark hole, the moment it went inside Ellie felt a jolt as a bolt of white light shot out of the centre of the darkness. It flowed through her spirit form, into the Man's form and then down into the centre of the folly tower. It looked like a bolt of lightning, but it was sustained for a period of time, as if the power would not dissipate or burn out. For the first time Ellie felt true energy flowing through her.

"This is the end for you girl," he cackled, clearly battling with the pain. "Nothing can save you now, not even your faith in symbols."

Ellie looked down, the bolt of light was scorching the tower, bouncing round inside it searching for something to latch on to. She looked at her body on the hilltop, still motionless. Then back at the Man, he appeared to be shuddering with pain now, Ellie on the other hand could not feel anything. Small fires were breaking out around the folly now, the bolt of light was getting wilder and out of control. Whilst Ellie did not know what would happen next, she did know that if it failed or she fell, she would lose, she needed to finish this. Then it came to her, the reason why her plan would work, she was right. They were both trapped here because one of them had to choose who should stay. The prison would not take two souls because the person who had activated it, the one who had started the energy flow this evening, the willing party was laying south to north. A simple change of direction. As soon as she thought this, she acted, there was no time to waste seeing if he realised this too. She forced her hand further into the hole and pointed the other at the Man floating beside her.

"See, you didn't take into account choice."

"Choice?" he asked in a fear filled voice.

"Yes, choice. By bringing me here, allowing me the choice of what to do you have put me in control. That's my body down there, this is my soul here. Both willingly given by choice. As such, I can choose you to be incarcerated here. One soul to be bound for eternity, and I choose yours."

As she said this, she reached out and plunged her hand into where the Man's heart would have been. The moment she did so he screamed in pain. The light grew brighter and Ellie could just make out his voice over the bangs and flashes.

"This is not over; this will not hold me forever!"

Yes, it will, Ellie thought to herself and twisted her fist inside the Man's chest. There was a loud bang. The Man's spirit split into what looked like dust and was sucked into the black hole above Ellie's head. She immediately removed her hand from it in panic, as soon as she did so it snapped shut and sent a wave of golden light out in a circle. It hit the sphere and flowed all the way down its sides to the ground. Once there it moved into the centre towards the folly where it gathered at the tower. From where Ellie was, she could see it gathering in the way morning dew does on grass. Without realising, Ellie began to float down towards the tower. She did not seem to have control anymore, down she floated, inside the top of the folly tower where she was immediately pulled into the stone and pushed back down towards the arch. After moving through the stone Ellie was left floating on her back directly above her physical body. Looking up at the tower, she could feel a build-up of energy coming from below, from her physical body. The static charge built, she could feel it building and building. It hurt this time; Ellie could feel the pressure building at the base of her spine. At the moment it became unbearable she screamed in pain; her arms outstretched to the sides like a cross. Her back arched and with a final scream she felt the energy burst out of her body, dissolving the necklace as it did so, through her spirit form and into the arch. This was passed through into the tower where it sent a bolt of light from its base into the sky exactly where the hole was moments before. This lasted for a few seconds, Ellie screaming in pain and the folly pulsating with energy sending bolts of light into the sky. Each time it hit the barrier with energy, the purple sphere rippled and sent the energy back down to the ground and into the folly again. Then, nothing. Ellie saw the purple bubble dissolve, the beams of light fade and the pain in her body subside. She relaxed, and as she did, she floated down and felt her spirit be absorbed back into her own body. There she lay, motionless with her eyes closed, feeling the cold breeze on her skin and the damp floor on her back.

Ellie did not know how long she lay there for; she was not aware of anything until she could hear voices. Keeping her eyes closed, Ellie strained her ears to listen.

"What happened?" a soft female voice said. "Someone call an ambulance or something, we have to help her."

"We couldn't see anything, it all looked normal from our side," a male said.

"Is the fact that we are all still here a good thing? Is it over?" a second female asked.

The conversation then split into several different ones, and Ellie was unable to make any of it out, but she was aware of someone speaking on a phone, explaining how their friend appeared to have passed out and needed help. She did a sense check of her own body, she could feel her arms and hands, her legs and feet were there too. Her breathing felt normal and she was not aware of anything hurting dramatically. Concluding that this meant she was probably ok, she decided to open her eyes but not move. Looking up, she could see her two friends Annabelle and Simon, along with the four council members. All chatting and discussing what they had, or rather had not seen. Ellie smiled to herself, they had not noticed she was awake yet and she mused about how long it would take for them to do so. They all looked ok too, no marks or bumps and scrapes, indeed they all appeared as if they had just been out for an evening stroll. Finally, Annabelle noticed she was awake. They made eye contact as Annabelle glanced down at Ellie and for a moment, they just looked at each other, Ellie had never appreciated how beautiful her friend was and also, how relieved she was to see her again. Then, Annabelle spoke.

"Ellie!"

She flung herself to the ground and hugged Ellie, who responded and squeezed Annabelle into the ground with her.

At this, the others stopped talking and looked down at Ellie, Simon put the phone down clearly happy that they no longer needed help. After a second or two, Annabelle let go and sat back on her knees, Ellie lifted herself up onto her elbows and looked around. It was still night, but she could see the devastation on the ground all around them. She was lay under the arch, exactly as she remembered it. The stone of the arch and tower of the folly was blackened and showed burn marks all over it. The grass on the top of the hill was scorched black and looked like it had been set on fire.

"So, this looks interesting," she said sarcastically.

"Ellie, what happened? We couldn't see anything except a feint purple haze, even that was hard to see!" Annabelle asked frantically, clearly desperate to know what had happened.

"Lot's happened," Ellie replied calmly, "But right now, all I want to do is go home and sleep. Can we do that, and I'll explain all of it in the morning?"

There was a pleading tone to Ellie's voice at this stage.

Annabelle smiled, "I think that is a fabulous idea."

There were sounds of agreement from the group. Ellie went to lift herself up, immediately Annabelle reached out to help. Seeing this, Simon did the same and Ellie was lifted to her feet by her friends with one under each arm.

"Thank you," Ellie said looking round at the group. "I have no idea how much of last night you saw or are aware of, or even if it worked! But I do know that we wouldn't have got as far as we did without your help. Thank you," she started to well up at the end of this, she truly meant it.

Nobody said anything, there was just a silent understanding between them all. The group turned and started to walk down the crest of the hill with the folly on, Ellie supported by Annabelle and Simon following behind the council members. "Annabelle, can we hang back a minute?" Ellie asked.

Annabelle stopped and looked at Ellie, a sparkle in her eyes, "Sure, I have her Simon you can let go."

Simon did so and carried on down the little peak of the hill, "I'll wait around the corner, shout if you need me," he called back.

Ellie turned to face Annabelle and stood on her own, a little wobbly, but she did it.

"Annabelle, you're amazing and I couldn't have done any of this if it wasn't for you."

Annabelle smiled, her hair blowing in the gentle breeze, "You did it all Ellie, we just helped."

"Yes, everyone helped but you gave me strength and something to fight for and hold onto. I've been fighting with so much lately and focused on so many things that I missed something that was right in front of me."

Annabelle tilted her head to one side slightly, "What's that then Ellie?" she asked kindly, a small smile on her face.

"I'm feeling brave after all that, so I'm just going to do this," Ellie said.

She reached forward and brushed the hair out of Annabelle's face. Then pulled Annabelle towards her and kissed her. To Ellie's relief, Annabelle kissed her back and the two embraced and held each other on the top of the hill. For those few moments Ellie forgot all about the evening's events, she could relax and be happy, this was the most natural feeling in the world to her. Simon was her best friend; Annabelle was so much more.

CHAPTER 19

The next morning Ellie woke in her bed, she lifted herself up onto her elbows and looked around. Her room was normal. The sunlight was coming through the curtains and shining on the floor. It was illuminating the blow-up bed where Annabelle had slept. Ellie smiled to herself at the memory of the night before, she shuffled forwards to the end of the bed and lay down on her front. Annabelle looked so peaceful sleeping, Ellie smiled a wide grin and chuckled, the feeling of butterflies in her stomach unlike anything she had experienced before. For now, their kiss was their secret, how long for would remain to be seen. After a few moments she got out of bed and went to the bathroom, when she returned Annabelle was awake and sat up facing the bathroom door.

"Hey, you," she said when Ellie appeared.

"Hey, you too," Ellie replied, walking over and sitting cross legged in front of Annabelle. "About last night, the bit at the end on the hill," Ellie started.

Annabelle put a finger on her lips stopping her from talking.

"Ellie, you don't need to say anything, I'm glad you kissed me. Means I don't need to make the first move anymore," she grinned. "I have tried to give you enough hints lately! I told you that the person would know when I wanted them to know, guess it took saving the world and an apocalypse for you to realise eh?"

They giggled.

"Can we keep it quiet, and just see what happens for now?" Ellie asked nervously. "Kind of want everything to settle down again before, you know," she looked down at her feet.

Annabelle reached forward and lifted Ellie's face by the chin, she lent forward and kissed her on the cheek.

"Whatever you want Ellie, I've waited a while, a little longer won't hurt," she smiled.

Ellie smiled, "You're the best Annabelle."

The two hugged.

"We best go find Simon and get some breakfast," Ellie said.

The two girls got up and threw on some comfy clothes and headed downstairs for breakfast. Simon was a step ahead of them, having slept in the spare room he was already downstairs and eating with Katherine and Nicholas. The two girls entered the room beaming and ran over to Simon to bundle him into a hug. Ellie had explained to all of them what had happened, how the spirits were actually one and the same. The energy from the stones, the folly and Ellie herself, how she had become a spirit for a time and had seen her own body before forcing the Man into the prison space between worlds. To the credit of her family and friends, they all listened politely and let Ellie finish her entire story before asking questions. Ellie had been right though; the purple sphere had hidden it all from view and the only way anyone would know now is because of the scorched stone and burnt grass around the folly.

"Your antics have made the local news," Katherine said.

The three stopped and looked up, "What?" Annabelle asked.

"All the marks on the hill and folly, the scorched ground and burnt stone. It's in the news," Katherine continued. "The council are reporting it as a fire that was started by a group of youths. Not a million miles away from the truth I guess," she added with a wry smile.

Ellie turned and could see the headline on the local news on the TV, there were cameras and everything up on the hill now.

"Mow Cop is on the map now then?" she asked the room.

"Yes, still as gorgeous as the day we moved in though," Nicholas replied, putting his arm around his wife. "Everything is back as it should be, I think, apart from a few burn marks up there of course," he gestured out of the window.

He and Katherine had made up, seemingly the surge of energy over the hill combined with Ellie's efforts had repaired that particular rift.

"I think we should go up there later, take stock of it all," Simon added.

"Agreed, Sophie will be here soon, so we can all go up," Ellie replied.

They had arranged for the council and Sophie to arrive around the same time, this was so they could all discuss what had happened and how to move forward. This served several purposes, the council wanted to know what had happened and Ellie and her family wanted to stop the council from being pests. A win-win as Ellie's mum would often say.

Around early afternoon they were all gathered around the dining table in the Fields family home. Unlike previous visits this was a calm one, everybody was there for the same reason and was relaxed. They all sat and listened whilst Ellie told the tale of what had happened, this was the second time she had done this now and it was becoming repetitive for her.

"Now he has gone I think we can all go back to leading normal lives. I certainly want to do that," she looked at Annabelle, then at her parents, "I can't wait to just have a normal life for a bit."

Everyone stayed silent for a moment, then Douglas spoke.

"Eleanor, you have done so much for us in such little time. When you first came here, we treated you the way we have always treated newcomers, especially those that we believed to be special to the council and its cause."

Ellie raised her eyebrows, everyone else turned to look at Douglas.

"We accept," he continued, "that doing things the way we did may have not been the best approach. Which is why, as promised the council is disbanded and we will no longer be preaching the Man Of Mow story to anyone. All the old ways will cease, no more meetings or secrets. Only normal fences and extensions you'll all be pleased to hear."

The room was filled with chuckles and muttered words of thanks and appreciation.

"Do you really think he has gone, and it is all over?" Kenny asked.

"Well, the stories have been told and fulfilled, Eleanor has closed the gateway between worlds, he is trapped or destroyed we don't know which. I think we can be safe in assuming that it is all over. Eleanor would you agree?"

Ellie pondered this, "I think so. He did say that it would not hold him forever, but he was just screaming anything at that point so I'm going with yes it's all good."

She smiled at the group, there was nothing else she could say even though she herself was wondering the same thing.

"Good enough for me," Simon added, "Means we can all relax and have a Merry Christmas soon."

This brought laughter to the room. Ellie agreed that it would be nice to have a normal life for a little bit, and time to enjoy it would be amazing.

After a short while the council took their leave and left, leaving Ellie with her three friends to prepare for a walk up the hill to the folly. Even though it was a clear sunny day, there was a winter chill in the air, so the group wrapped up a little more than previous walks, and set off up the hill. The walk was a slow gradual one, they were not in a hurry and wanted to savour the moments as they went. The four walked two by two, Ellie with Annabelle at the front and Simon with Sophie behind. After about twenty minutes they turned one of the last corners and could now see the folly properly. Ellie stopped and paused to look up at it.

"You ok?" Annabelle asked, the others stopped behind them and looked up as well.

"Yeah, just, thinking. Will I ever look at it the same way again? We now know it was never just a folly, it's odd you know?"

Annabelle looked from Ellie to Simon, to Sophie, and back, then replied, "Yes, completely understand. But now, thanks to you it is just a folly and can be enjoyed as such," she smiled.

"Now come on I want to see the damaged you caused Eleanor Fields!" and she started moving again, virtually dragging Ellie be the arm with her as she went.

They continued slowly waking up the hill, when they turned to go up the last steep set of steps Ellie noticed and pointed out the scorched earth.

"Look! Is this where the purple sphere stopped and started

into the ground?" she stopped and touched the grass where it went from green to black. "It's completely different and a perfect line," she added.

"It goes all the way around in a circle too," Sophie added. "You really went to town up here didn't you?"

Ellie grinned, "We did, yes," she stood and peered around the corner, "Are people really buying that this was some kind of out control fire that stopped in a neat line?"

Ellie was confused by this, it was such a neat circle around the peak of the folly hill, how could anyone believe it?

"Guess we believe what we are told don't we? I mean, we believed it was just a folly until recently," Simon responded.

Ellie nodded, "Ok, shall we go on up then?"

She took a step forward over the line into the scorched Earth and led the way up the last set of steep steps to the peak of the hill, the folly level. The ground was scorched here too, the grass and stones on the ground were black and almost unrecognisable. Ellie turned and walked towards the folly itself, walking by the arch she reached out her hand and touched the stone.

"No vibrations," she called back, she had not been expecting any but felt the need to share it as she ran her hand along the stone.

"Is that good or bad?" Annabelle asked.

"The song said it was a good thing," Simon commented with a grin, everyone turned to stare at him. "What? You're not telling me you've never heard that song?" he asked the group.

Ellie grinned and the others chuckled, there was a change in mood amongst the group of friends now. It was as if everyone could breathe and relax once more, be normal and do what they wanted to do without worrying. Ellie carried on up the steps alongside the wall, past the arch and to the tower. When she reached the gate she peered through, remembering that the last time she did she was face to face with him the night before.

"Is that the end?" she asked the empty tower quietly, as if the stone would answer her. "I hope so, I don't want any more pressure or decisions to make. Just a normal life please."

"Talking to yourself is considered strange in some cultures

you know," Annabelle commented as she approached from behind.

She put her hands round Ellie's waist and rested her chin on her shoulder, "You're not going to keep anything from me from now are you? If anymore weird stuff happens, I want to be the first to know, understand Ellie?"

Ellie turned and faced Annabelle who kept her hands round her waist, "You will be the first to know, I promise," she kissed Annabelle on the cheek. "No idea where this will lead you know, us I mean. Never had a girlfriend before, never had a boyfriend either. I mean I've had friends that are girls and boys but never."

Annabelle put her hand over Ellie's mouth, "Ok, you don't need to literally tell me everything," she chuckled. "We will just see what happens ok, but first we should probably tell them," she gestured behind her towards Sophie and Simon.

"You're right," Ellie said, then moving to the side to see around Annabelle called out, "Sophie, Simon, we need to tell you. What the heck?" Ellie cut short what she was saying.

She tugged on Annabelle's sleeve to turn her around. Sophie and Simon were locked in a kiss themselves, to Ellie's utter shock and surprise there they were right in front of her plain as day.

"Excuse me!" she shouted, "This is a decent place we don't need that sort of thing thank you," she teased, she was shocked but also sort of pleased.

"Sorry, but if you can do it why can't we?" Simon asked.

Ellie and Annabelle looked at each other, flushed a shade of pink, and then looked back at Simon and Sophie.

"How did you know?" Ellie asked.

"Saw you last night," Simon replied. "And heard you talking too, and I'm not stupid."

Simon and Sophie were walking up the steps to Ellie and Annabelle now.

"Besides, figured we were all friends and made a good team of sorts, so why not?"

He grinned, clearly pleased with himself putting his arm around Sophie.

"Well just be careful Simon, Sophie is a handful," Ellie playfully jabbed Sophie on the arm.

"Hey!" she pushed back, "As for you Annabelle, look after my Ellie, she is a sensitive beautiful person."

Annabelle looked at Ellie, "I will Sophie, I will."

Ellie pondered this, "Hang on, let me get this straight. I move to the country leaving my best friend behind. I then make a new best friend, that's you Simon," Simon grinned, "Oh shhh. Who then ends up going out with my old best friend? In the meantime, I save the world and get the girl," she squeezed Annabelle's waist, "In true Hollywood style and then the four of us just get on with our lives? Is that about right?"

She was beaming by the end of this.

"Not a bad summary of a few months I think," Annabelle added. "Been a good few I'd say," she looked up at the tower, "It is still beautiful, despite the fact it now looks like it burnt down a million years ago."

"Yeah, strangely beautiful," Ellie agreed.

"Ok, enough hill walking tower stuff, can we go eat now?" Sophie asked.

"You can take the girl out the city as they say," Simon grinned, and turned to lead Sophie back down the hill.

Annabelle went to follow, reaching out for Ellie's hand.

"Can you give me a minute?" Ellie asked.

Annabelle's smiled, "Sure, we will start walking slowly."

She left.

Ellie turned to look at the tower once more, the evenings events had changed her she hoped for the better.

"That was a tough few months," she said to the stone, not a whisper but not loud either as she wanted to keep this between her and the folly. "You taught me a lot about myself, and for that I am grateful. But for all the pain, confusion and anger you caused you got what you deserved. Our world is safe, and I truly hope that Imaginari is too. The energy flow you showed me should be moving the same way it always was, meaning both worlds should be fine," she reached out and put her hand on the bars of the tower gate. "The really sad thing though, is I think if you had tried to go a different way, there could be a way to give you what you want without destroying either world. You were so focused on your path that you didn't even consider other options," Ellie took a deep breath and let go of the gate. "So, this is me saying goodbye. I'm going to have a normal life now, going to live in this village, our village, and do normal things. Without interruptions from spirits or whatever you really were. Goodbye."

With that, Ellie turned and walked back down the steps by the folly wall, with a cursory glance at the ground beneath the arch she noticed that the patch she had lay on was not scorched. A perfect human body shape in green surrounded by black burnt ground. "How are they explaining that?" she mused out loud as she walked by. Ellie jumped the last few steps, as if doing so was a final farewell to the crazy life she had led recently. She turned to look up at the folly once more, she knew she would look at it many times over but wanted this to be a farewell to these specific memories. She smiled, turned and walked down the steps where her friends were waiting for her. Then they walked, two by two down the hill back to the Fields family home.

The end of part one in The Book Of Imaginari.

ABOUT THE AUTHOR

Richard Hayden

At the time of writing The Book Of Imaginari (it began in 2019), Richard lived in the village of Mow Cop where it is set. He would often visit the folly and look out over the surrounding areas – it is this that led him to the inspiration for Imaginari.

Part one – The Folly On The Hill – took around four months from concept to first draft, with parts two and three taking a similar amount of time afterwards, they are coming soon.

The book was written for pleasure, creating it would fill his spare time and this opportunity was increased massively during the pandemic of 2020 – the goal being to create something that at least one person would find and enjoy reading it.

Let him know what you think of Imaginari, he can be contacted on Twitter and Instagram (@R_C_Hayden) and on Facebook (Richard Hayden Author, @rchaydenauthor), he would love to hear what you think of the story.

Printed in Great Britain
by Amazon

58893120R00154